A shot hit the heel of Shelby's boot, then one ricocheted near his head. Thaddeus Kele moaned, hurting bad. A shotgun blast kicked up dirt into his eyes, blinding him for the moment.

Shelby grabbed the Colt's Navy pistol Thaddeus Kele had inside his belt and fired again. More men fell—dead as dry flies in December snow.

"Click. Click," the Navy said 'empty' to Shelby.
"That's all she wrote, Cinque. We gotta run!"
"Ain't no place to run, Sergeant Shelby. We's surrounded . . . !"

WEST OF

PARADISE RUN

J. J. R. Ramey

BALLANTINE BOOKS • NEW YORK

All rights reserved under International and Pan-American Copyright Conventions. Published in the United States of America by Ballantine Books, a division of Random House, Inc., New York, and simultaneously in Canada by Random House of Canada Limited, Toronto.

Library of Congress Catalog Card Number: 89-91649

ISBN 0-345-35700-0

Manufactured in the United States of America

First Edition: December 1989

Prologue

During the years 1861–1865, the North battled the South in the Civil War—the bloodiest clash in U.S. history—the war that would determine if the states that had seceded from the Union would become a separate nation bound by slavery, or if the slave would become a free man.

The Civil War marked the first time in American history that men of African heritage were engaged in extensive combat service.

On July 17, 1862, the U.S. War Department created the Bureau of Colored Troops to handle Negro Enlistment. In Louisiana in 1862, General Nathaniel P. Banks formed "Corps d'Afrique," a Negro Army Unit, and Blacks, paid ten dollars a month, signed up by the thousands to defend the nation that their kinfolks had built with blood, tears, and thankless oppression.

Negro soldiers saw the war as a chance to plot their hopeless destinies. These Black men-in-blue were brave under siege in several major battles: Point Lookout, Virginia; Fort Pillow in Tennessee; and at Milliken's Bend, Louisiana. Almost 200,000 Black men had fought for the North by the time the war had ended.

On March 1, 1865, by order of Brigadier General Hollingsworth Williams, U.S. Army soldierscout Sergeant Jonathan Frederick Shelby, a Yankee by circumstance as well as motive, headed north out of New Orleans, then west on a vital intelligence mission along the Red River into northeastern Texas. His destination: Red River Station. Should the war move west toward Rio Grande, the Union would be ready and Jon Shelby would lead the way.

But Shelby found trouble where the desperadoes

roamed, in the lawless land of Texas—a land where rattlers and roughnecks reigned supreme—a land where dying was cheaper than living.

Sergeant Shelby dreamed of one day soon becoming a cowboy and of running cattle into towns like Dodge City and Ogallala, by way of the Texas trail. One day he knew he would find the land of his dreams—once the war was done and his people were totally free. But first he had some fighting to do. . . .

Chapter

One

The crackling, dry sagebrush weaved and rolled atop the skin of the dusty soil. The wind swirled along the plains and plateaus in the wild expanse of a land called Texas. The sun shone bright along the rim of the golden horizon. Vultures, their two-toned, blackish wings spread six feet or more, hovered dangerously across the land. These indiscriminate birds of prey would fill their bellies with the flesh of lesser varmints, and ofttimes man. While blood congealed upon their pointed beaks, their red heads glistened in the late wintertime light.

Two strangers were headed west, and since their mission had begun, each day had been long—too long, in fact. But by now the leader and his pal had gotten used to the relentless cycle of hot, dry days and slow, uneventful nights.

It was March of 1865, and the War Between the States had yet to be won by either side. The brother-against-brother war had begun in 1861, when Confederate regulars fired on Fort Sumter in South Carolina. Since then life had grown harder than either the North or the South had ever expected; it was especially difficult for the Southern gentleman who had built his fortune on the blood and toil of African slaves in the land where cotton was king.

No Southerner ever dreamed God's good fortune would end. But the men of the industrial North, the Yankees, knew that in a pinch the South would have no chance to defeat their ranks in battle, and they prided themselves on having drawn the Southern states into a war that was destined to change the status quo in their favor for a long time to come.

3

The rumble of distant Rebel cannonfire still echoed within the strangers' minds, yet they were too far west inside Texas to really hear the guns that took their toll on lives in nearby Louisiana. It was easier for an ordinary man who could lay down the burden of thought for a few moments and pick up the load again when he saw fit. But for the fighting men of the Union and the Confederacy, the war was a never-ending trauma, a once glorious dream become all too bloody and real for men who had been Mamas' boys not too long before.

The pair of Union fighting men rode slowly toward a place they had located on their primitive map, the once lawless town of killers and thieves, a place called Clarksville, Texas. The stranger in charge was one Union soldier scout named Sergeant Jonathan Frederick Shelby. He had accepted the mission to map and peruse the land that lay between New Orleans and Red River Station, Texas. His run from southern Louisiana should have been a practical, straight shot north and then west, but his orders had taken him off track for a brief stop in Natchitoches.

But that was all part of the job, and he was proud of the Union blue uniform resting upon his back. This man was dark-skinned, a Negro, a Black, an African—and so was his partner—and that made all the difference in the world. In 1865, men of color were not supposed to read, lead, and certainly not wear the white man's blue—not ever in a world where he was an outcast, thought to be what he had never been, inferior at every given level.

Shelby's rank was corporal before he was ordered by the army to scout territories west. Brigadier General Hollingsworth Williams had insisted he was the man for the job. The general was a strict man who, believing that "rank and privilege" came first in times of war, gave the rank of sergeant to the young but seasoned Black man.

"It's better to have it and not need it, than to need it and not have it. The rank, that is, Shelby." Williams paused to let his words sink in and then continued.

"You've got your orders, soldier. Prepare for your mission. See Lieutenant Bridges for your supplies. That'll be all." He paused again before he stressed the new title now owned by the Negro soldier. "*Sergeant* Shelby."

Of course, there were some white officers who had tried

4

to trouble Jon about his new rank. One man in particular, a Lieutenant Hamilton Bridges, found Jon's promotion sickening and had taunted the Black man in front of his peers. Jon had withstood Bridges's insults for a time, but when the young officer had called him "nigger boy" for the third or fourth time, Jon just couldn't help himself. With one swift motion he had laid the white man low. Sprawled out in the dust, Bridges had been the laughingstock of both Black and white soldiers, and from that point on, he'd avoided crossing Shelby's path.

The incident with Bridges had happened several weeks ago. That time was long gone. At twenty-two years old, Jon told himself that he'd seen change too many times to dwell on what had been. Better to pay attention to what was happening now and be prepared for what might come his way.

Jon sighed. He knew the War Between the States was really one of greed—the Northern white man after control of the Southern gentleman's cotton country. And until the Southern majority bowed and behaved, the fight would go on. Black folks hailed the Civil War as "God's way of making rights from wrongs." But Jon knew they failed to see beyond the smoke.

Jonathan Shelby was a soldier who respected both man and nature as long as they respected him in return. His hair was long and thick and combed back to hang over the nape of his muscular neck, which was covered, as usual, by a bandanna just in case a dust storm cropped up at the most inconvenient of times.

His eyebrows were heavy—the better to sift away the grit and airborne debris of the range from his deep-set eyes. His hands were large and thin, just perfect for swatting mosquitoes at night and dry flies at high noon. And the hairline scar that rested laterally above his left eye was the first gash to open and spurt blood whenever he got into a fight.

Jon's deep, brown, cautious eyes lightened and pleaded for trust whenever the need arose, as it did quite often in the war-torn South. His nose was large, but it fit his face well, and his skin was a dark shade of bronze, a tinge of vermilion after days under the hot Texas sun. The color didn't wipe off, so it must have been real, concluded the

5

Indians, who were awed by his color from the start.

Shelby always shaved close when he could find the time, but at the moment it didn't matter that his beard was two days old. He had a job to do—deliver a secret document to Red River Station, Texas, after scouting the territory for future reference. "Can't trust that confounded wire machine to secrecy," Brigadier General Williams had said. "It's highly sensitive material. That's why you are delivering it by hand, soldier. If you decide to take the job, that is."

Sergeant Jonathan Frederick Shelby, a Yankee by circumstance as well as motive, accepted Brigadier General Williams's challenge—because he was a U.S. Federal soldier and proud to be one.

Most African men found failure when they attempted to stand up strong and proud in a white man's world, yet there were some men, like Shelby, who relished the challenge of any man in any world, as long as it was fair and square.

He was mean when he had to be, but his heart was naturally filled with compassion. Jon's chocolate-brown skin set him apart from most other men out on the range or in the battlefield. He had read somewhere that one out of every three cowboys was Black, but he was different from them: he was a Union soldier, fighting to end the scourge of slavery.

Shelby hoped his friend and older confidant, Private Daniel Walton, understood the danger of their mission. He loved his companion, who hailed from Atlanta, Georgia; but a good soldier never let his feelings get in the way of a job at hand.

"You been awful quiet, Dan'l," said Shelby, leaving out the "ie" in his companion's name by way of his Tennessee accent. "Ain't like you not to talk me damn near to death on a long haul like this."

"Thought I heard some horses whinny across the way," answered Dan'l. "Let's head over toward that ridge. Something tells me, Sarge, there's trouble a-brewin'."

"You call me 'Sarge' again, Dan'l, they'll be trouble right here," snapped Jon. "Never did like nicknames, never did."

"Didn't mean no harm, Jon," said Private Walton. "Jes' can't get used to calling a superior officer by his first name. Before you, all of my commanding sergeants were white. Guess I jes' like to hear the word roll offa my tongue, I reckon. I'm proud of you, Jon, being a sergeant and all. Didn't never think I'd live to see the day one of my own would move up in rank in the white man's army. Never did think that. Shore enuf, didn't."

"Sorry, Dan'l. Guess I lost my head. I'm so sick and tired of my folks being called out of their names by white folks, I reckon I'm fit to be tied."

"I knows what you mean about them names, Jon. Makes me madder than a honeybee without a hive when I hears us bein' called something we ain't."

Jon Shelby smiled, knowing if his friend had an itching that something was awry, he had better take note. Dan'l Walton's intuition was seldom, if ever, wrong. Jon yanked rein, and his roan, named Easel, responded quickly.

The Black sergeant squinted his eyes as he wondered what had Dan'l so anxious. Can't ask questions now, Jon told himself. I chose him to come along; he's still the best man to cover my butt if trouble gets on our tails. If I hadn't listened to him back down Louisiana way, that bullet that went through the hollow of my hat would have landed inside my thick skull.

Sergeant Shelby and Private Walton rode slowly toward the legendary Red River. There was still a good piece to go yet. When Walton slapped his unusually smart Appaloosa into a trot and moved ahead of him, Jon knew he had heard or seen something that deserved immediate attention.

The young Union scout led his blaze-faced roan in line behind his brave friend. When they got near the crest of a ridge overlooking a well-traveled road, they both paused. "Reckon I lost the scent, Jon. Shore have."

Shelby had already dismounted and was lying on his belly to conceal himself, inching closer and closer to the edge of the hill.

"What you see?" asked Dan'l, crawling up beside Jon.

"Stagecoach comin'. Yonder ways, around the bend." Shelby indicated the direction with a nod of his head.

"Stagecoach ain't never been no problem. Come on, we's got to get goin' to Red River Station."

"Reckon you're right. Thought it was something else we

7

should be privy to. Got worms in your britches, Dan'l," said Jon, laughing.

As they headed toward their mounts, Jon suddenly eyed some movement on the other side of the ridge. "On second thought, Dan'l, we'd best hang around and see that that stage gets through the pass."

"We's under orders to head west up the mighty Red, Jon. We starts nosing 'round into other folks' business, we git trouble shore enuf. Got enough trouble with them Rebels. Shore don't need no more."

"May be Union folk or property on that coach. I got orders to help them if they's in distress. See them bushes over yonder on the other side of the valley?"

"Yup. What about 'em?" said the private.

"Saw a something move there from left to right," said Jon.

"So?"

"So, it looks like somebody done seen what we seen. We better stick around, just in case we's needed."

"Ain't our job to protect them folks. They's got to make it on their own."

"We'll head that stage off before it gets to the pass," said Jon firmly.

"Waste of time, I say, boy!"

"That's an order, Private. I'm in command here," said Shelby, squinting his eye toward Walton in serious fashion.

"Yessir, Sergeant," he said, then hawked and spit, obviously not liking the order one bit. "We'll head 'em off like you said, Sir!"

Shelby and Walton walked their horses off the hard Texas rock, making nary a sound. Jon stopped just long enough to adjust the bit within Easel's mouth. He had selected a curbed bit with the split-ear headstall, the most comfortable piece of gear for the horse. For a moment he allowed himself to reminisce. It was not long ago that he had broken the roan down. That had been in Shreveport, where he and Walton had stopped to deliver a dispatch from Brigadier General Williams. He had fallen in love with the animal when he first laid eyes on his lovely coat at the local livery, and the steed, Jon felt, had fallen in love with him in similar fashion.

Easel started to whinny, but the Black man held his hand over the muzzle, talking him out of a frenzy. "It's all right, Easel, take it easy, boy. We got to be quiet, you know, as quiet as a broke-leg dog in a swamp full of Louisiana alligators. That's it, boy." Easel calmed down.

Across the valley, the bushes moved again without apparent reason. Someone or something appeared to be lying in wait. The experienced scout didn't know what to make of it, and it was then that he remembered General Williams's words as he prepared to leave camp in New Orleans. "Remember, Shelby. You're the best damn scout I've ever had, but stay on your toes. You're headed into Texas—there's no other place like it—where the law could be the enemy, and the enemy could be the law. It's no-man's-land to some, the end of the line for most others —especially good men like you. You're headed to a place where there're no rules and no real laws, except the law of a man with his finger on the trigger. Shoot first, son, ask questions later.

"Even the men who wear badges may not be the ordained law. If someone confesses too fast that he's the law, assume up front that he's lying. Most true lawmen get killed in the land of Texas and their badge taken as a trophy, like a Medal of Honor. Ornery scoundrels. Do I make myself clear, soldier?"

"Yessir, General," Jon had replied, but he hadn't seriously thought about General Williams's words until now.

And since he respected Brigadier General Williams as a fair man, he decided to heed his advice. Some white men were good men, with not a tinge of bigotry in their bones. Shelby had decided when he first laid eyes upon the General that here was a man deserving of his trust and devotion.

It was the same in 1865 as it had been all along. A smart Negro had to learn to read a crooked Black and a prejudiced white simply by the look in their eyes. Shelby had learned this as a child, and his experience had matured him. True, sometimes he was wrong about a Negro's intentions since he always tried to give a kinsman the benefit of the doubt. But he was never wrong about the motives of most white men. Can't hate a good white just 'cause he's

9

white, he told himself. Can't let myself fall into a bigot's trap. I'd rather die and go to the devil first!

On the far side of this Texas valley, atop a ridge that was flanked by deep, thick trees and underbrush that seemed out of place in an area that was mostly level, were grouped men of differing heritage and motives. The leader of the band was a wild man from farther west, a place called El Paso just south of Fort Fillmore in New Mexico and south also of the Laguna de los Chihuahua range in Mexico. He had killed many times before, often only for some hardtack and an old saddle, or maybe a mess of wormy beans here and there. The outlaw had robbed stages, too, though he thought them no real challenge. Robbing the rig on its way into his trap was like lifting eggs from a hen fast asleep.

The outlaw lay low to the ground and belched final instructions to his men. They were men who could never lead, and when they met up with this fuzzy-faced outlaw who bragged about his leadership of his gang, that had been enough to convince them to join. Most of them had killed many times. There was a thrill about taking the life of a man that few killers could explain. And they hoped to kill again.

The desperado gave his orders a second time, wiping fresh new slobber from the corners of his mouth onto his filthy flannel shirtsleeve. He had a wild look in his left eye, and his right eye winked a lot. The men thought it was his way of looking tougher than the devil on Monday morning. "You boys got that?" he asked as the men prepared to rob the stagecoach moving their way.

The leader of the desperadoes was called Wooly Samples, and he was a master at planning and executing robberies and killings. Although he wasn't the smartest of Texans, he always got away. That reason alone had many would-be robbers and killers seeking to join his band. He was a mean brute who hadn't seen a tub of water or a bar of lye soap almost since his mother had bathed his ornery bottom some twenty-five years ago. Those were the days when the only excitement in El Paso came when Mexican vaqueros crossed the Rio Grande and stole from the ranchers along the border, or when white men did the same thing down Mexico way to even up the score.

But that was all in the past, and the future was what Wooly had on his mind. "Now if we get scattered gettin' away, we'll meet on the other side of the valley. That way we can all leave together."

"Then we can split up the loot," said killer Ace Wiggins.

"We ain't splittin' up a d-damn thing, boy," said Wooly. "We got expenses, you see. After the bills been paid, we get what's left."

Ace Wiggins and four of the other six outlaws had never worked with Samples before; in fact, they had never robbed a stagecoach. Their reputations were for killing and stealing more stable booty, like paper money and gold from the nearest bank. It didn't matter much to them whether the take was from the Confederacy or from them damned crazy Yankees.

"Get ready, boys, stage'll be here directly," said Wooly. "After this job, we can lay back and live like we's rich."

Racing up the dusty road from east to west, the Harris-O'Leary stage kicked up dust like an infant tornado dancing across the prairie land of Texas. Inside were six unsuspecting passengers, including a little boy, each with a lifetime of plans and dreams. Their destinies grew nearer to a head.

Jon Shelby looked across the horizon and knew intuitively that the stage was in trouble. He jumped up on Easel's back and motioned for Walton to fall in behind him. "Kick some spur into that horse, Dan'l. We's got to warn that stage before it runs into that ambush."

"Don't see no sense in it. You's the boss, though, I reckon," said Dan'l, racing up behind Jon. Walton saluted his friend and added, "Yessir, Sergeant Shelby. Yessir."

Jon and the private slid easily and quietly away from the rocks that had hid them well. In a moment, they urged their horses to a full gallop, hoping to arrive quickly at the cut-off point in the middle of the pass so that they could stop and warn the stagecoach.

The Harris-O'Leary stagecoach was still several miles

away from a fateful rendezvous with uncertain destiny. The freight and passenger line had offered, both before and after the war, a most dependable means of travel for men, women, and even young children traveling alone, regardless of their political affiliations. But the world was different now, and anyone could lose his life traveling west, especially in a land where self-appointed soldiers made their homes, and their guns played God.

It was true that mostly Yankees traveled that stage line since the rebellion had commenced back east at Fort Sumter in 1861; it was clear to those who protected the stage's contents, and to those who sought to steal it, that money and gold were legal tender in the world of the blue or the gray.

"And where might you be heading, Mrs. ah . . .?" asked the man inside the stage to the young woman sitting opposite him. She wondered now why he hadn't spoken to her before, but that was the way with some travelers, she surmised. The less said, the better.

He was a businessman from Mobile, headed to Texas to become rich at whatever he found suitable for the taking. No line of work was out of the question, as long as he didn't have to work too hard at it.

"Faraday. Eva Faraday. And your name, sir?" asked the young woman, who was expecting her first child in the very near future. Her Southern drawl, laced with a British accent, was deep, innocent, and refreshing to the easterner.

"Taskman's the name. Robert Taskman," the well-dressed gentleman said to the young woman. "I daresay, ma'am, that you ought not be traveling at this time. Alone, that is."

"I beg your pardon," snapped the young woman, feeling only the impertinence of his observation and none of its concern.

"I mean, ma'am, that riding out here all alone in the wilderness when the Union is a-pillaging and killing innocent civilians seems mighty dangerous, you bein' without an escort. You bein' in the family way and all."

"My husband usually travels with me on our excursions, sir," replied Eva Faraday, easing a handkerchief from between her milk-laden bosoms.

Taskman looked around the coach, viewing the folks

12

who were all asleep or pretending to be asleep. He hadn't really paid much attention before to either of the two other men or the other woman; the boy-child apparently traveled alone. He had napped during the first leg of the lonesome trip and just now, upon awakening, had he noticed the cute filly sitting across from him. It was unlike a young husband to virtually ignore his expecting wife. Most responsible men in these times of war and lost hope cherished the thought that many sons would be born to them before their tenure on earth came to an end.

"I don't mean to pry," said Taskman, "but would one of these gentlemen here be your husband?"

"My husband was killed back East, sir," answered Eva Faraday, her eyes tearing. She wiped the droplets of despair from her rosy British cheeks. "He was killed in a skirmish with the Union Army back on the Mississippi River near Memphis."

Feeling pained and wishing he had never brought up the subject, Robert Taskman reached for the woman's free hand and tried to soothe her. "I'm terribly sorry, ma'am. I..."

"There's no need to be, sir. Any brave man would have given his life for the Confederacy."

Eva Faraday was a true Southern belle if there ever was one. She was young and beautiful, the pride of her British heritage. Yet she was troubled, knowing that the war had destroyed what hope she had once fostered. There was only one consolation in her life.

"You must be devastated, Mrs. Faraday, ma'am," said Taskman.

"You see, I'm carrying the child of Hollis McGrath Faraday. That means that his family must be kept alive. That is why it is so important that I flee the East to safety at my father's home in Dallas. He's the District Sheriff and I know no matter what the future brings that he will protect me and my child and make certain that my son will be raised in the tradition of my own family."

Once again, Taskman noted the British accent beneath her Southern drawl. In many ways, American and British English were still very similar, he thought. Her lovely voice temporarily took his mind off his troubles.

Chapter

Two

Sergeant Shelby and Private Walton topped the last hill between them and came out on the open road where they could cut off the stage. They relaxed, but only for a moment. Their troubles weren't over yet. For all the driver and the shotgun knew, the two Black soldiers could be bandits themselves, only dressed to look like legitimate keepers of the peace. Shelby and Walton were ready for a difficult job.

"They got to come this-a-way, Sergeant. So I reckon all we's gots to do now is wait."

"I like the way you think, Dan'l. Sometimes I think you're reading my mind."

Jon Shelby had joined the Union Army to fight for what he believed in, the freedom owed his people. When he had first left Tennessee, he hadn't known what to expect. Growing up, he had somewhat escaped the tyranny of ruthless slaveholders and their kind. His folks, Jemeliah and Hallie Shelby, had been dealt the trump card when they were bought by the Thatcher Morgan family and immediately set free in 1842. "I've decided, Jemeliah. I'm setting you and your clan free. The paper'll be a-drawn up within the week, maybe as soon as tomorry, I reckon. Tell your folks, Jemeliah."

That was a glorious day for the Shelby family of Tennessee, yet thousands of other Negroes remained enslaved.

Shelby had always known that Negroes, Indians, and Mexicans topped the list of those that white folks loved to hate. And when he discovered that Mexicans were at the very top of the list, and that Indians were one notch below them, he almost cheered that his kind was number three.

14

"Here they come," yelled Walton, breaking up Jon's daydream.

"Hope you ain't mistaken. I'd hate to be chasin' nothin' all this way. I'll run up ahead; you plant yourself in the middle of the pass."

"So I'll get run over, huh?" complained Private Walton.

"You buckin' orders, Private?" Jon said.

"Naw, sir, Sergeant. I'm on my way," said Walton, racing straight toward his ordered destination. Although he hoped Jon wouldn't think hard of him for questioning his orders, he knew deep inside that they were friends for life.

Easel ran hard and straight ahead toward the fast-moving stage. The sergeant didn't know who ran the stage line, but he hoped they had respect for the Union blue, or if not, for the men trying to save them from harm.

A flicker of doubt teased across Jon's mind as he charged. Maybe Dan'l was right, maybe he was jumping to conclusions. Sometimes he wished his devotion to the Union wasn't so taut and sure. Right now, he wished they had kept their momentum moving westward, up the mighty Red River, delivering his top-secret dispatch to Red River Station.

Often Jonathan Shelby the man wondered what was inside his leather satchel. But the soldier knew the code, and the only way not to reveal secrets under torture and threat of death was not to know the contents of the message. He dared not peek at the contents of this urgent dispatch. He would live by the scout's creed or die by it.

Over the hill echoed a loud, booming noise: the Harris-O'Leary stage had appeared above the horizon. It was moving so fast its wheels sometimes left the ground. The wooden and metal-wheeled horse-drawn buggy rocked with speed. When the driver saw a figure waving his arms, he thought only one thing: An ambush again. This time they were prepared, armed to the hilt.

When the shotgun-toting Black man riding guard on the Harris-O'Leary stagecoach spotted the two riders ahead, he rightfully thought of nothing but the obvious—a hold-up in progress. He had ridden with his partner, Fell Cooper, since the beginning of the war, and both had seen their share of robberies. Each time, the guard and the driver got the worst end of the ordeal.

"Looks like we got trouble, Fell," said Olu Graham to the driver.

"May be, may not be, Olu," said Fell Cooper, his Irish brogue still deep and distinct. "If me eyes ain't playin' tricks on me brain, laddy, seems to me the men's dressed in Union blue."

"Can't be too sure these days, especially in this dad-burned land of Texas," said Graham. "I got my weapons cocked and ready. Slow down a might, we'll let 'em have their say 'fore we blast 'em to kingdom's come!"

The swirling air suddenly rose from a tender whirl to a menacing, dust-raising wind. When the stagecoach made its final approach, the driver lifted his foot to mash in the handle of the brake, which brought the buggy to a complete halt.

"Howdy, stranger," yelled Jon Shelby, watching the guard slowly raise the double-barreled shotgun, the heel of which rested securely against the back of the seat.

"What can we do for you, son?" said the obviously older Olu Graham. "We got a schedule to keep, and you're gittin' in the way."

"My name is Shelby, sir. Sergeant Jonathan Frederick Shelby, Union Army, Company C, Fifteenth Regiment of the Ninety-ninth U.S. Colored Troops, Corps D'Afrique, Louisiana Division."

"Ain't never seen no colored soldier before, much less a nigger sergeant. You 'spect me to believe that, boy?" said Graham.

"I ain't never seen no colored man riding shotgun, neither, but I see you sittin' there in the shotgunner's seat, so I have to believe what I see. At least for now," said Jon.

"What be your business, lad?" asked Fell Cooper, who respected almost any uniform, no matter who had it on his back.

"I expect some folks plannin' to come down on y'awl just up ahead between them rocks. My orders are to see any civilians, especially Union folks, get through the territory safely."

"Sure and that'd be grand of you, then," said Cooper, pulling rein. "Yer man and I hold no fight with the Union.

But if you don't mind now, we'll make it on our own. Good day to you boys, and God bless."

The Black soldier couldn't see the other folks in the shadows of the coach, not from his angle. He did see one man clearly—Robert Taskman, holding his head outside the coach window like a little child. He pulled it in when the coach lurched ahead.

There was once a time when folks riding alone in barren, wild country welcomed a helping hand if danger was deemed near. But the army sergeant reckoned that since the war, that time had passed. General Williams had warned him that Texas was like no other land on the face of the earth. From that point on, Jonathan Shelby vowed to take the extra precautions that could spell the difference between life and never seeing his mother and father again.

"What's the word, Sergeant?" asked Private Walton.

"They didn't believe me, Dan'l, or he didn't believe me," answered Jon, peeved at the Black man who had spurned his warning.

"You're talkin' in riddles, Jon. Don't know what to say."

"Never mind, Dan'l. We'll just have to stay close in case they *do* get ambushed. "Let's hope we's wrong."

" 'We'? 'We's wrong'? Why is it that whenever you could be wrong, you include me, too? And whenever you's right, it's all your doin'?"

Jon Shelby cut his eyes toward his companion and offered a wide smile, showing a mouth full of white, well-kept teeth. Then he yanked rein and raced full speed ahead. But Daniel Walton just shrugged his shoulders and let out a laugh, then kicked some spur into his horse. "Let's go, baby. We gots to save us some white folks."

Ahead at the pass, Wooly Samples's men—two of his regulars and five new men, all killers and robbers and murderers—vamped down upon the Harris-O'Leary stagecoach with a vengeance. Their guns were blazing, and sparks and shrapnel flew across the wide-open space like feathers at a chicken-plucking contest.

Wooly was the first to arrive within killing distance of the stage. Driver Fell Cooper got shot in the right shoulder. Olu Graham was lucky at first, but not for long. Soon a

17

pellet from a Sharps carbine breechloader tore into his side, but he was man enough not to be deterred from trying to save his cargo of passengers and riches.

Outlaw Ace Wiggins ran alongside the team of fine horses pulling the Harris-O'Leary stage and positioned himself on the blind side of both Olu Graham and Fell Cooper. They never knew the stagecoach had slowed to a crawl until it was too late.

"Must be a hunnerd of 'em," yelled Cooper to Graham.

"Shut up and drive, white man," said Olu Graham. "We gots to git outta this mess."

And at that moment a bullet ripped into Cooper's neck. Blood flew from the gaping hole so fast that the man never knew what hit him. Graham knew Fell was a goner, and before he could catch him he fell off the stage's perch and hit the hard Texas soil with a thud.

Jake Moody, one of Samples's men, laughed out loud when he saw that their job was easier than anticipated. Jake was the meanest one in the bunch. He looked away from the coach and saw two riders racing his way, red-and-yellow gunfire spewing from the barrels of their rifles. He knew it was time to kill up some more do-gooders.

"You cover the left side of the coach, I got the other side," yelled Sergeant Shelby.

"Right-o, Jon," answered Private Walton, happy to be in another fight with his favorite commander.

Jon fired his Colt's Navy at one outlaw, who fell off his horse. Then the sergeant took aim at another fellow, and the ball of hot lead sent the man flying to the ground. Shelby chased a third man into a thicket but lost him without a trace. By that time, he heard the stage grind to a complete halt. One of the hombres grabbed Eva Faraday's arm and dragged her into the bushes. Jon heard the woman screaming loudly, but could not see her. He tried to put a bullet into another man's heart, but missed. He raced Easel back out into the open and saw two outlaws wrestling with the second woman. One cowboy slapped her to the ground, grabbed her purse, and point-blank fired a bullet into her chest.

Jon raced back into the thicket as fast as Easel would carry him. Without warning, the horse tripped over a tree stump and sent Jon flying head over heels into a thorny

18

thicket. He landed on his back but was fortunately cushioned by the thick underbrush. The fall had saved Shelby's life; Wooly Samples had had his rifle sight aimed at the soldier's bobbing head.

Suddenly the horse team pulling the stage bolted at the sight of a rattler and took off down the road. When one of the wheels hit a large rock, the stagecoach bounced up and tumbled over several times, sending the remaining four passengers hurtling through the air. The boy died instantly of a broken neck. One outlaw ran up, fired shots into two of the men, and then rifled their pockets. Another shot Robert Taskman, the finely-dressed easterner, and stole his fancy duds.

Again, a woman screamed. The yells were coming now from within the thicket of trees and nearby. That was when Jon saw one no-gooder ripping the clothes off Eva Faraday, who was lying spread-eagle on the ground. The outlaw sprawled on top of her and muffled her words of fright with his lips as he mockingly kissed her and slapped her around. The Black sergeant leapt back onto Easel and was headed straight for the scene when he heard the outlaw cry out. The pregnant woman had evidently bitten his lip, and he was riled. The man yanked his pistol from his holster, took the butt and slammed it into her head. Then he stood, pointed the weapon at her middle, and pulled the trigger. The man had gone plumb loco, and he fired again into her naked chest and then let go a round into her head.

Shelby jumped off Easel, slid to the ground, and inched his way toward the scene, dodging bullets on the way. Finally, the killer had had enough; he wiped the blood from his mouth, pushed the pistol back in his holster, and looked around. Suddenly, he spotted the man in blue half-hidden but coming his way. He ran fast into the woods, where he mounted his horse, and headed out toward the upended stage.

"Look out, Dan'l!" Jon yelled as loud as he could, but it was too late. The man who had just killed an innocent woman had taken aim and pulled the trigger once more—and when the fire and smoke billowed from the barrel of the outlaw's gun, Daniel Walton, who'd been kneeling beside the first murdered woman, was slumped over heavily, a red spot forming on his midsection. Jon knew the private had been mortally wounded.

He tried to race toward his friend, but gunfire pinned him down. The only thing he could do was crawl back into the same thicket where he had seen the pregnant woman brutally murdered. It was the best and safest way to get to Dan'l. And as he made his way, Jon got a good look at the man who had shot Private Walton and murdered the innocent woman. It was a face he would never forget.

Tears welled from his eyes as he grabbed an Allen revolver lying nearby and crawled on his belly, firing into the band of outlaws who were racing toward their horses with several leather satchels and a strongbox that contained the gold and legal tender they had first come to get. The cowards raced into the nearby forest, sporadic gunfire covering them as they made their escape.

The Union sergeant ran to his partner, calling out his name. He cradled Daniel's head in his arms.

"Dan'l. Dan'l . . . You all right?" he wailed.

Private Walton's eyes were closed. A thick line of blood ran from the corner of his mouth, and his nose was clogged with blood. Thick, red stuff bubbled with each shallow breath. The death rattle was announcing the kill.

"Looks like you gon' have to come get me on the way back, boy," Walton murmured. "Reckon I's gone the last mile of the way."

"Don't talk like that, Private. Can't no bullet break us up. We's a team. You can't get out of this war that easy," said Jon.

"Tell . . . " Daniel Walton coughed up more blood.

Jon grimaced at the sight of his best friend's twisted flesh and ground-up bone.

"Tell what?" he asked.

"Tell my wife Ellie—if you can find her at the end of the war—that I still love her and . . . and . . . that . . ."

"Dan'l, Dan'l . . . You can't leave me," Jon pleaded.

"That an order . . . Sarge?"

"That's an order, Private."

"No. It's the end, Sarge." Walton reached toward his vest pocket.

"What you trying to do, Dan'l?"

"My vest pocket. Ouanga... Baka... in my pocket. Take it. I'm giving you my lucky talisman."

"You ain't goin' nowhere. You keep your own luck, friend."

Private Daniel Walton smiled, a peaceful smile, and he was suddenly a young man again. "You's my Sergeant. You's my ma—"

So ended the life of young Jon Shelby's best friend. Tears rose in his eyes as the weight of Walton's lifeless body grew heavy in his arms. He hugged Walton to his chest, then laid his head down softly on the ground. When he looked up, his eyes were red with fire. "You goddamned bastards, you're gonna pay for what you did to Dan'l!" He let out a loud yell that echoed through the valley.

Across the brown thickness of underbrush, a coyote rustled within its den, a prairie dog ran for cover, and a flock of quail fluttered at the call. The men still hiding out in the forest couldn't make out what it was they had heard. It was then that Jonathan Shelby vowed to kill the man who had killed Daniel Walton.

Chapter

Three

The blistery-hot and sultry sun dropped fast toward the edge of the world. The last few rays of golden light bounced boldly off the mighty Red River as a bullet sang dangerously through the trees, destined to kill. The ornery, menacing words of Wooly Samples accompanied the whining voice of his bullets as they rang through from the darkening thicket.

Hot lead from his Henry .44 rifle flew fast between his every syllable. "Might as well give up, fella. You think you're huntin' us, but we's huntin' you. Ain't but one a' you and a whole bunch a' us. We know where you are, and we'll come in and git ya. All we want is some victuals and that pack hoss a' yours. We'll have to take your shootin' irons a' course on general principle, ya understand."

Wooly snickered and continued his yapping as juice from a wad of tobacco oozed down the corners of his stinking mouth. "I just might let you live if you act right. Seems fair to me. I hate to shoot a man 'fore I see his face. I like to know who I'm killing, know what I mean? So you'd best come on out, boy, 'fore I lose my patience directly."

Guns, not words, kept law and order out on the trail, but words coming from a rifle-wielding, hidden-in-the-bushes cowboy meant trouble, especially when two of his shots damn near blew a man's ear off. As the sun melted into the pink-and-blue yonder, Jon Shelby crouched in the thicket and planned his attack. He calmly rolled a smoke for later, passing the time while he waited to kill the son of a bitch who was trying to kill him.

There had been eight outlaws altogether. He had killed

two, so there were six of them left to hunt down. The bastard who had murdered his best friend would be the one to die next. The rest of the outlaws could live. He'd leave them with the law in the nearest town for legal judgment.

There were lots of traits Jon hated in the white man, but he had to admit that on some levels they were to be commended. For one thing, whenever the Union Army occupied a Confederate town, it would run things smoothly until decisions could be made in Washington. Thank goodness for that, the Black man thought.

Some men could have let Dan'l's death go, but that was not Shelby's way. He was on the hunt now, and he would claim revenge as his own for the first time in his life. Revenge was a concept he had never before understood. No one understood it better than he did now.

Jon looked around him in a full circle and then gazed into the heavens in search of strength and God's help. In the year 1865, a Black man needed all the help he could get, from anywhere he could get it. And Jonathan Shelby needed help if he was to survive now.

Shelby was one of the best scouts ever born; he didn't know it, but it was a fact. And he had often been called the best darn scout under pressure in Civil War Louisiana. He tried to keep up with the white man's side of the issues of the day; by lifetime association, he made certain he understood the Black point of view. He often grew weary, even angry at times, when he felt his fellow Negroes paid too much attention to complaining and wasting time, rather than studying the enemy and his tactics for personal and community gain. It was Jon's curiosity that made him both a good scout and a good human being.

Inside his leather wallet folio, Jon had a newspaper clipping that explained the new Thirteenth Amendment to the Constitution. It was from one of Frederick Douglass's speeches made right after the Washington politicians voted in favor of the glorious amendment. The folks of one of his Northern partners had sent it to their son not too long ago, but the boy, who was just sixteen, gave it to Jon because he knew the Black man was a thinker, and most thinkers were politicians, especially many of the Blacks Jon's age. The Black man wished he could comfort himself with the words of the amendment now.

23

Grudgingly, the three or four broad beams of bright light still shining around the branches of a sturdy oak gave way to nighttime darkness. It was time to make his move.

An expert tracker and master of incognito weaponry, Jon checked and loaded his weapons and filled his pockets with spare rounds. Soon after joining the United States Federals down Louisiana way, he had learned to stock his belt and boots with hidden weaponry. He stashed his Remington new model Army .44 in his belt. The gun was a more accurate and sturdier weapon than similar percussion shooters made by Sammy Colt. The weapon was well balanced to suit his large hands, a must for deadly accuracy. But the Spencer seven-shot carbine, served by a spring-loaded clip in the stock, was his favorite. Once he'd settled for an 1860-model Henry—also a .44—but the well-worn Spencer had stolen his respect, and although it was old, Jon kept it clean and well oiled for times just like these.

Inside his left boot he felt the bulge of a Colt derringer, hidden for emergencies. Lightly rubbing his other ankle was the heel and guard of a razor-sharp bowie knife, fifteen inches long. It had saved his life on numerous occasions. Up his sleeve was a damn-near-new, straight-edge razor he used to scale and cut up fish, untangle blackberry vines, and chop off the heads of slimy green snakes. The last time he'd used the deadly blade was only days ago, to cut a noose from around an Indian's neck down in Natchitoches.

Though he was well armed, it appeared that he was not just the hunter, but the hunted as well. There were still six of the outlaws alive and bent on killing for survival. From the darkness, the angry, cut-throat leader, Wooly Samples, continued his taunts. "You got a death wish, boy. We's comin' in after you. Can't say I didn't give you fair warnin'."

The desperado gave the verbal signal, his men let go of a hail of flashing gunfire, and the pungent odor and foggy cloud of gunsmoke filled the air. Shelby felt the angry presence of one of the cowboys. Jake Moody, a yellow-haired boy out of Austin on the Colorado River, had Shelby in sight. Moody had killed his first man by shooting him in the back while he was swimming in a river. Since then, he felt a surge of power whenever he killed, like a

24

rattler squeezing a mouse to death until it was too darn dead to keep from being eaten. Moody suddenly changed his position, and Jon lost the sense of his enemy for the moment. But he smiled, knowing the outlaws who were gunning for his life lacked plain good sense. They had let the sun drop three fingers below the horizon before making their move, evening up the situation considerably.

Though the sergeant was unsure of the number of guns he faced, one thing was certain. The battle was less than one-sided now. The odds were in his corner. For on his sleeve were three golden striped V-bars, the distinguishing marks of sergeant in the United States Army. He felt proud each time his fingers touched the fabric. The provoked infantryman was convinced that his life would be spared. Somehow, he knew he would live through another battle. Hunted animals in the wilds learned early on to outwit the enemy. As a Black man and as a soldier, Shelby had learned a similar lesson.

Now he inched his way through the heavy underbrush, crawling on his belly as bullets raced through the trees. Some ricocheted several times, no doubt in search of a second chance at their mark. As he crawled, Jon determined that the men were inexperienced trackers. They talked too much, letting him know their precise locations.

There was a deep-throated grunt when he sneaked around a clump of undergrowth and clobbered one of the men with the butt of a Colt revolver he had confiscated during the stage robbery. He grabbed up a handful of the man's hair. It was cowboy Ace Wiggins, caught and snared.

But Wiggins wasn't the one who had killed Dan'l Walton, so Jon decided to let him live. He tucked Wiggins's Lefaucheux pistol behind him, between his belt and the small of his back. He tossed the varmint's Starr carbine breechloader into the thicket for later retrieval.

Hearing the man's groan, the outlaws whispered loudly to each other through the brush. "Ace. Ace! Why ain't you answerin' me . . . Jake?"

"Over here, Wooly," answered Jake Moody.

"Didn't I tell you not to call my name out loud? You let the whole danged world know who I am," hissed Samples.

"Sorry, Wooly. Didn't mean no harm—" Jake Moody's

25

sentence was cut short as a bullet flew through the woods and popped him between the eyes. Wooly's eyes were splashed with Moody's blood. He yelled and wiped his face and pushed Moody to the forest floor. Jon knew his bullet had hit something human, but he didn't know who had been hit. "A lucky shot—shore was—but it shore as hell did the trick," he whispered to himself.

What Jon Shelby didn't know was that he had just killed Dan'l Walton's murderer.

Another shot. Hot lead flew fast from the Spencer, and by now Jake Moody was deader than beef on the table. The Union sergeant ran silently between the trees, then stopped short. Manny James, one of the remaining outlaws, gave a startled yell that was muffled instantly. The eighteen-year-old son of a butcher man saw stars when a hot, ebony-brown arm wrapped around his neck and tightened like an iron vise. A sleep hold cut off his wind, and he almost passed out from lack of air. James didn't give up easily, so Jon bloodied his nose with a convincing left hook. He was unconscious as his feet and arms were bound with leather lash cord and his mouth was stuffed with dry mulch, bugs and all. Jon used the boy's own red bandanna to bind his mouth. It would keep the darn fool from bawling his head off in case he woke up too soon.

The oak trees swayed under the fingers of wind that blew sometimes hard, sometimes soft, through the early Texas dusk. But Wooly Samples heard a noise that was not the wind, and rather than suspect it could be his prey, he yelled out like a buffalo calf calls to its dead mother.

"Hey, Injun Wolf, you there?" said Samples.

"Here," whispered the Natchez Indian called Yelping Wolf, touching his boss's shoulder.

Wooly jumped. "Dammit, Injun, don't you sneak up behind me like that. I could'a blown your hot-damn fool head off."

"You're faster at talking than shooting, Samples. You are all mouth and no brains," answered Yelping Wolf.

"When we catch that boy out there and kill him, I'll show you how fast I am, Injun. I'll shoot them feathers from 'round your neck 'fore you can say Injun squaw."

"You would never survive as a Natchez, Samples. If I

were that man out there in the bushes, you would surely be dead."

"But you ain't him—so shut up. I'm in charge here. We got him pretty much licked now. You circle around and head toward town. Look up them boys I told you to—their names are on that list I gave you. Find them, then find us. You know where the meetin' place is," he snickered, "don't you, Injun dawg?"

"Call me out of my name one more time, Samples, and I swear I will kill you," the Indian replied as he disappeared into the moonlit night. Samples aimed his pistol at Yelping Wolf's fading back, cocked the hammer, then laughed and decided the red man would live—this time. But only because his services were needed.

Back inside the safety of the thicket, a sneaky grin spread across Sergeant Shelby's stubbly face. He knew the tables had turned and he, the hunted, was once again the hunter. Jon crept up close to another killer. The red-haired outlaw wheeled around and fired his Colt. The Union man jumped from the dark into the light of the rising moon, then back into the dark. Hank Parsons's first shot missed, and the second misfired. Shelby's bowie knife swished through the air into the man's chest. Parsons fell backward, his legs kicking spasmodically. In a moment, he was dead.

Wooly Samples heard the not-too-distant commotion and began to sweat like a freshly drunk man with time to waste. Suddenly it occurred to him that maybe he wasn't that great a leader after all. "Manny? What's wrong, boy? Manny? Shit. Damn fool done gone and got into trouble agin." Samples squinted through the dark woods toward where he had last seen the lone rider dismount before the sun went down on the other side of Texas. Suddenly he realized he could barely see his hand in front of his face. But he spoke his mind anyway. That was the Wooly way.

"Hey, fella, my patience done plum gone now. Say your prayers, boy, 'cause I'm a-gonna let you have it." He emptied the 1849 Colt's Navy he'd stolen from a man he'd killed on the same road Captain Marcy had taken in his eastern Texas travels between Toyah Grange on the Rio Pecos and Fort Belknap near the Brazos River. He continued his yapping, reloading his weapon, which was relatively accurate at twenty paces. "Gon git that boy if it takes

27

ever' bullet I got!" Wooly cussed. "Why ain't you talkin', boy? You's dead or sumpin'?"

The Negro soldier sitting in the bushes listened and smiled, saying to himself, you want me to talk, hombre? Listen to this. He fired rapidly into the thicket. Bullets flew past Wooly's head like mosquitoes near a summer pond. Hot metal singed the Texan's right ear.

"Wanna play rough, hey, fella?" whispered Samples, his milky sweat growing colder with each moment. He was scared, affected badly by his inexperience in fighting blind warfare. That was the bad part of the fight for Wooly Samples. But his fear would work to Jon's advantage.

The last shot had not come from in front of him, but from the side. It was time to change his plans, thought Samples. Another bullet whizzed by his head. It seemed to hover for a short spell before hitting the tree behind him. Samples yelled out, "Where you at, boy?"

Jon Shelby inched his way on his belly through the brush. He had located his next victim. Wooly was the name of one of the outlaws. He had heard someone say it earlier, and if Wooly turned out to be the leader, his throat would soon be cut. And if he was the varmint who'd killed Dan'l Walton, he would get shot at least once, maybe even twice, if his gizzard had the itch.

Suddenly Wooly smelled it—the metallic odor of fresh blood. The metal kissing his neck skin was from a sharp, killing knife, and the blood smell coating his flared nostrils was his own. He guessed a man never really got to smell fresh blood unless he was about to die. Of all the men he had killed, he had never scented the smell of death, if there was such a thing.

The white man's neck burned from the salty sweat running into the fresh wound carved by the knife of the man he should have caught and slaughtered long ago, as Jake Moody had slaughtered Dan'l Walton.

"It's prayin' time, cowboy," Jon said to Wooly Samples. "You move, you're dead!"

Chapter

Four

The Black man watched intently as a figure about a quarter mile in the distance sped away on his obedient roan stallion. He had to be one of Samples's men, the one Jon hadn't seen before now. There was something about the way the man looked in silhouette that was familiar, but he nixed the idea as poor eyesight in the dark. Now there was one less fool to tackle, he surmised, as he tensed and refocused on Samples's face.

"You's a ugly son of a hound dog, ain't you," said Jon. The blade of his bowie knife broke the skin, and blood brightly coated the steel along the edge. Sweat poured from Wooly's brow, his cheeks commenced to shaking, and his smart-alecky grin turned terrible.

"You . . . you wouldn't slit the throat of an unarmed man, would ya?" asked the pale, bony-faced, bubble-nosed outlaw.

Shelby eased his Colt from his boot. Now there was a knife at the killer's throat and a Colt's barrel up his nose. One slip and a squeeze, and Samples's life was history.

"Never killed an unarmed man in my life. Reckon there's always the first time," drawled Jon. He had purposely kept Samples from seeing his face. What Samples couldn't see would frighten him far more than what he could.

"I could put a bullet in each one of them bloodshot eyes of yours. Blood might shoot out too fast, though. Wouldn't want that. Then again, point-blank shots don't never miss the mark, neither. Of course, I wouldn't want to get even a speck of blood on my new vest here. I only wear it for killin yaps." Jon looked down and blew an invisible piece of lint off the watch pocket slit. "I paid a pretty penny for it down Louisiana way. Said ain't another one like it, excepting in New York, and that's two thousand miles away."

"You wouldn't kill me, would ya, friend?" interrupted Wooly. His voice was desperate.

"I ain't your friend, boy," snapped Jon, grinding his teeth. "I'm the worst enemy you've ever had. So, good-bye, boy. Good-bye!"

Shelby cocked his pistol, got a new grip on his man, and eased his face into Wooly Samples's view. Samples's bowels grew hot as he saw the man who was about to take his life. A crazed gleam of revenge shone in Shelby's eyes. Wooly's words broke as he spoke. For once in his ornery life, he didn't know what to say, especially to a Black man ready to kill.

"But, but . . . I ain't got a chance," Samples whispered, swallowing fast.

"You didn't give me no chance . . . nor my partner. I wish you were the one who killed Dan'l. I'd have a field day chopping you up, but you don't look like him."

"It waddn't me, nigger. It waddn't me," Samples protested.

"What did you call me, boy?" growled Jon.

"Nigger. That's what you is, ain't ya?" cried Wooly.

For a moment Jon was so angry, he couldn't think straight. He was quite sure by now that most whites thought the only word they could use to address a Negro was "nigger." This outlaw was probably calling him the only word he knew. It wasn't hard killing an intelligent bigot, but killing an ignorant bastard wasn't worth the time or trouble, since he figured he'd have to explain his earthly actions to God on Judgment Day.

"Which one of you killed Dan'l?" yelled the sergeant into the face of the quivering outlaw.

"I don't know, nigger. . . ."

Jon backhanded Wooly with the butt of his gun. "Don't call me that no more. Get it?" He hit Samples again. "Get it?"

"Yeah, I get it," murmured Wooly.

"Now where's that killer?"

Wooly feebly shook his head toward the dead man lying next to him.

"Jack Moody's your boy, nig—Uh, I seed him do it."

The dead desperado was lying on his face. Jon yanked him by the shoulder and turned him over. He recalled this man's mug and knew his job had been done. For a moment Shelby relaxed inside and sighed silently. The deed of revenge was completed. But with his next breath his anger rose again when he remembered the look in Dan'l's eyes when he died. Jon turned toward Samples with a look of murderous rage.

"Give me one good reason why I shouldn't slit your throat from ear to ear or blow another nostril inside your ugly face, or both, you dry-mouth son of a bitch." Jon paused a long time, the meanness making his face a horrible mask. Suddenly, without warning, he smiled like he had gone plumb loco. "You got no cause to worry, friend. This bowie's my huntin' knife," he said, easing the razor-sharp knife back into its sheath. Another, sharper blade slid down from inside his shirtsleeve. The straight-edge glistened as it slid into his hand. "This here's my throat-cuttin' knife!"

Wooly Samples panicked as the barrel of Shelby's Colt snaked its way up his over-size left nostril and a blade sawed across his neck. The sharp-edged metal was cold, and it blocked the flow of life-giving air to his pea-size brain.

"You shoot a white man, nigger, Texas Rangers go' hang you 'til you's dead, darkie," Wooly managed to gasp.

"Maybe so, peckerwood. But any man who thinks he's brave enough to put a bullet in this here body—color aside—deserves to suffer before he dies. And that means you!"

The cold, bloody-red edge of the blade tickled Wooly's throat. He gagged when the knife tore through the stubby beard again, and he feared it was headed toward the bone beneath the skin. Shelby gritted his teeth, slowly, precisely squeezing the trigger of the gun holding Wooly Samples's life in balance between life and death. The man holding the knife spoke his words clear and distinct, like a preacher in sermon on Sunday morning.

"Anyways, slime, I ain't seen no Rangers around these here parts since I arrived—ain't heard a' none, neither. The way I see it now, boy, your ass is all mine!!"

Chapter

Five

The aroma of hot coffee and sizzling bacon filled the clean, fresh morning air, one of the brightest days ever recorded in Texas. Shelby felt good about sparing the outlaws' lives. It also pleased him that Dan'l's death had been avenged indirectly and not in the terrible rage that had overcome him with Samples. Right action had prevailed in the end. The campsite near the Red River was home for the moment, and with the arrival of this beautiful morning, Shelby let himself feel a moment of peace. He had stayed awake all night, keeping an eye on his three prisoners and watching out for Samples's other man to return.

Jon surveyed the area with a slow wandering of his eyes. Fresh spring rains two nights before had given life to that which had seemed dead. Today the rains were gone and the skies were clear. Yet there were still thousands of pencil-thin tributaries trickling rapidly across the dry land toward the larger body of water. Still, the river of the people was navigable for light draft boats and sailing switches for as far as the eye could see.

Jon allowed his eyes to roam farther and higher. On the northern bank of the Red River he spotted the awesome silhouette of a man on a mighty stallion. Shelby assumed that the lone rider on the other side of the river had seen the smoke of his campfire or had at least gotten a good strong whiff of the salt-back he had not long ago cut, fried, and devoured. He wet his index finger and pointed it toward the blueing sky to measure the direction of the wind. About fifteen miles per hour, gusts near twenty, north by northwest.

The sergeant knew he could easily trick a regular cowboy and skedaddle, pure and simple, even with his prisoners. But if the rider were an experienced tracker or an Indian, their temporary home was a trap. He couldn't take a chance on staying put for too long.

After the dead killers were laid to rest, Shelby and his felons would hightail the camp and head toward the nearest Union occupied town. Jon had checked his maps and army papers again during the night and had determined to make for the town called Clarksville. There he would let the law handle these scoundrels in the proper way. But he knew that nothing in this land was a sure thing for long—not when Lady Luck was a river called Red.

"I still can't believe you's a nigga, no matter how many times I look at that black face a' yourn," snapped Wooly. Jon was quiet.

"Ain't you gon' share some of them victuals with the rest of us?" Samples asked as he vainly attempted to wipe sleep from his eyes with his shoulder. Shelby stared at him without a trace of emotion or respect.

"Can't you talk, boy? Anyhows, what's your name? I told you I'm Wooly Samples. My boys here is Manny James and Ace Wiggins. There's other fellas out there somewheres gon' git you. Why, I bet they're plannin' our rescue right now." Samples paused and snickered.

"Now me and my boys, we's a-might hungry. I get a taste ornery when I ain't had at least a tin of coffee first thing in the mornin'."

Ace Wiggins, his head bandaged up and dried blood all over his face, had a terrible time sitting up straight. "Big-time stagecoach robber Wooly Samples," he grumbled. "I should'a known better than to trust you. Now look at the fix we's in."

"Shut up. No matter what happened, Ace, I'll git us out if it's the last thing I do." Wooly spat angrily as if to prove he still had the power.

"It probably will be," groaned the bloody-mouthed Manny James. He hawked and spat greasy globs of viscous blood into the dust. "I'm awfully sick, Wooly. Feels like that damn nigga boy done scrambled up my innards like quails' eggs. I need a doctor sumpin' awful."

"Now you just close your mouth, Manny, 'fore I give you a fistful a' knuckle pie, ya hear!"

"You don't tell me to shut up. . . ." Manny lunged toward Wooly, and the two men went at each other like battling rams. Shelby watched the fools fight with their hands tied behind them, one hard head banging against another. He finally set his plate down, carefully finished chewing his food, and got up to stop the men from hurting themselves.

"You fools stop your bickerin'. Thought y'awl were partners. Might as well be enemies. Now straighten up. I could have killed the lot of you back there in the thicket, if I had a' wanted to."

"Damn, nigga," said Wooly, looking around and off into the forest. "We should'a been rescued by now. I wonder where Hank and the boys done gone to."

"Two of your boys died at the stage robbery, in case you didn't know. Buzzards takin' care of them, I reckon."

"Where's the other two you kilt last night, spooky?" asked Wooly.

"Over there." Shelby nodded his head toward a clearing nearby. "Next to them shovels."

"Shovels?" Samples squinted at his captor.

"Yup. Shovels you and your boys is goin' to use to put them six feet under. Now get up and get a move on. I ain't got all day to spend at two no-accounts' funerals, let alone three."

"I ain't diggin' no graves! Niggers 'spose to do what white folks says—darkies can't give a white man orders. Darkie's job diggin' graves, I say," snorted Wooly.

"Times changing," said Jon. "Pretty soon your kind be taking orders from Black folks . . . just like me!"

"I'll leave Texas first." Wooly growled his defiance.

"If you wasn't so 'tied up,' you could leave now," quipped Jon. He pulled out his pistol, cocked it, and pushed the barrel up under Samples's neck, where it hurt. "Convinced now that them boys need burying? Now get going or there'll be three graves instead of two!"

Shelby eased the trigger down and motioned with his head toward the figure of a man still patiently waiting on the riverbank. "That one of your men?" he asked Samples.

"Maybe it is." Samples paused and eyed Jon carefully. "And maybe it ain't."

"Your mouth's goin' to get you into a heap of trouble,

Samples," Shelby said, biting into a thick piece of fat-back bacon. He picked up his coffee cup. "I'll make another pot so you can have some when y'awl finish diggin' them graves."

"Can't work on an empty stomach," said Wooly.

"No work, no food. Get it, boy?"

"Ain't no darkie nigga boy gon' call me 'boy' too many times and git away with it! I'm a white man, and I deserves respect!"

"The man with the gun is the one who gets respect. I got the gun. You know the rest." Shelby smiled and sipped his last swallow of coffee. Always the best, he thought. "That means you do as *I* say or get shot. That's Shelby's rule number one."

"Let's do as he says, Wooly. Don't look like we got much choice," said Manny James.

"Yup. The sooner we starts, the sooner we'll git through," agreed Ace Wiggins as he staggered to his feet. Manny James helped him get steady, and each one waited calmly while Jon untied their bonds. Slowly they approached the dead men. One had a bloody wound in the chest from Shelby's knife—that was Hank Parsons. Jake Moody was the one with a hole the size of a fat man's thumb between his eyes. Moody was Dan'l's killer, but he was dead, and there was nothing else to do with a dead man except bury him six feet under.

"Gon' get you, dark boy, for killin' my men. Ain't fair, just ain't fair," Wooly grumbled.

"You call holdin' up that stagecoach, ambushing them drivers, killing six innocent people, including a boy and a pregnant woman, and stealing the lifelong savings of decent men and women fair, Samples? And what about those good, honest citizens you killed up in Fort Smith when you robbed that bank? If I's a lawman, I'd swear to see you hang by your neck 'til the buzzards pick your bones clean. I hate scum like you, Samples. The sooner the world is rid of varmints like you, the better off we'll all be."

"I ain't no bank robber, nigga," snapped Wooly.

Jon reached inside his saddlebag, pulled out a scroll, unrolled it, and showed it to Samples. The outlaw flinched. He knew what the paper would say. "This here Wanted poster I found in your saddlebag says you are!"

- Samples got quiet, and the men proceeded with the task at hand.

While his prisoners toiled, Jon took out a small folio filled with papers he'd collected over the past few years. He flipped through it briefly. One clipping in particular caught his eye. It was from the writings of Frederick Douglass, an old newspaper article about the Underground Railroad. It told of John Brown's efforts to free the Negroes in Kansas. Jon was glad there were men like Douglass, a Negro, and Brown, a white man, to carry on the cause of freedom.

The Black man was also honored that his middle name was that of Frederick Douglass himself. He wondered if a hundred years from now Black folks would remember names like Abraham Lincoln, author of the Emancipation Proclamation, and Dangerfield Newby, who fought to liberate the slaves. He wondered if they would remember Harper's Ferry in 1859, where John Brown met his match with federal and government troops, hung by the neck for what he believed in. Jon had always admired great men, and he felt that in his own way he was standing up for what he believed in. He would die if he had to, like John Brown, fighting for the cause of freedom.

Outlaws Wooly Samples, Ace Wiggins, and Manny James dug only shallow graves for their friends. Jon put away the folio and laughed when he saw their shabby work; he knew the animals would probably dig them up that night, and to a hungry coyote or a foraging wolf, the dead meat of a man was simply dead meat. The three remaining outlaws were too mean even to say a prayer over Jake Moody's and Hank Parsons's graves. Wooly made a grunting sound, and just that fast the funeral was over.

Watching their poor ritual, and then retying his prisoners, Shelby was left with a hollow feeling inside his craw. He had dug Dan'l's grave under the moonlight the night before and given final rights to his friend. His eyes watered when he thought about how abruptly a man's life comes to an end. He felt weak inside whenever he thought of Dan'l, and he would always think about his friend until the day he himself was laid to rest in the belly of God's fertile earth.

Shelby looked again into the rising sun, then over to

where the man and horse had been standing. He was gone. The forest was still; even the crickets and bullfrogs had stopped their yapping. The soldier's instinct told him that something was up. Only Indians moved so quickly, so quietly. . . .

Out of the forest came a yell. The first shot hit the coffeepot and bowled it over into the fire. The wetness on live coals hissed, and hot steam rose real fast. Shelby hit the ground, pulling Jake Moody's Joselyn from his belt. The outlaws, thank the Lord, were tied and as immobile as hogs on a log. It was plain to Jon that a rescue was in progress. One rider galloped through the camp at full speed. Shelby fired, and the man fell dead off his horse. Another attacker seemed to come out of nowhere, brandishing a sawed-off ten-gauge shotgun that made a heap of noise in the hollow where they were under attack.

"You gon' let us get slaughtered!" Wooly shouted to Jon.

"Be quiet or I'll shoot you myself!" Jon had lost all patience with these men. He could take a lot of pushing, Jon Shelby could, but when he finally got riled, he'd un-leash a driving fury that no one could stop. He had never really liked guns. Guns often made cowards look like men. He preferred hand-to-hand combat, where the winner could walk away satisfied and the loser could walk away alive. But as the bullets whizzed by his head, Jon assumed that since Texasland was such as it was, there was no walking away for both sides. Sometimes the good man won, and sometimes the good man got killed.

A bullet hit the ground near Shelby's head. He aimed his Henry rifle and fired twice. Two men fell from their horses. He peered through the dust and the smoke and saw the familiar roan stallion standing perfectly still in front of him. The rider was an Indian who motioned for his men, what few were left, to cease fire.

"Shelby! Jonathan Shelby. What brings you to be here?"

"Yelping Wolf. Was that you on the high hill over there?" said Jon, nodding toward the north side of the river.

"It was me," answered the Indian. "What are you doing with these outlaws?"

"They ambushed a stage, killed up a bunch of folks, and stole the strongbox. Did my pardner in."

"Which one did it?" asked Yelping Wolf.

"Jake Moody, they called him. He's over there under that shade tree."

"You got him," said the Indian, with a grin.

Jon smiled. "I got him."

Wooly laughed, suddenly convinced, although he was still tied up, that liberation was at hand. He yelled his words, talking too loud as usual for the occasion, but that was Wooly's way. "Well, there you is, boy. I know'd you's gon' show up eventually, Injun. Now untie us." He turned his body around so Yelping Wolf could cut the rope binding his hands. "Well, what you waitin' on, Injun! Shoot that nigga and git us outta this mess."

Yelping Wolf looked down at Samples from high atop the roan. The Natchez Indian was dark-skinned. His face was bold and attractive, and within his skull sat two of the deepest coal-black eyes that anyone ever wanted to see. He was a bold man, who sported an array of multicolored feathers hung proudly around his neck atop a loosely tied bandanna. His close-fitting breeches were of light brown suede, with tassles along the seams that dangled like pods from an early sporing mimosa tree.

Yelping Wolf was the only Native American in the bunch of hard-fisted men. His shoulders were broad, his arms muscular, his hands strong, and his chest stood high and mighty. A most powerful frame of young, strong bones lay poised beneath the skin white men haphazardly called "red."

Yelping Wolf sat perfectly still, while Samples made a fool of himself.

"What you waiting' on, Injun? Take that Yankee nigga's weapons and we'll divide up that loot and we can all go our separate ways."

Yelping Wolf turned and looked at Shelby again. "You need some help, brother?"

"I think I can manage," Shelby replied, removing his hat and wiping his brow with his shirtsleeve. He surveyed the outer horizon. "I'm takin' them into Clarksville up the road a few miles, where their debts'll be paid in full. Then I got to be on my way. Heading west, up the muddy Red.

I'll turn 'em over to the marshal. They's wanted, dead or alive! There's a reward on their heads for robbery and murder."

"Now you wait just a gall-durned minute. Ever since I's jes' a young feller, I ain't cotton to no law," Samples whined, almost singing his words to the Black sergeant. "Being it is that Injun dawg here is one a' my men, you'll have to take him in to the law, too, nigga Union man. I mean, it's only fair, don't you think, Injun dawg?"

"Is that the truth?" Shelby turned to Yelping Wolf with a quizzical look.

"I was with him, yes, but I did not have anything to do with killing innocent people. That was his doing. I never wanted any killing. I am not a violent man."

"Shore he ain't," Wooly laughed. "He was the lookout . . . and a piss-poor one at that. Never could trust no Injun when it came to pullin' off a job."

The Natchez Indian leaped off his horse and strode toward Samples. His jaws were tight with fury, his muscles flexed for a barehanded kill.

"What you gon' do, Injun? Remember who's boss. . . ." Samples's words were cut short when Yelping Wolf backhanded him. He grabbed Samples by the collar and began to beat him. Shelby grabbed the angry Indian and stopped him before Samples was dead.

"You'll kill him, Yelping Wolf. Now stop it! You's in enough trouble as it is."

"This man deserves to feel what he does to others." Yelping Wolf looked sickened.

"Stop it. And let's get the hell out of here," said Ace.

"You see, Manny? Didn't I tell you Injuns was no good? . . . Ace? Y'awl seen him. Guess you boys'll believe me now. Yellow Injun attacked an unarmed man with his hands tied behind his back." Samples grinned through his bruises.

"I could kill you any time, hands or no hands, Samples," said Yelping Wolf with a deadly calm in his voice.

Shelby looked toward the perimeter of the valley and spoke up, taking charge of the situation. "Ain't no need of fighting here. We'll head out directly and let the Clarksville law take care of this matter."

Wooly Samples was downright upset, peeved at his

treatment by a tall African man in blue and a two-faced red man in feathers and tassles. Blacks were tolerable as long as they stayed in their place, thought Wooly, but Indians were despicable—so bold, proud, and stubborn. Samples hated that. He had sworn to himself ever since his best friend died by the points and shafts of Apache arrows that he would kill every Indian in his sight. But he had soon learned that out on the range, having an Indian ally was smart business. If he could use an Indian or a Negro to further his cause and help him out of a ruckus, why not? A man needed no good reason to shoot an Indian or a Negro in 1865 Texas. If one got out of line, Samples could simply get rid of him.

But he had decided to wait until the time came to split up the money before taking care of Yelping Wolf for good. And the others, too. Thousands of dollars in gold and notes for four men meant an easy life for a brief spell, but it would set up one man for damn near his whole natural-born days. Providing he didn't live *too* long.

Yes, sometimes white men got in the way, too, thought Wooly angrily. Killing Manny and Ace in the process of becoming rich was worth the weight on his conscience. Hell, I ain't never had a conscience in the first place, Samples thought, so killing two men and an Injun would be easier than taking titty from a baby. "No ghosts would dare to haunt a man without a conscience," Wooly's pa, Avery, had said to him when he was just a snip. "But ghosts ain't alive, and the man who scares a ghost may soon be one himself!"

Maybe he would never fight and become a hero in the War Between the States like he had planned, taking the Medal of Honor home to his pa for icing on the cake, but Wooly surely expected to at least have enough loot to fix him and his old man for a normal lifetime. The "El Paso Kid"—Samples's own secret identity—lusted for fame and good times before heading west toward the setting sun. I owe it to myself, his second mind whispered from time to time. And I'm a-gonna have it, or my real name ain't Horace Lee.

Chapter

Six

Sergeant Shelby and Yelping Wolf looked at their prisoners with a mixture of pity and contempt. The Black man and the Amerian Indian were fighting the same fight. They were bound together by blood spilled and by the struggle for respect in the bloodstained changing world of 1865.

Back east the Civil War raged in all its final glory. Thousands upon thousands of men, both Black and white, had lost their lives in battle. Jon often thought about the rivers of Negro blood that had been spilled along the way to freedom. Sometimes it seemed to him that any number of individual deaths was worth the price of liberation for the generations to come.

His heart warmed when he thought of the African-American heroes such as Frederick Douglass, who spoke out boldly for the cause of freedom. His chest swelled with pride each time he thought of the physical courage and bravery of Negroes such as Captain P.B.S. Pinchback, and Major F. E. Dumas, who had led the Corps D'Afrique to many important victories. And each time he thought of these men, he was glad that he had joined up early in Louisiana instead of waiting for Black regiments to form in Tennessee, Kentucky, and Alabama. And even if he had to die, others would live to experience and enjoy the fruit of his labors. And his soul would bask in the glory of having been a part of the second great American war for freedom.

Shelby and his prisoners broke camp and headed out toward Clarksville, Texas. Samples, Wiggins, and James feared they'd be hanged if word of their bungled stagecoach robbery had leaked into the nearby town. Their hope for immediate freedom had dwindled when Yelping Wolf refused to set them free.

Though it was still early, the temperature out on the Texas plain had already hit the high seventies, and the sun's rays beat relentlessly upon the heads of the group. The men grew drier and drier as their slow crusade moved toward the outskirts of the Texas hot-hole called Clarksville.

"There's the town up ahead," said Sergeant Shelby to Yelping Wolf. "Reckon you'd better hold up here. Wouldn't want them to hurt you. After all, anytime I save a man's life, I expect him to live long enough to pay back the debt."

"I appreciate your saving me from that lynch mob down in Natchitoches. I'd have been dead if you had not come along when you did."

"You know I's joshin' about you owing me. I'd do it for any man I didn't have a gripe against." Shelby looked into the cold eyes of the Natchez. "Where're you heading?"

"I am not sure. But I am leaving these—these men. I have much to think about. Maybe the white man's world is not for me."

"What's wrong with staying with your own kind?" asked Jon.

"I left my people when I was just a boy. I was too young to know what I was doing."

"Home is always the best place to start looking for yourself," said Jon. "I wish to God sometimes that I could have lived in my native land. You can go back home if you want to, Yelping Wolf. It's not that easy for me.

"You be here when I come back through?" Shelby asked the Indian.

"I will be close, yes."

"Any partic'lar place?" asked Jon.

The Indian shook his head, tightened rein, whispered a word to the roan, and was off like the wind toward the nearest hollow. Soon he was lost to sight over the horizon. Shelby knew he would see him again.

The rays of the hot yellow sun shimmered as they seared the sandy earth, forming rings of visible heat that swayed before Jon's dry eyes. Sergeant Jonathan Frederick

Shelby was in the land of Texas—or Texasville, Texas City, Texasland—whatever a man chose to call this place.

Sergeant Shelby and his prisoners rode on slowly toward Clarksville. There was a proper method of traveling into small, out-of-the-way towns and Indian villages, and Jon Shelby knew it. He knew he was one of the best scouts partly because of his ability to talk with most friendly folk as well as with hostile strangers. And because of his social abilities, Shelby often became privy to information that remained carefully guarded from most. And this was essential because an army scout's job was vitally important to the strategy of all commanding officers. Not knowing beforehand the character of new terrain, places of ambush and good holes to hide out in, a regiment of fighting soldiers was helpless. A good scout obtained such information for his commanding officer, often merely by respecting an Indian's wish to be asked in friendship for permission to trod his land. Shelby learned the disadvantages of invasion and force, and by nature he respected the Indians' sacred grounds. In turn, an Indian was more inclined to listen to a Black man's word than to that of a white man. Jon rarely had trouble with hostile Native Americans. Blacks and Indians shared a similar, tragic cause in this land of freedom.

It was amazing to Shelby that deep within the bowels of Southern racial hatred, his skin color could afford him passage where no white man could go and live to tell about it. Unbelievable as it was, there had been times when he had changed into civilian clothes, and after having told Rebel scouts that he was on an errand for a Confederate general, they had let him through their lines undeterred. In this way, he had been able to spy on the enemy operation for the U.S. Army and gain valuable intelligence for Brigadier General Williams.

In spite of racial prejudice, Jon thanked God that he was a Negro and not something else. Brown skin's better than light skin anydays, he often told himself with a laugh. Brown skin don't show dirt nearly as fast as light skin does!

Manny James and Ace Wiggins were both wondering why they had let a fool lead them to the gallows. Only God could know the answer. But Wooly Samples, scrambled brains and all, had always had the knack for pulling off a job and getting away with the loot. He was the man to have on your side when a caper was being planned. How could they have known they'd be caught—and by a Black man at that! The two desperadoes grew tense when they saw the town of Clarksville in the distance. They knew their lives were worth less than a dead dog's bones.

"I doggie, Ace. Will ye look a-there, we's almost in town," said Manny James to his partner. "Let's see you get us outta *this*, boss man Wooly!"

Jon listened to the outlaws yapping, but their words were of no concern to him. He thought of Dan'l Walton and how he had left him so far behind, deep in that cold, wet grave. He once thought he could shake the hollow feeling that comes with loss, but he had learned the hard way that love and devotion could mean much more to a man than a cold drink on a hot day, and when they're yanked away so sudden and cruel, even a good man might start to wonder what God was all about.

When Dan'l died in Shelby's arms, he vowed to himself that the men who shot him would pay with their own lives. Now Jake Moody, Dan'l's killer, was dead. Jon had one more task before the ordeal could end: to deliver the Samples gang to the Clarksville marshal.

Shelby was glad that Clarksville, Texas, was under the control of the Union Army. Without his white friends in blue, he could never take white men to justice, and he would have to let the hombres go free to wreak havoc on more innocent people. He turned to look at the wanted men again. He wanted to hate Wooly Samples, but somehow he just could no longer muster the energy.

Thick, yellow beads of sweat popped up on Wooly Samples's forehead, but since his hands were tied behind his back, he couldn't wipe them away. The sun's rays were fierce and relentless. It's bright, white light punished those who refused to seek shade. Only those creatures that moved out of its way deserved to live, and those who sat still too long got cooked alike.

"Y'awl think I'm a-scared ta be hung!" screamed Wooly. He was wetter with sweat than a fly in a bowl of soup. "Well, I ain't. A man ain't afraid to die, and I'm a man, I tell you! Why, I'm more man than the two of you put together. I'm more man than *fifty* of them no-account niggas."

"Betcha wish you'd never robbed that bank and that stage, don't you, Samples?" Shelby grinned, rubbing the end of a dogwood twig across his teeth to keep them clean and white. "Keep yourself clean, boy, ya hear?" his grandmother Mara had told young Jon. "Be jes' as raggedy as you please, but as long as I'm alive ain't nun a' my kinfolks stinkin' none. White folks gots too much soap for niggras to be stinkin' like sum ov 'em do!" Looking at Wooly, Jon wished the outlaw had met up with his grandma Mara.

"You really think they'll hang us?" asked Manny James.

"They might have been more forgiving if you hadn't robbed that stage over yonder at the pass."

"Ah, they ain't heard about that yet," Wooly grinned.

"Good news travels slow, Samples. Bad news spreads like wildfire. Ten to one them folks in that town we's ridin' into done heard. And if they ain't, I'm a-making sure they do!"

"Trial!" yelled Wooly. "Trial, trial! Can't hang a man without a trial."

"I'd say my prayers, if I's you, boy," answered Jon with a sober nod.

"You's thinking about 'darkie hangin's,' boy. Only nigga toes like you get hung without a trial."

"Trial's mighty swift around here, I hear tell," said Manny.

"Yup, Wooly," added Ace Wiggins as the men drew closer to the first building in the town of Clarksville. "You might see your Maker 'fore the sun goes down."

The first structure Jon Shelby and his prisoners saw was the Baptist church of Clarksville, on the right-hand side of Main Street. The nameless town barn sat on the left side of the street beside a large community smokehouse, which was busy smoking up fresh ground pork sausage, lean shoulder hams, and whatever else the folks of Clarksville decided to put inside for some curing and worm killing.

Jon noticed that businesses in Clarksville, a small but well-developed horse town, appeared to thrive. There was

45

McKinney's General Store, Flatt's Haberdashery and Dry Goods, the telegraph office, and Bonham's Feed Store. Unfortunately, Bonham's was often empty of grain supplies due to robberies out on the trail. These places of commerce were located between two buildings of lesser respect: the Lazy Day Saloon, a gambling squat and house of ill repute, and the Clarksville jailhouse. Within spitting distance was the bank, and at the far end of Main Street Jon spotted a newly constructed hanging post. A crowd stood around its towers, witnessing with obvious relish the local law's brand of revenge. In the dangerous and uncertain scheme of life in Texasland, Clarksville, like so many other western towns, was no place to lay one's head too long.

Several other smaller sheds and storehouses were peppered along the dusty Main Street. Some of the stores had names posted, and others were as nondescript as a sack of dried-out beans.

The crowd of Clarksvillians gathered around the gallows began to disperse, and the cries of the hanged men's kin echoed down the far reaches of Main Street. Wooly heard the cries and knew there'd be no one to mourn his own passing. His death would be entertainment on an otherwise dull day. Samples searched his little mind for a way to bribe Sergeant Shelby into letting him and his gang go free. First he had to get on the Black man's good side. Impressing another white man wasn't so hard, thought Wooly. All he had to do was talk bad about darkies, but he couldn't do that with a darkie. He figured the best way was to be straight and honest and to forget about tact and delicacy. Hell, he had none of those things anyway.

"How much you want, nigga? Just name your price and you'll have it. You darkies used to bein' sold. All y'awl can be bought—for a price, that is."

Jon eased his horse over toward Wooly and backhanded him as hard as he could. The outlaw fell hard from his horse. Jon jumped down off the roan and yanked Samples up by the collar.

"The name is Shelby to you, fool. You want to talk, you call me by my name, or you'll keep falling off that horse until you's dead. Get it?"

Coughing and sniffing up snot stringing from his nose, down over his thick, parched lips, Wooly finally caught his breath and tried to talk sense to the dark-skinned man, but it didn't seem to work. He still couldn't figure out what else to call a nigga, except . . . well, a nigga!

"I got lots of loot, boy . . . ah, Shelby, nigga. I can't spend all a' that loot by myself. A piece of the pie is yours, if you let us go. There'll be no bloodshed, no jail . . . and no hangin'. What you say, darkie Shelby? We got a deal?"

"Too late, Samples," said Shelby. He was disgusted by this man's lack of pride. "That looks like the law and a posse comin' now, at full steam. Word does travel fast about bank robberies, stagecoach holdups, and killing innocent people. I suspect they done already had your trial, white man. That just might be the Clarksville marshal coming to carry out the sentence before the hangin' rope gets cold."

A group of men rode slowly up the street toward Shelby and his prisoners. When they were close enough to speak without shouting, the leader tugged rein and tipped his hat at the motley crew.

"Howdy, strangers," said the lead man.

"Howdy. The name is Shelby. Sergeant Jonathan Frederick Shelby, Company C, Fifteenth Regiment of the Ninety-ninth U.S. Colored Troops, Corps D'Afrique, Louisiana Division. At your service, sir."

"I ain't never heard them many names spoke all at once before. Ain't never seen no darkie, colored soldier in a uniform before, neither. A nigger sergeant . . ." The man laughed as he pulled off his hat and wiped sweat from his brow with his arm. "You 'spect me to believe that, boy?"

"I'm a man of my word, sir, and I know you respects the current Union authority in this here town. And you be who, sir?" asked Shelby.

"Richards the name. Marshal Cotton Richards. I'm the law in these here parts. Thank you kindly. What can I do for you?" Richards paused and rubbed his face. "Sergeant."

Shelby unrolled the Wanted poster and handed it to Cotton Richards. "I hear there's a warrant out for these here men for robbing a bank up near Fort Smith. They killed some bank folk there and ambushed a stagecoach several hundred miles up in Indian territory, too."

"Where'd you find 'em?" asked Cotton Richards.

"They robbed a stage and killed up a bunch a' folks not too far from here, Marshal. Took no prisoners. Killed my pardner in the process."

"So y'awl the cutthroats that shot the district sheriff's youngest gal! Wasn't she the one expectin' his first grand-baby boy?" asked Cotton.

"You heard?" said Jon.

"I heard," said the clean-shaven marshal to the sergeant. He spit into the dust, squinting his eyes while he looked over the men. "You boys do that?"

"I didn't know she's important! If I'd a' known she's somebody important," said Wooly, "we wouldn't a' kilt her. Coulda kilt somebody that waddn't important, I reckon."

Richards turned back to Shelby. "I ain't never seen no colored sergeant before. Shore ain't never seen three white men bein' brought to justice by no Black man in Texas."

"Things a-changin' here in the South, Marshal."

"Texas just ain't your typical Southern territory, son. Some folks say it's better to be wrong sometimes in Texas, if you can back it up, than to be right and abiding by the law anywheres else."

"Some folks say a lot of things that ain't right," Jon replied. "And that ain't wrong, right, Marshal?"

Cotton Richards frowned and scratched under his arms. He didn't look dirty to Jon, and no strange odors had leaked from under his garments. He was a strong-looking man, not too large and not scruffy, either. His brown hair was well trimmed, his face was unworn, and his square jaw gave him possibilities. His shoulders were narrow, but he could hold his own in a fight. He grinned out of the corner of his mouth when he figured out what Jon had said. He knew it was time to change the subject.

"You still ain't told me what you need. I'd be much obliged if you did, 'cause the sooner you tells me, the sooner you can git outta town!"

"You can lock these men up, see that they get a trial, if you got someplace to put 'em."

"We got a jail—least, that's what we Clarksvillians like to call it. It's good enough to hold them that's done wrong, been known to delay those who think they done right. But if you take my advice, you'll get outta town 'fore the sun hits high noon. Cemetery's already filled to the brim. Ain't got no room for no outsiders in Clarksville."

Suddenly the crackle of a gun blast echoed through the shallow valley that held the town of Clarksville. Jon instinctively flinched, expecting a barrage of cannonfire. But he realized that his reaction came from the shell shock he experienced ever since the battle at Vicksburg. His olfactory senses even manufactured a false smell of gunpowder and steaming-hot, mutilated flesh. That was a smell Jon Shelby sought to forget, but mere talk of the War Between the States brought memories of death ever fresher into his world. He had witnessed firsthand the exploding mass of a man who a second before had shared a smoke with him, their lips drawing on the same short butt. Sometimes the explosions bounced from side to side within the walls of his skull. Jon hoped that one day they would end, but somehow he knew it would take a long, long time to forget. For now, he tried to refocus on the marshal and his men.

Riding straight down the middle of Main Street, Imus Wixey drove his black buggy up beside the men standing like fools under the hot sun. Some folks called Wixey "Reverend," since he preached on Sundays at the local church, but most folks called him "the Funeral Man." Wixey was head undertaker in a town that really needed two. The only ones who didn't call Imus anything were already six feet under.

Wixey looked closely at Sergeant Shelby, Marshal Richards, and the rest of the strangers, and seemed to perk up for a moment. He knew the war was still going on, and when he saw the uniform upon the body of the African, he knew that for a time to come there'd still be a great demand for his services.

Three coffins filled with the remains of hanged outlaws were in the back of Wixey's wagon. He went around to the wagon and opened the wooden caskets. The burly varmints were sprawled out in most uncomfortable fashion, laid to rest in cheap pine boxes, compliments of the grand state of Texas.

"What'd them dead men do, Marshal?" asked Wooly Samples, swallowing thickly.

"We suspect they burned several houses tryin' to hide

49

their murderin', stealin' ways. Then again, they may have been innocent," answered Marshal Richards. "Hell, we couldn't think of nuthin' else to do with them, so we hanged 'em to make room in the jail. But since they were the only strangers in town, and most strangers in Clarksville get shot or hanged, it musta been them who committed the crime, I reckon. Anyways, whether we's wrong or not, three women in town just had baby boys, so we lost three no-gooders and gained three more young-uns. Guess it all evens out in the end."

"Suspect!" yelled Wooly. "Suspect? Suspect they did it! When you hang a man, seems to me you oughta know fer sure if he's guilty or not. And what about the judge? Where's the got-damned judge?"

"Judge!" Richards laughed. "Ain't seen no judge round these here parts in quite some time."

"You can't take the law into your own hands like that, Marshal," said Wooly. "Ya jes' can't . . . can ye?"

"Reckon we can, 'cause we did. Ain't no judge been round these parts since we hung Judge Dennison McKay for makin' hay with Bingham Farley's youngest gal, Kathryn. Such a pretty white gal, she was."

"You hung the judge!" cried Wooly.

"Yup. Money and land calls the shots round here. You got money or land, and you got power in Texas. Only then you get the benefit of the doubt. Old man Farley had all three. If you's broke, why, you hang 'fore the mornin' comes!"

Shelby opened his mouth to speak, but Marshal Richards pulled his Colt's Navy, cocked it, and pointed it at the sergeant's face. And in rapid succession, at least a dozen rifles cocked and took aim at the African's middle.

"Been nice talkin' to ya boys," said Richards. "Hope y'awl can come back someday under more sociable circumstances."

Wooly blurted out some cheap words, as he usually did when he was scared. "Lotta money gon' go to waste if we die, Marshal. It's out there in the woods somewheres. This here smart-ass nigga man in blue didn't know where to look. Be mighty pleased to share it with you . . . ah, your purty little town, Marshal, bein' me and my men might not live long enough to use it."

"I said git or else I'm liable to fire this here pistol. Last man I shot between the eyes didn't feel a thing until he hit the ground, colder'n yestiddy's hambone."

"How'd you know he didn't feel nuthin' 'til he hit the ground?" inquired Wooly.

"'Cause when I blew in his ear, he jes' laid there, starin' into space," said Richards, laughing at his own joke like a man with nothing better to do. He looked around, and suddenly all of his men laughed, too. The joke had obviously passed them by, but it was clear that those who laughed at Richards's jokes kept their jobs and the ones who didn't got fired. "Now if you don't turn around, I can't promise you'll be that lucky.

"Anyways, folks hear the shots, they'll hang ever' stranger in town 'til they find the guilty party." Marshal Richards paused and smiled wide, inching the pistol toward Shelby's head in point-blank range. "And y'awl boys is real strange!"

Chapter

Seven

Wish he wouldn't hold that gun so close to my hide, Sergeant Shelby thought. Guns had been known to go off at the strangest of times, and too often a Negro was in the line of fire. His life was on the line now, and that was the first priority at the moment. He hadn't needed the Union teachings about war to tell him how to recognize danger. Survive at all costs was a commanding officer's unwritten creed. But make certain your men are safe. If *they* die, all is surely lost.

Marshal Cotton Richards's demeanor suggested a man of principles. But whether those principles included sparing the life of a Black man in blue was anybody's guess. And the Union soldier didn't care for guessing at a time like this, when his enemy was about to pull the trigger. The dedicated sergeant had, above all, a mission to carry out, and a bullet inside his brain would slow things down considerably. Shelby desperately needed time to get a bath, a bottle, and some sleep. Soft-soaping Marshal Richards was the best way to accomplish this task; otherwise he would have to make the run to Red River Station on empty, not a good way to complete the last leg of an important mission. And what if he had to take his prisoners along, or worse, set them free? Many a dangerous man was tamed by having his ego soothed with flattery, and Richards was a prime candidate for this sort of calming down. The Union soldier began his slick talk pronto. His gift of gab would save the day—he hoped.

"I'm sure glad to know you run this fine-lookin' town with an iron fist, Marshal. In fact, these here outlaws

52

would probably escape a less secure town lawman, don't you think?"

"Sweet-talk won't do you no good, boy. I've heard enough a' that to fill up a good-sized cistern, I reckon," answered the marshal with a wave of his hand. "Your words don't mean a good cuss to me."

Jon wasn't deterred. "Bein' that the Union Army done took over this town and left you sole authority over the civilians in these here parts, why, it's plain to me that you's a man to be reckoned with. I'll even bet a six-foot spit the good folks of Clarksville be mighty proud of their marshal if he had these criminals behind bars."

Wooly sat up straight on his mount. The sun was baking what brain he had left to a pulp. "I ain't no criminal, nigga! I jes' ain't, I tell ya!"

Shelby continued to speak, stopping only for a second to frown at Wooly Samples. "As I was saying, Marshal, if I have to move on to another town in my worn-down state of alertness, these killers might just figure a way to jump me and hightail it off and do some more killing and robbing. They might even come back to this prosperous town of Clarksville, knock off your bank, kill a citizen or two, then go gunning for the lawman. Why, Marshal Richards, that'd be a crying shame, wouldn't it? I mean, a peaceful little well-marshaled town like Clarksville deserves to stay peaceful, don't you say, Marshal, sir?"

"Stop beatin' round the bush, boy. I never did like niggras who talked too much. Say what you gotta say and be done with it," said Richards, easing the hammer in on his Colt.

Shelby grinned like a man who had just snared a prize mammy bobcat. He knew he would soon have Richards eating out of the bowl of his hat. "I'm trying to put these men somewhere safe, so I can get a bottle a' whiskey, a bath, and some shut-eye. I been up all night watching these varmints, to see that they didn't escape. I'm plumb tuckered out, Marshal Richards. Surely you been in my shoes before. I mean, upholding the law in this fine town is mighty tough, even on a good strong lawman like yourself. District sheriff be mighty obliged to you if you brung in his little gal's killer . . . and she expectin' and all."

Marshal Cotton Richards, an ambitious man in his

mind, bought the sergeant's talk and decided to cooperate for a spell. He knew, too, that if this dark man was indeed a soldier of the Union Army, he had the power to call on the Union Yankee headquarters in town for assistance. Rather than embarrass himself in front of the Union men and the townsfolk, who looked up to a man with a badge, he decided to back down, if only to save face and hold on to what little power he still retained. Richards didn't want the world of Clarksville to know that he had taken the marshal's job practically under the gun after the banker Hamilton Featherstone threatened to call in his loan if he didn't pay up. He needed this job to pay back the loan, and then he could hightail it out of Clarksville and head north to Montana or west to California.

"We do try to keep law and order in Clarksville, soldier. Maybe I been a little hasty, darkie ... Sergeant. Sure. Come on into town. It ain't much, but you kin git what you want at a decent price, I reckon. And you kin even git outta town just as fast as you come in. Get my drift?"

Before Shelby could answer, a small man on horseback galloped toward the band of men clustered in the middle of Main Street. The man didn't start reining his horse until he was almost on top of them, and for a minute Jon thought he'd ride right over them all. The man called Marshal Richards bellowed at the top of his lungs. The distraction was perfectly timed.

"What's the trouble, Fats?" asked Marshal Richards, pushing his Colt back inside his new leather holster.

"It's Jipson Tandy agin, Marshal. Drunken devil's been shootin' all the *O*'s and naughts outta signs all over town, he has. Knicked old Pete Freeman's kid's arm. Poor little fella, but he's all right, though. Doc O'Reagan patchin' up the boy right now."

"Well, why didn't you *stop* Tandy?" Richards asked impatiently.

"I tried! He even took a shot at me. Musta thought I looked like a naught, 'cause I shore don't look like no *O*, but I guess there ain't too much difference 'tween a naught and an *O*. Then again ..."

"Shut up that yappin', Fats! What'd you do when he shot at ya?"

"I came to git you." Fats replied matter-of-factly.

"Why didn't you stay and fight?"

"I ran outta bullets, Cotton."

"Why didn't you go git some more?"

"He's 'tween me and the jailhouse."

"I thought you wanted to be marshal one of these days, Fats," said Richards. A disgusted, embarrassed look clouded his face.

"You knows I do, Cotton. You knows I do."

"You can't be a good marshal and run from trouble!"

"The way I see it, Cotton, it's better to be a live deputy than a dead would-be marshal. As quiet as it's kept, I ain't as stupid as I look. Ands I ain't gittin' shot by no lazy drunk in a two-bit town on the edge of nowheres for nobody, unlessin' I was marshal."

"What's bein' marshal got to do with it?" asked Richards with a suspicious squint.

"Marshal gits shot and the whole town calls him a hero. Deputy gits shot, they say he's no-account."

Shelby muffled a grin as Richards wiped his face with the bandanna around his neck. The marshal shook his head and looked as disgusted as a fly stuck in sorghum molasses.

"Fats, this here colored fella says he's a sergeant for the Yankee army. This here's my . . . ah, deputy, Fats Griffin. These here strangers are bank robbers and killers. They's wanted up in Indian territory, here in Texas, too. See that these men git locked up. Show him"—Richards pointed to Shelby—"where everything is in town. He'll be stayin' the night, then movin' on by, say, high noon tomorry. Right, Sergeant?"

"Sumpin' like that. I got business to attend to."

"Come to think of it, Fats, I ain't heard no shots in town. Only noise I heard was that dynamitin' and blasting outside of town," said Richards.

"Tandy ain't plumb stupid. Every time he heard 'em blasting, he commenced to firing his pistol. Reckon old Jipson's smarter'n you thinks, say, Cotton?"

"Shut up, Fats, and follow orders. Now where the hell was Tandy when you last saw him?"

"Still shootin' the O's and naughts out of ever' sign he could see. He was reloading outside Whipple's Shoesmithin'. Ain't too many O's in Whipple's sign—'ceptin the *O* in Shoesmithin'. Don't take too long to shoot one *O* out. No tellin' where he done gone to now. Probably 'sleep somewhere's, I reckon. That's the way I always end up after a drunk."

Marshal Richards looked plainly disgusted. "Excuse me while I do some lawmakin'," he said to Jon, remounting his contrary Appaloosa. Shelby never did like those horses. Too ornery. All of those bloodlines mixed up in one animal kept both horse and rider in a frenzy most of the time. He had to admit, though, Dan'l Walton's Appaloosa had been a dandy, almost as smart as Easel, that's why he brought him along to Clarksville.

Richards yanked rein and kicked some spur into the animal. Horse and rider spun around several times, and Richards cussed out loud. Then, hitting the wind like a bolt of lightning, they were away in search of Jipson Tandy.

"I ain't never seen no military man who was a nig—" began Fats.

"I know, I know," said Shelby. "But you's seeing one now, Deputy. So, can we get going 'fore I pass out in this here hot sun?"

"Follow me, boys!" said Deputy Fats Griffin. "Bank robbers, huh? Killers, too. I doggie, you boys jes' in time. Hangin' rope's mighty empty without a neck in it."

"What you mean?" snapped Wooly.

"Well, fella. We wore our other hangin' platform plumb out, 'cause we only had room for one lynchin' at a time. But hangin' became so pop'lar all of a sudden with the district judge 'fore he got offed himself—God rest his soul!—we decided to build us a brand-new hangin' tree. Judge hisself ordered us to do it, shortly 'afore he died.

"We almost hung a woman not too long ago, but old Campy Weems's boy, Collier, decided to marry her up to keep her alive. Hear tell old Mary K. Court beats him up pretty near ever' night. Well, anyway, to git back to what I's sayin'. Yup, we got us a brand-new toy that guarantees the peace in Clarksville. And this time we's got enough ropes to hang half-a-dozen men at the same time."

"Y'awl must do a lot of hangin' around Clarksville," Shelby commented dryly.

"Shore do. Why, for a spell there"—Fats laughed —"seemed like ever' stranger come through town did sumpin' wrong. Had to hang the lot of 'em, one by one, 'til they's all sent to their Makers."

"We's innocent 'til proven guilty!" Samples cried.

"Last time we hanged an innocent stranger before was when the Yankees come to town. We'd a' hung them, too, iff'n they hadn't been the current authority, like they is now. Don't mean no harm, Union man." Fats gave his balding head a quick bow in Shelby's direction.

Jon looked at the three men he had brought to justice. Yes, all three were guilty of trying to shoot him dead, but all men deserved the right to speak on their own behalf in a court of law.

Sergeant Shelby was weary. Although he had never felt faint in his life, he did so right now. A cold drink of water would quench his thirst, a swig of whiskey might bring him back to life. He hoped the cordial deputy would stay that way. He badly needed to rest, to get some shut-eye soon.

"Well, boys," said Deputy Fats, "might as well get a move on. Word spreads fast when strangers are in town. By the time we gets you boys settled in, folks gon' wanna know who y'awl be. And when I tell 'em 'bout tomorry, they'll be mighty pleased. Right now, though, the safest place for y'awl's in jail. Clarksville folk been known to take the law into their own hands while the law stood by and watched."

"What's happenin' tomorrow, Deputy?" asked Wiggins.

"Plain as day to me. You see, our populace been used to peace and quiet. They hates gossip and danger. And you boys create a whole lot a' gossip." Deputy Fats Griffin pulled off his hat, wiped the sweat from his forehead with his cotton shirtsleeve, and pointed toward the crest of the far hill where Imus Wixey was digging graves. "By this time tomorrow, maybe sooner"—Fats paused to snigger—"you boys gon' be deader than pork chops on the table. Lonesome Hill gon' be your new home."

Chapter

Eight

Several young boys were noisily playing gunslingers outside the Clarksville jail as Deputy Fats, Jon, and their prisoners approached. A thick-boarded structure of oak with one window on either side of the heavy, rough plank door, the jail was the newest structure in the bustling township, but it had already housed its share of killers.

Jonathan Shelby was surprised at the number of Negroes he saw in the town. There was a peppering of Black faces all throughout the crowd. Some of them looked worn, as if slavery had taken the best years of their lives, while others were smooth and proud. Jon wondered how many of them were slaves and how many were too scared to be free.

The riders dismounted their horses, and Deputy Fats led them inside the jailhouse, ushering Samples, Wiggins, and James into cells on the far side of the largest room that served ably as the lockup's front office. When the deputy finally got Samples to give him his name, there were snickers from his buddies.

"Y'awl laughing at my name?" growled Wooly Samples. Manny James and Ace Wiggins replied in unison:

"Yup. Shore does look like it, don't it."

"Everybody got a first name," Wooly snapped.

"Horace Lee ain't much of a name, Wooly. Ain't fit to be a stagecoach robber's name, neither," said Manny James. They laughed, trying to ease the tension of a morbid situation.

"If yore name is Horace Lee, then where'd you git a name like Wooly?" asked Deputy Fats, muffling a snicker.

"None a' yore dang bidness."

"See them chaps he got on," said Ace Wiggins.

"Them's woolies, Deputy Marshal. Seems our 'leader' here wears 'em year round, even when it's a hunnard degrees in the desert. Ain't never figured out why a sensible man'd torture himself like that. Wool chaps is for the wintertime. Just don't seem fair to his body. Anyhows, that's how he gots the name Wooly, I reckon."

Though Sergeant Jon Shelby had delivered his prisoners to the Clarksville jail, somehow he still didn't feel that justice had been fully served or that Dan'l Walton's untimely death had yet been fully avenged. Shelby would feel at peace with himself for a moment, but when he closed his eyes Jake Moody's face continued to haunt him. He wished he could have met the Moody fellow on the battlefield, where he would have had the license to kill him face to face. He tried to toss the uncomfortable feelings behind him, but he knew it would take time to get over the death of Dan'l Walton. He guessed such a big loss took a long, long time to heal—more time than he could spare right now.

The Black man washed his face in the cold water provided by the gracious Fats Griffin. He felt somewhat better, and as he wiped his face with the rough towel, he eyed a bunch of moldy Wanted posters. The placards had evidently arrived long ago, but Richards had seemingly failed to check their contents. A good lawman always reads his dispatches, but maybe Cotton Richards was a piss-poor manager instead of a "man to be reckoned with," as Shelby had so tactfully put the phrase earlier that day.

By the time Shelby's shuffling hand got around to one particular Wanted poster, it was suddenly yanked out of his hand by Deputy Fats. Jon barely got a look at the wanted man's face. All he had seen was the grainy likeness of a heavily bearded man in Confederate duds. His name was Monte Devlin. But it was the look in the criminal's eyes that Sergeant Shelby would never forget, that stood out clear from the otherwise fuzzy picture.

"This is law bidness, bluebelly. If we'd a' wanted you to see these posters, we'd a' hung 'em up somewheres in public."

"Didn't mean no harm, Deputy. What'd that fella on that placard do, rob a bank or something?" asked Jon.

"Nope. Say he shot his commanding officers in Wilmington, down on the Cape Fear River at Fort Fisher. Then he hightailed it west to escape a court-martial and hanging to seek his fortune. Says so on the outside of the roll. We didn't have to open it all of the way to tell that. I've talked too durn much anyhows," said Fats. "You interested for some reason in particular?"

"Nope," Shelby answered honestly. He didn't know at the time that the more he knew about this man, the better it would be for him. Shelby hadn't fully learned that being extra inquisitive kept his mind active and afforded him an edge when tangible surroundings became intangible. "Tell you what I am interested in—getting these horses some oats, shod, and a rubdown. Got a livery, ain't you?"

"Down Main Street a ways, past the Lazy Day Saloon on the other side of the street. Walk west. Ya can't miss it. It's on your right."

"Thanks for the cooperation, Deputy Griffin. It's mighty appreciated," said Jon.

"I like you, soldier. As for your affiliation, why, it can go to hell. Folks around town calls me Fats, Sergeant. Some call me Deputy Fats—all depends, I 'spect, on how respectable they's feeling at the time they calls my name."

"Any trouble, Fats, I'll be at the nearest sleeping place. You do have a hotel, don't you?"

"Chelsea—down the street a piece," said Fats, never once thinking that the African wasn't at all like the other strangers that came to Clarksville looking for a good time and a bottle to while away the lonely Texas night.

"Thanks," Shelby said.

"Best rotgut in town at the Lazy Day, too, soldier. What'd you say your name was agin?"

"I didn't. But to a friend, it's Shelby." He tipped his hat. "Jonathan Shelby."

Shelby walked out onto the primitive wooden sidewalk that was still under construction. Clarksville was not as busy as it had been when he rode into town, due mainly, Jon guessed, to the pounding heat that beat down upon the town like a yellow hammer of blinding light.

He patted Easel on the nose and decided to first check in with the Union Army. He would return for the horses only after his army business was completed. He noticed Easel

60

had a bruised and bleeding fetlock, but a little care would make the young roan better than new. Shelby believed in the value of an obedient and intelligent animal. Easel was a wonderful horse, smart and with a good memory. Just over three years old, he was fourteen hands high and a beautiful red color with a classic blaze face. His injuries would need tending to fast or maggots would infect the wound. The last thing Jon wanted was to shoot a good and faithful mount in the middle of a hanging town. He'd better be on his way.

The sun inched even closer to the earth. Overhead hung a bristling array of savory red, passionate yellow, and bright orange-and-gold clouds. Not a drop of rain was in sight. Clarksville seemed actually peaceful as evening approached. Jon savored the excitement of setting foot in a new town. It was one of the best feelings a man could have, like tasting a bit of another and maybe better life.

With blazing speed the mood changed. Two bodies flew from between the flapping doors of Houlihan's Lazy Day Saloon. The two men were dusty from the trail, and it was plain to Jon Shelby, as he watched one of the men draw his pistol and start back inside the drinking joint, that he wasn't the only stranger in town. Suddenly a bullet landed at the man's feet, causing him to leap like a jumping bean.

"What'd you go and do that fur! I's just gonna teach that cardsharp a lesson," whined Cheat Perkins, daytime handyman, nightime varmint. His blond hair and mustache glistened under the Clarksville heavens.

"That's what I's afraid of. Get your hat, you're spending the night in the pokey," said Marshal Richards, who had just walked up on the brawl.

"Who says?" growled the drunken cowpoke. It was the first time he'd had some happy juice since he left Dodge City. He was a short, bow-legged spit of a man who wanted things his way when he was drunk and was as quiet as a field mouse when he was sober. Cheat Perkins's face was red. He was drunker now than a skunk.

"I says." answered Richards evenly.

"And who is you?" Perkins cocked open his eyes as best he could.

Richards pulled the left side of his vest open, revealing a shiny badge that read "U.S. Marshal," and when he said,

"The current authority," that was all it took for Perkins to think twice before pulling the trigger of his old Colt Army revolver. His pa had given it to him back in 1860. It was a more accurate and stronger weapon than any equivalent Colt percussion instrument made to date.

"What if I don't see it that way?" Cheat said.

"There've been a few that haven't seen it my way," said Marshal Richards, "until they's dead, that is. And of course, by then it didn't matter who I was."

"It don't matter to me none now . . . and I'm not dead," said Perkins.

"Not yet you ain't."

"What you mean, lawman, 'not yet'? Ain't dead now and ain't a-gonna be."

"Reckon we'll have to change that, lessin' you snap to your senses, boy," Richards said, removing the leather thong wrapped around his pistol's cocking mechanism. "And if you're thinkin' 'bout firing that six-shooter, either forget it or pray to God that hell ain't too close to Clarksville."

Cheat Perkins's partner was Sam Breakers. Sam and Cheat had come together while making the cattle run from Houston up from Brownsville and San Antonio into Fort Worth, Indian territory to Caldwell, Wichita, Newton, and Dodge City in Kansas. Breakers was a tall fellow with coal-black hair and eyebrows. He was a reasonable man, even when his belly was full of rotgut and his mind on a bright future. "He's had enough, Marshal. Ain't no cause to git all riled, now. Cheat here didn't mean no harm."

Shelby saw the tiredness in Richards's eyes. The man had seen a lot in his day. But there was something about this dark-haired, clean-shaven man that failed to level out. Something told Shelby to keep an eye open and an ear to the ground. As the threat of a good gunfight died out, the folks of Clarksville dispersed and got back to doing what they had been doing before the disturbance.

Jon was stared at and frowned upon as he strolled toward the Union Army station. He checked in with a rush. The scowls and bitter words never bothered him none—white folks always got scared of colored folks they couldn't immediately touch and whose pride they couldn't rifle all to hell. The white men manning the station, though, gave him no trouble. All he had to do was fill out a report, which took more time than he had wished. The Union men wanted news from the war back east. He filled them in as best he could and walked back toward the center of town, taking a look at the sights along the way. He would take care of Easel and the other animals, then take care of himself.

A large sign hung above the wide double doorway that was the entrance to the Clarksville livery. The words burned into the wood read:

LIVERY AND WHEELWRIGHT
Zeke and Savage Stevens, Prop.

Jon walked to the door and called out. Somebody was piddling around in the back of the shop, which smelled of fresh fescue and manure. It was a new-looking structure made of long, thick oak planks, not airtight, but it no doubt served its purpose. There was a photograph of Confederate President Jefferson Davis hanging in plain view of the doorway with a brand-new horseshoe hung above it, evidence that one or both of the Stevenses had hopes the South would win the war.

The corral out back was usually full of abandoned horses, as it was now—mostly roans, Appaloosas, several dappled mares, a long-legged sorrel, and even a few draft horses sixteen hands or larger. The large remuda was due to the high rate of hangings in the town. Dead men never needed their horses. Everybody knew that only live men saw fit to ride out of town when their needs had been met.

"Anybody here? Got some work for you, blacksmith," Sergeant Shelby yelled, noticing how well kept the stable was.

"I'm here, mister," hollered a young voice. Small footsteps scurried toward the front of the establishment. "Yessir. What can I do for you?" the small Black boy asked.

"Got six horses and a mule need a good feedin'. Rub this here roan down. Them others, the marshal will pay you for," the Union soldier told the young boy. He rubbed Easel's nose and patted him. "You take good care of this here one, son. Easel is the best horse I ever had. Check the fetlock and joint—a little creosote oil might help it heal. Some neat's-foot oil on my saddle wouldn't hurt none, neither."

"Ain't never been a problem, sir."

Jon noticed the boy perk up when he saw the stripes on his sleeves. "What's your name, boy?" asked the sergeant.

"Cinque, sir. Cinque Kele. Thaddeus Kele's youngest. I'm ever' bit of twelve years old," said the boy.

"Sergeant Jon Shelby's the name."

"You's a Union man, ain't ya, Sergeant?" asked Cinque.

"Yup."

"Gon' be stayin' long, Sergeant Shelby?"

"Don't reckon I will," said Jon, noticing the boy stand up taller as he became more comfortable with the stranger.

"What brings you to Clarksville, Sergeant? Ain't much here but a bunch of dust and some bear grass and arroyos to keep ya company."

"Got some law business, then I'm headed on assignment farther up the Red."

"Oh." The boy looked down, not knowing what "assignment" meant. He figured it was something the soldier had to do and that it must have been important or such a strong, tall, Negro man wouldn't be doing it. If there was one thing Cinque Kele had learned in his short time on earth, it was that African men seldom, if ever, did more than was necessary to complete the job at hand. And he had learned that, unlike Black men, white men generally talked more than they worked, but when they *did* work, they did a good job. If they ever finished what they started. Boy! thought Cinque Kele. A real live Negro sergeant, and he looks like a big *me* instead of being white like all the rest a' them Union soldiers!

Chapter

Nine

Cinque Kele was disappointed that he had run clean out of questions to ask Jonathan Frederick Shelby, who was the first Black soldier he had ever seen in his life. Pappy Thaddeus had warned him about being too curious a long time ago. "A boy can get into big trouble asking questions, Cinque. especially a little nigger boy like you in a mean white town like this."

Shelby reached inside his vest pocket, pulled out a small leather pouch, and turned it upside down; a gold coin dropped into his hand. He tossed it to the boy. "Do them horses real good and you'll get another one of these when I'm ready to go, you hear?"

"Yessiree, bub," Cinque said, biting the coin. "You can count on me, Sergeant. Your animals be taken care of directly or my name ain't Cinque Kele."

"What kind of name is that, anyway?" asked Jon, curious himself.

"It's African, sir. My mammy give it to me afore she died in a Rebel raid."

The boy looked down at the ground again, and his bright face darkened.

"Sorry to hear that. She's still with you in spirit. Remember that. You're a smart boy," Jon said. "You'll be all right."

"Yessir. I can read and write as good as anybody." Cinque paused and wrinkled his forehead. He had trouble saying the word. "What's 'spirit,' Sergeant Shelby?"

"Remind me to tell you one day. Right now, where can a man get a cold drink, a bath, and some victuals? I'm tired of hardtack, salt pork, and jerky. Want some real food to stick to my ribs, know what I mean, boy?"

"Cinque's my name, sir. You been calling me 'boy.' Pappy Kele says don't let nobody call me out of my name. That's why my mammy gives me a name, I reckon, so as you wouldn't have to call me boy!"

"Right, Cinque. Mind if I change my boots? These here are still wet from wading a creek."

"Mr. Zeke would mind, but shucks, he ain't here. So that makes me the boss. You can change whatever you like as long as I'm here!" Cinque paused, folded his arms, and looked glassy-eyed out into the street, past where Jon was standing. Something had caught his eye across Main Street.

"About that drink?" asked Jon.

"Houlihan's Lazy Day Saloon's the place for liquor, and I hear the Chelsea Hotel serves up a fine mess of greens and pork belly and apple pie. LaDonna's Place has the *best* victuals, though. Whiskey ain't bad, neither," the boy added knowingly.

"You ain't been drinking whiskey, have you, Cinque?" asked Jon.

"Naw, sir, not me." It was not quite the truth, but it was close enough for Cinque to tell a stranger. "Antonio— that's my big brother—said it stunts a young-un's growth. And I want to grow up and be big and strong just like him . . . and you, Sergeant. Just like you!"

Jon smiled. "Be seeing you, Cinque. Take care of my critters now. I'll be back in the morning, 'bout sunup."

"You ain't plannin' on wearing that Union blue and stripes inside the Lazy Day, are ya?" Cinque said protectively.

"Never thought one way or another about it," said Jon.

"Might be best if you pull that coat off, Sergeant. Folks round here don't cotton to the Yankees' uniform. Riles 'em up real bad. Some men been known to get drunk and shoot at anything colored blue. Wouldn't want you to be the target of some stray bullet, sir."

"Ain't nobody going to shoot at me," said Sergeant Shelby evenly.

"Our kind don't usually go inside the Lazy Day, only

sometimes when they's with a big white man everybody's a-scared of," Cinque added.

"Thanks for the warning, Cinque. But these ain't 'usual' times, know what I mean?"

"I reckon so, Sergeant. You's a real brave man. Ain't nothin' more you can do now but go inside the place, I guess."

Shelby ruffled Cinque's wooly hair and thought about Manama Jelani, back in Tennessee. Her hair was nappy and finely grained, just like Cinque Kele's.

Manama Jelani was one of the few Negroes who kept several of the old African languages alive. Manama's folks back in Cabin Town had passed down the knowledge of the old country to her. She spoke some Wolof, Fulani, and Mende, and she taught those who were interested and those who promised never to reveal the sacred words to anyone except another African. The ceremonial vow of secrecy was set in blood, near a stream of sparkling water, on the last Sunday in August in an odd-numbered year.

The soldier scout had forgotten many of the words she had taught him, but he vowed to renew his teachings if he made it back home alive. Jon smiled when he thought of the beautifully innocent Manama. He hoped his young friend was doing well with the war going on. He hoped she was still alive and would enjoy peace and freedom if and when it ever came.

The sergeant knew that if he ever needed a friend in Clarksville, Cinque Kele would fit the bill to a *T*. Young-uns sometimes were the loyalest of friends. One day Jon hoped he would have a boy, maybe two, after his cowboying days were over, when he had had his fill of running cattle up north by way of a western trail. But now it was time for self-preservation. He tipped his hat at Cinque Kele and walked out of the Clarksville livery feeling a little bit better about the world.

Sergeant Jonathan Frederick Shelby wore shining, new black government-issue boots, with a garnish of silver spurs. Missing were the generous jinglebobs that he would have worn into an establishment such as Houlihan's Lazy Day Saloon if he had been a civilian. But when his size twelve boots hit the wooden sidewalk, it was plain that a man of substantial power and authority was on his way toward a cold beer and a whiskey or two.

Jon soon learned that Houlihan's Lazy Day Saloon was also a dance hall and gambling squat, a place where men got drunker than a gnat in a swamp. Damn shame, Jon thought to himself, while some men enjoyed fun and games, hundreds of Mamas' boys were out losing their lives on the battlefield in the War Between the States. It was only a matter of time before General Lee would surrender the South; every good Union man knew that. But for now it was tit for tat until the last man down was dead.

Shelby checked his pistols, derringer, and boots for adequate weaponry as he always did before a potential conflict. He was just about to enter Houlihan's Lazy Day Saloon when a body came flying through the double doors like a rag full of fresh cow chips. The odor rising from the sprawling man wasn't much different.

"And stay out, you lazy cowpoke! Next time I'll send you to the devil without a head!" bellowed an angry voice from inside the Lazy Day.

When the dust had cleared, Sergeant Shelby walked through the doors, his boots clunking louder than he had intended. No matter how tough a man was, a stranger never sought a high profile in a new town. He'd live a lot longer that way. But there was simply no way a Black man in blue could go unnoticed inside a bar in a mad Rebel town like Clarksville.

The Lazy Day Saloon was near full of rough-looking customers. Generous ornaments adorned the dance hall: wide, elaborately etched mirrors, crystal chandeliers from New York, a large glossy mahogany bar. There was a banjo player who also played harmonica. Jon noted that even his pockmarks had pockmarks. The seating seemed about as comfortable as the back of a longhorn beef in a blizzard. But drunk cowboys and cattle rustlers didn't care where they sat. Some of them got so boozed, they didn't know from one moment to the next whether they were sitting or standing.

Jon walked up to the bar amid the stares and low muttered remarks. On his way he laid eyes on the first woman he'd seen in several weeks, a redheaded Irish woman, all gussied up and glossy, probably sweet-smelling, too. "Whiskey," he said. "Your best, barkeep."

The long-haired, bushy-mustached man hesitated before he spoke. "Don't usually serve your kind here, mister."

Jon looked around the room. Several of the patrons were dressed in blue, just like he was. "I reckon all these folks in here dressed in blue are having milk?" Shelby ventured calmly.

"But they—" the barkeep said as the sergeant cut his words short.

"I said whiskey, bartender. I been on the trail too long to be standin' in a drinkin' hall without a drink a' my own. Now I don't want no trouble. Just give me that whiskey and be done with it." Jon stared unflinchingly at the man behind the bar.

Randall Pickens pretended to reach for a bottle. What he laid his hand on was the heel of a Remington revolver, fully loaded for times just like these, when a tinhorn got a bit too rowdy to reason with and when squaring the odds meant living or dying.

Pickens often thought about the war raging between the States in the East, and he thought about how the country would be when the Negroes were freed. He was convinced that Negroes were nothing more than rustlers, thieves, and whiskey guzzlers. These dark folk were from Africa, but where such a land was, Pickens never did know. He'd been told it was a place across the Atlantic Ocean, where all the men were black as coal instead of white as lilies.

Randall had often looked at his own skin and wondered why people called it white. He was actually pink, sometimes red, depending on how hot or cold it was. There were plenty of times when the color issue had merit, thought the Lazy Day bartender, but when there were so many folks around of all different shades and creeds, talk of color often turned good sense into nonsense.

Randall often recalled what he had been told about the Negroes. "Can't never tell when a darkie might turn on you and hurt your feelings or try to take your life," Pickens's granddaddy on his father's side had once told him. "So always be ready to defend yourself, boy, whenever a nigger's around."

But Pickens's dearly beloved granddaddy had been

wrong about one Negro man, Randall's friend, Bobbin Sheffield. No white man ever lived who was a better man than Bobbin, he often thought to himself. Since Sheffield had saved Randall from getting trampled by a herd of stampeding cattle last year out on the O'Malley spread near Clarksville Pass, Randall had grown to respect men of color, however begrudgingly. Still, caution was advised when dealing with a new darkie. This Negro might cause some trouble.

"I'm afraid this is the only thing I got for you," said Pickens, and in one motion he pulled and cocked the pistol. The Remington was ready to kill. Shelby saw the weapon's reflection in the mirror behind the bar. Quicker than a rabbit's run, he hit Pickens's hand with his own, knocking the gun to the floor. Grabbing the barkeep by his white shirt collar, Shelby pulled him across the bar. Everyone in the place scooted chairs, jumped up, and ran hard for cover. The women screamed as they always did when fisticuffs broke up the fun.

Shelby punched the barkeep a good one, and then he heard a pistol cock and fire. Both men froze. The strong smell of perfume close by told them that the one who had fired the shot wasn't an ordinary gunslinger—no cowboy worth his boots and spurs would wear *that* kind of stuff.

His fist in midair, poised to put Pickens's lights out, Shelby looked up and saw the tall, buxom redhead, the smoking barrel of a Colt's Navy in one hand, a more accurate Remington revolver in the other.

"You boys's breakin' up my place. Them's good glasses and chairs." She smiled at Shelby. "Wouldn't want y'awl to git hurt none wallowing around on the ground, now would we, darlins?"

"Sorry, ma'am. I didn't mean to disturb your property," said Sergeant Shelby. "All I asked for was a bottle, and this 'barkeep' started a ruckus." Jon let go of Pickens, who scampered back behind the bar.

"He's lyin', Miss Kate. Nigras always lie. He's—"

"Hush up, Randall," said Kate.

"But Miss Kate—"

"You back-talkin' me, Randall Pickens?" asked the redhead, who was obviously the boss or someone in real high authority.

"No, ma'am, Miss Kate. Naw . . . I'll serve this here darkie, but I ain't a-gonna like it none, shore ain't," answered Randall, embarrassed at being defeated by a woman. White women got more respect than anyone out on the range, that was a fact. "Make a white woman cry, and you stand to be kilt. That's all we white men got is white women," Randall Pickens's granddaddy had said.

The woman turned toward the stage, snapped her fingers, and when the piano man hit the first lick, the chorus girls danced across the stage as if nothing had ever happened. The evening fiesta in the town of Clarksville had begun, and no one would stand in its way.

"You can put them guns down now, ma'am," said Jon, "if you don't mind." Kate laid her weapons behind the bar, where she sat most of the time when she wasn't busy upstairs "entertaining her guests."

Pickens reluctantly set a bottle and a shot glass upon the heavy, mahogany countertop. He was shaken up a might, but he would have no problem finishing out the night. Randall would soon figure a way to kill the African who'd made him look like a fool in front of his friends and his idol, Miss Kate.

Sergeant Shelby picked up the bottle of whiskey with his left hand, and raising it to his mouth, he yanked the cork out with his teeth. He eyed the woman who had saved someone's life, maybe his, maybe Pickens's. "Mighty obliged, ma'am. I'd a' hated to hurt that boy. Sometimes I don't know my own strength."

"Happens all the time, cowboy," answered the redhead with a shrug.

"I ain't no cowboy. Not yet, anyway."

"Forgive me, I should have known that Union blue meant otherwise. I'm Kate Pearson. Owner of this here establishment. What be your name, soldier . . . you do got a name, don't ya, fella?"

"Shelby, ma'am. Jonathan Shelby." He cut his eye toward Pickens.

"United States Army." He started to give his rank, company name, and the like, but he recalled Cinque's warning. In a Confederate town, folks were obviously Rebel sympathizers; no sense in rubbing his rank into their pride.

71

"You passin' through or plannin' to stay a while?" Kate Pearson asked.

"Marshal Richards says I'm leaving round sunup tomorrow mornin', noon at the latest."

"Richards is a fool!" It was an unusually sharp remark for a woman who seemed to hold her temper well.

"That fool's got a badge . . . and a gun."

"You be the feller who caught them bandits, aren't ya?" Miss Kate asked.

"That's me."

"They the ones killed the district sheriff's onlyiest daughter?"

"Yup!" Jon was enjoying the whiskey burning his gullet on the way down. He was slightly wishing the woman would run out of talk, but she didn't.

"Wasn't she expectin' a young-un?" asked the talkative Miss Kate.

"Hear tell."

"You got reward money comin', stranger."

"Don't think so," mumbled Jon.

"You brung 'em in, didn't ya?"

"Yup."

"Who they gon' give the bounty to, then?"

"Don't know, ma'am, don't know."

"Suit yourself, stranger," said Miss Kate.

"I will."

Jon looked carefully at his female companion. Kate Pearson was a big-boned woman with a shock of the reddest hair and smoothest pale white skin any white man would want to see or feel. She owned Houlihan's Lazy Day Saloon and ran it better than any man ever could or ever did. Her eyes were blue, eyebrows thin and light, and her lips were rosy red with a slight, natural pouting expression. Her dress was white ruffled lace. Her bustline was firm, full, and tempting, and her waist was small and surprisingly uncorseted. She was a fascinating woman. All the men in Clarksville town had agreed to that.

"Got a place to stay?" asked Miss Kate.

"Nope," Jon answered, taking another drink.

Miss Kate watched as Shelby stared intently toward one of the more animated gambling tables. He had always been good at winning the upper hand, and in cards some folks thought his luck was cheating. But no matter how closely they watched him, he was never caught taking what wasn't rightly his. And since he never cheated, he expected the next fellow to do the same. "Do unto others as you would have them do unto you." The words echoed through his mind, words he often quoted from the Holy Book. He hoped he hadn't misquoted.

"I know a place where you can have a good time, soldier. Companionship, if you know what I mean. Female companionship," said Miss Kate.

"Maybe later. I got an itchin' that needs scratchin'."

"LaDonna's Place. Should I send word you be a-comin'?" she asked.

"Got rooms and victuals there?"

"That . . . and more." Kate gave him a wink.

"Maybe later," said the sergeant. "Maybe not."

"What's your fancy?" asked Kate Pearson, the business-woman inside her coming out of hiding.

"Your gamblers look like cheaters," he said.

"Sometimes looks is deceiving." And she was right; no one knew that better than Jon Shelby. "You callin' my houseman a cheat?"

"I call it like I see it, ma'am. Think I'll play a few hands, if you don't mind, and if I win, you can tell Miss LaDonna I'm on my way."

"Call me Kate . . . and I don't mind."

Jon grabbed the whiskey bottle by the neck. Suddenly a gun cocked, and a sharp, cold rod poked into the small of his back.

"Put that bottle down, you got-damned nigger. I ain't never shot a man in the back, but you's a nigger, so it don't make no difference. I'm Jipson Tandy. Who the hell are you, some-a-bitch?"

It was Kate Pearson's old man, the trifling and forever drunk Jipson Tandy—the O's and naughts man who now thought Jon was disturbing his woman's peaceful business. Tandy was so drunk that he could barely stand. What kept him from falling on his face, Shelby couldn't figure out. Shelby was brave and strong, but he was no fool. With a man this drunk, in a town like Clarksville, *his* blood could be spilled in the wink of an eye. And no one would much care. Jon Shelby used his instincts at times like these. He

73

would trick Tandy out of pulling the trigger, but he had to turn and face him first. If it was death Shelby had to deal with, he would confront it with a chance of winning.

Jon looked slowly around the room. Union soldiers sat and stared but failed to come to his rescue. They were fighting for the same cause, but now, here, it didn't matter one bit. Jon realized that he was more hurt than shocked at the reaction of his white compatriots in blue.

"What seems to be the problem, Mr. Tandy?" asked Jon.

"You's causing a ruckus in my woman's place a' bidness, ain't ya, nigger?" Jipson Tandy asked in a voice thick with drink.

"Naw, sir, Mr. Tandy, I'd never do nuthin' like that in your pretty woman's place. Naw, sir, not me."

"What you doin' inside a white folks' drinking hall, anyhows?" Tandy's breath almost caused Jon to gag.

"Jes' passin' the time, havin' a drink a' this here fine whiskey," the sergeant said. He always talked in down-home Negro slang in a dangerous situation like this. White folks seemed to soften when they heard a Black talk in a subservient fashion. Ask Miss Kate, sir. Go on, ask her."

"That's right, sugarplum," Kate said. Tandy staggered when he heard her stick up for the soldier. "He's right, Jipson. Now put down that gun afore ya hurt somebody, lad," she pleaded.

"I ain't a-gonna do it! Naw, sir. I'm killin' me a darkie tonight. Causin' trouble for a white man's white woman in a white town, jes' can't let you live, boy. . . ." Tandy's sentence trailed off as he seemed to catch a nap between his threats, but he woke up when a hound dog barked outside in the street. Jon thought for sure he would pull the trigger. "Why, boy, I used to be the terror of Clark'vull. Had ever'body comin' from miles and miles around just to try and outdraw me. Now say yore prayers, boy. I'm puttin' a bullet in yer gizzard."

Shelby grabbed Tandy's pistol by the barrel, jumped out of the line of fire, and twisted the man's arm behind his back as the gun went off and put a smoking hole in the spittoon sitting at the base of the bar. There were several bullet holes there already.

Kate walked over to help Tandy up from the floor,

where he was crying near pure rotgut tears from his red-and-yellow-splotched eyes. He was sickly drunk, and he spoke not in rhyme, but in song:

> Wanna find me a nigger
> Jes' let me be.
> Gonna keel me a darkie,
> Jes' wait and see. . . .

Jipson Tandy was singing, laughing, and crying at the same time when Randall Pickens and haberdashery owner Simpson Flatt took him away, his boot heels dragging on the splintering knotty-wood floor.

Kate motioned to Pickens and Flatt to get Tandy to bed upstairs on the second floor. She waved her hand again, and the music began. In a moment folks at the Lazy Day were laughing and drinking and swearing that the South had won the war. The Union men sat to themselves and were unconcerned about the Rebel banter. *They* knew who would win the war. They only hoped that General Grant would lead the way to victory before the rains came.

Miss Kate looked at Sergeant Shelby, embarrassed. "Sorry 'bout all a' this soldier. Guess trouble comes in pairs. Why don't you take in a game or two, help ease your nerves a bit, lad."

"He your man?"

"You could say that."

"You couldn't do much worse."

"I know," the saloon owner answered, looking down as if to hide her shame. "I reckon I feels sorry for him, soldier. He was some highfalutin gunman, heck of a rancher years ago. Locusts hit his farm in fifty-six, he went bankrupt, ain't never been the same since. His wife left him and went north on a whim and a prayer with some two-bit politician. J.T. lost all of his courage. He tried to find it in a bottle."

"Sad story. . . . Maybe you need a change of scenery. Ever think of leaving Clarksville, movin' west? Word is, a woman like you could do well in, say, San Francisco. Goin' there one day myself."

"Word could be wrong," Kate answered boldly. But she

softened the rest of her reply. "Never thought about it, leavin'. Mighty big step, Shelby."

"Best to make a big step fore you get too old to enjoy it, ma'am . . . not that you's old or anything." Jon paused and looked up toward the top of the stairs and then back at Kate. "I still think you could do better."

Chapter

Ten

Jon tipped his hat and walked off toward the gambling table that was close to the middle of the floor. He felt sorry for Kate Pearson. She was such a lovely specimen of womanhood trapped out in the middle of nowhere. There was no place for her to go on lonesome nights but to bed and back downstairs in the morning to a bunch of cowpokes and no-accounts smelling of puke and last night's onions making wind.

Funny how a good woman could latch on to and fall in love with a bungling has-been drunk—even when she had the pick of the litter at her disposal.

Shelby looked around the room as he walked, checking for exits and corners. "After you find a way out of a strange place, Jon, be sure you check them corners, they tells you what to look out for," his father, Jemeliah, had told him on numerous occasions when he saw that his only son was itching to go to war. "Don't you never mind anything else. Keep a bearing on them corners and doors. They'll save your life ever' time!"

The large room where the whoopie was going on in the Lazy Day got brighter as the smoke got thicker. A man filled up one of the many bright coal-oil lamps, getting ready for the long day's evening into night. The saloon gals were plentiful, almost one for every two laps; they buzzed around the room like yellow jackets in a barrel of apples. They knew the look of love was gold.

There were five poker tables in the Lazy Day Saloon; all were busy winning and losing for first one cowpoke, then another. Each fellow was armed and ready to catch a cheat. The airy shuffle of the cards and the clink of shining coins was proof that money was changing hands. Kate Pearson grew richer by the clink. Ever since he discovered that gold came from God's earth for the digging, man had committed just about every straight and crooked act he could think of when the prospect of owning nuggets by the pound was in view.

Shelby could tell by looking at the wide gaps between the thick planks of the walls that in winter these old geezers had to down several jugs of sour mash or a pint of killer home brew not to feel the cold. Of course, when the spring and summer came, for most men the drinking habit was largely replaced by the daily routine of farming—growing wheat, oats, and cotton—and by the tending of livestock, pigs, and cattle. But for folks like Jipson Tandy—and there were many—it was drinking time all the year round.

Shelby approached the table he had eyed from the moment he had entered the Lazy Day. Just then, a well-dressed paunchy fellow with a gold pocket watch chain hanging from his vest threw his hand down on the table. He stood up and yelled, "I'm damned tared of all this here a-cheatin'. I ain't won a hand since the sun went down!"

"Seems the sun's always down when you pick up a card, Hamilton. You got more bad luck than a dead man. Now be a good loser, will ya, these boys here're ready to lose their money, too," said Drew Murdock, the gambler man, sitting easy with a fresh cigar in his mouth.

"Sumpin's wrong here. I think them cards is marked, and I ain't leavin' 'til somebody pays me my money back!" yelled the big-bellied fellow.

"Ain't no cause to git all riled, Hamilton. We all have our days. Some days we win, most days you lose. I never know'd you to be a bad loser; then again, I ain't never know'd you to win, either," said the fancy-dressed Murdock, puffing slowly on his cigar. Most of the folks let out laughs that flooded into the street. "You done lost a lot of gold this year alone, ain't ya? Why, Hamilton, you must be losing your touch."

"You shut up, Drew! I didn't say it was you, but somebody's been cheatin—" The fat man named Hamilton cut his sentence short. Chewing ferociously on his stubby, unlit cigar, Hamilton looked up at Jon. "Well, now, I

78

reckon you's waitin' for my seat, hey, boy?"

"You's got that right, Mister," said Shelby, turning toward the rest of the men at the table. "Gentlemen, seein' that your friend here's leavin', I'd be much obliged iff'n you'd deal me in, if it's okay with him."

The fat man puffed out his chest. "Now *wait* a minute. Do you know who I am?"

"Don't reckon I do, since I just got into town today."

"Hamilton Featherstone's the name," said the fat man, poking his finger at his chest, "and I'm the local banker here, I am. Nobody just takes my seat and be's done with it, especially no stranger."

"Sorry, Mr. Featherstone. I'll just wait 'til you lose the rest a' your gold, then I'll take your spot."

Somebody yelled out in the back of the saloon, "He done lost all his gold, fellas!" The crowd laughed. "Banker man's broke. You might as well quit now, Featherstone. When I come to get my loan tomorry, I want it in cash!" Cowboys and dance girls continued to laugh, and the banker steamed.

Hamilton Featherstone huffed and puffed, yelled some cuss words at the gambling table, and lumbered toward the Lazy Day's exit. His head and face were large. He had a pug nose, and his clean-shaven skin and thin lips gave him the look of a man who preserved his every wind for eating. Nevertheless, Hamilton Featherstone's life revolved not around food, but around all-powerful gold and any single note deemed legal, spendable tender by the Confederacy.

Hamilton stopped at the door, looking like a duck-necked squash. "I'll get my money back, Murdock. You know it, ha, you know it!"

Drew Murdock, a tall fellow with black hair and a thick mustache, didn't reply; he just kept smokin' on the largest Mexican cigar Jon Shelby had ever seen. He wore the finest in silks, and his suit was brand new. The beige-colored fabric matched his eyes, which were small, like dots, and he was proud of that distinguishing feature.

Drew had accidentally killed two men up in Indian territory, but his reputation traveled faster than he did. So by the time he arrived in Clarksville, folks saw him as someone to be feared. He became a man the easy way, killing men without a prayer, but what he did best was shuffle cards and roll those dice, and he always cheated at both games.

Back at the gambling table, Jon Shelby and Drew Murdock introduced themselves, and Shelby laid his money on the line. Since Drew Murdock was the veteran at the table, he was the first to bark out the code of play. "Straight five-card draw, Yankee."

"Wild cards?" said Jon.

"Ain't none," Drew said.

"Bets and raises?"

"Of course," Murdock snickered.

"Capped?"

"I only play when the sky's the limit," said Murdock.

"You a sharp or something?" Shelby asked bluntly.

"I ain't no sharp. I just like insurance in case I git to winnin' big."

"Ever think about losing?"

"Nope!" Murdock grinned. "I want a chance to up the ante anytime I damn well please. Boys?" asked Drew, looking around the gambling table and shuffling the cards like the professional gambler his reputation proclaimed.

A small, yellow-skinned, just downright puny fellow said, "I ain't in it, Drew . . . dun lost most a' ma pot as it is."

"Reeves?"

"Too rich for me, Drew. Guess I'm out. Niggers been known ta git lucky."

"Now, have you ever known a darkie nigger to ever git lucky?" snapped Bobby Cassidy, killer Ball Cassidy's youngest boy.

"Onlyiest lucky nigger is a dead nigger!"

"I asked you in or you outta the game?"

"*I* ain't sittin' at the same table with no nigger. Don't want no coal soot to rub off him on me," said Cassidy.

"Now, now, Cass, don't be so unfriendly. That ain't the way to show our newly arrived Negra friend that Texas hospitality. Why, we welcome you with open arms, soldier, especially your money. I hope Cass didn't offend ya none." Drew Murdock's voice went from a pleasant drawl to a cold bark. "Now get out, Cass . . . and cool off."

Shelby could sense the tension within the group of men sitting at the table. Two gentlemen approached them.

80

"Mind if we join ya, Drew?" asked Chuck McCaskill, pointing to himself and his younger brother, Treat. "We jes' sold a shitload a' longhorns up in Dodge City. Got a pocket full a' booty we's itchin' to lose."

"Empty your pockets, boys," sang Drew Murdock. "'Cause y'awl gon' lose what ya got!"

The card game got under way, and Shelby continuously lost hand after hand. Soon he discovered that, like the fat banker, Featherstone, his losing ways had some help. Once Jon got a tinge that some sharping was going on, he decided not to quit.

It was Jon Shelby's first night in town, within Clarksville proper, and already he knew most folks were alarmed at his presence. He knew that most of the townsfolk regarded him as a miracle that had been made, no doubt, from molding by the white man. But Jon knew that he had been molded by Black men and women who were brave and strong, and he knew one day he would win against the odds of prejudice and oppression—if not against the odds of Drew Murdock.

Deep down inside, the townsfolk knew Jonathan Shelby was a harbinger of things to come. He was a tall, proud African man wearing the blue of the North. It was a damn shame most white folks were afraid of Black skin and the blue on his back.

If Jon had been a regular, nonuniformed Negro, the good people of Clarksville could have hung him, shot him, or done a number of other nasty things to insure that he was out of the way. But Jon Shelby was different. These Rebels wished they could kill the Negro who talked better than most Texans did. But that would never happen now, Jon thought, smiling inwardly. Slavery would end one day, and the white man would have to change his ways. And the fact that men brown and red and white were fighting for life and for liberty cheered Jon when he was tempted with despair. But the look on Murdock's face turned Jon's attention back to the game.

Simply by reading Murdock's face, Jon saw a man who would cheat on a widow's mama on Sunday, if Sunday came too soon. "I'd like a new deck of cards," he said abruptly.

"Whenever a man is a-losin', he always wants a new

deck on the table. I'd say you lack skill, partner," Murdock said with a sneer.

"Maybe I do, maybe I don't," replied Shelby, squinting his right eye at the man across the table.

"Winner's choice," Murdock said, smiling like a possum in the top of a tree. "And I'm the winner agin, soldier boy. I hope you ain't a sore loser, too."

Sergeant Jonathan Frederick Shelby was a man to be reckoned with, from his incognito weaponry and deadly accurate gunslinging to his sharp, accurate judgments in times of trouble, but right now he had to put up or shut up. He realized he was outnumbered as he slowly removed his left hand from the table and rested it on his Colt's Navy, the accurate one, the gun that had killed many times before in battle. "All right. Count them cards, out in front, nice and slow."

Drew dropped the argument, and so did Chuck and Treat McCaskill. Shelby watched intently as Murdock counted. Two cards were officially missing.

"Just as I figured; either one of you boys done stole a couple of cards, or two of you's holding one card apiece. I don't cotton to no cheat. Where I come from, that's automatic ejection from the game or a bullet where it ain't supposed to be. And I ain't ready for no bloodshed my first and only night in town. I suggest one of you boys cough up them shingles, else we's fixin' to war a bit tonight."

"Mighty bold, ain't you, Black man," said Drew.

"Just want to be treated right, that's all, sir."

Drew reached inside his finely tailored light beige suit coat and as quick as he could say "son of a bitch," Shelby blocked the barrel of the derringer and slammed it to the table. The weapon discharged a pellet into Treat McCaskill's brand-new Texas Star hat. He was peeved beyond repair.

"I 'spect, Mr. Murdock, if you want to continue breathing, you'd best come out of that other pocket empty-handed. There's a hair trigger on my Colt," he lied to the white man, "won't take much to send your nose through the back of your head."

Cold steel kissed Shelby's neck. The deadly noise from a hammer cocking back echoed throughout the now quiet room. A wide Cheshire-cat grin spread across Drew Murdock's face, and he spoke his words extra slow. The killer held the gun, snickering, ready to kill. Murdock reached down, picked up his derringer, and shoved it into Shelby's chestbone. "Looks like you lose the game," said Drew. "Now you gon' lose your life!"

Chapter

Eleven

"That's it, ease back on that trigger, nice and slow so's nobody'll get splattered all over Miss Kate's purty little saloon," said Drew Murdock.

Jon glanced over at the congregation of Union men, who moved not a muscle to help him. He was disappointed that the camaraderie of fighting men wearing the same colors meant nothing at all when one of their own was Black. He had to get out of this mess all by himself, but that was nothing new.

Having no choice now, Shelby surrendered to the unseen gunman poised behind him and ready to put a hole near his head. He laid the Navy down on the table, and as he did, Kate Pearson ran down the steps from the second floor. She looked like a lily in a brier patch, Jon thought. "What's the commotion all about, boys?"

Clemmie Ferguson, Murdock's man, was the one holding Shelby at bay. Not a smart cowpoke by any means, Clemmie was a short, muscular, dark-haired bull of a man with double thick eyebrows, black eyes set wide apart, a large nose, and lips that hung like a dog's. He was only nineteen, but the years out on the cold and dusty range made him look at least twice that. For all his dullness, Clemmie was polite and courteous whenever a woman was around. The burly redneck withdrew his pistol and became as gentle as a housefly in the dark when Miss Kate grabbed his right arm.

"Don't mean to cause you no trouble, Miss Kate. This here Negaroo fella claims there's been some cheatin' a-goin' on. He got no right to blow into town and cause a ruckus with friendly folks like us."

84

"Shelby, what's all this fussin' about?" asked Kate, a sympathetic ear awaiting his side of the story, hoping he'd tell the truth. She admired the Black man's courage. To rise above both Black and white men and become a soldier scout for the official U.S. Army took guts, Kate knew. But maybe she had Shelby pegged all wrong, maybe he was a troublemaker just like all the rest.

"Somebody's been holdin' out a card or two," Shelby said. "Puttin' it back when it benefits them, takin' it out when they stand to lose. I'm an honest man, Miss Kate. All I want is my money back from these cheating dogs. That's all, ma'am."

Drew Murdock jumped up from his chair, his face red and his feelings hurt. Ashes from his long cigar went flying all over everybody at the table. "Now see here! I ain't gon' stand for no two-timing, scatterbrained stranger to call me a cheatin' dawg, especially no tinhorn Ne-gra. I'd jes' as soon wallow in a pigsty as to be called outta my name, Miss Kate. I'm an upright citizen in the town of Clarksville and a white man to boot. I demands an apology."

For the first time since closing time the night before, Houlihan's Lazy Day Saloon was stone quiet. All of the patrons looked on intently to see what would happen next. More than a few were hoping for a fight, complete with blood and guts. Kate Pearson walked around the strong oak-based gambling table and calmly reached inside Drew Murdock's fancy lapel and pulled a card out of a hidden pocket. Then she eased around to his other side and slid a card from inside his fancy shirtsleeve. She had noticed both hidden pockets the last time they'd kept each other's company in her room last Tuesday. She'd known such information would come in handy someday.

Kate held up the cards for everyone to see. She cut her pretty blue eyes toward Murdock, like a mother staring down at a naughty child. Murdock removed his hat and, playing with the brim, hung his head in shameful remorse.

"You know my rule against cheatin', Drew," said Kate, her Irish temper beginning to flare. "You disappoint me. You know where the door is."

Drew Murdock had never backed away from any man in a fight, but Kate Pearson's words made him feel as dry as a worm in a drought. Without once meeting Kate's eyes,

Murdock stomped over to the door. Angry and embarrassed, not knowing what exactly to do about Shelby but thinking mightily about revenge, the gambler man looked back and yelled, "You boys comin' or ain't ya?" Two men followed, hats in hands, like dogs with their tails between their legs.

Kate turned to Shelby. "How much did you lose?"

"'Bout fifty dollars, I reckon," Jon said.

Kate Pearson picked up a handful of gold pieces from the pot in the middle of the table and handed a few to Sergeant Shelby. She stashed the remaining three or four hundred dollars inside her pocket. "This table is closed for the evening, boys. Go find another table or go home where you boys rightfully belong."

Kate Pearson's customers, men and dance hall girls, stood staring at their Miss Kate, wondering why their boss lady would side with a stranger, let alone a Negro scalawag.

"Now git," said Miss Kate, hands on hips, "all a' youse, 'fore I call in the marshal, I will."

Jon Shelby tucked the money inside his vest and bade farewell to the extraordinary Kate Pearson. Yes, thought Jon, she was a woman with a golden heart. "Well, ma'am, I reckon it's time to call it a night. Much obliged to you. I think I owe you one."

"Them three yella stripes on your sleeve means you're a sergeant, did ya say?"

"That's right, ma'am. U.S. Army all the way."

"My offer still stands, soldier," said Miss Kate.

"Offer?" Jon said.

"Fun and games." She nodded her head toward the door. "At LaDonna's."

"I figured this woman you's talking about done been taken for the evening," said the Union man.

"You figgered wrong. I told her you be a-comin, lad. She'll be waitin' for ya. Tell her who you are, she'll know what to do."

"Why you being so accommodating to me, ma'am?" Jon asked.

"I reckon I just want to show how I feel about the way your people's been treated. I never thought it was right, slavery and all. Sometimes I wish the South would lose this nasty old war. But I'm too loyal a Southerner for that."

Shelby didn't want to get tied up in another person's problems. Lord knew he had enough to deal with himself. So he just bowed his head to avoid hurting the hospitable woman's feelings.

"Which way is LaDonna's Place?" he asked.

"Out the door, take two left turns . . . you can't miss it," she said.

"Good night, ma'am," Jon said.

"Where did you say you was headed?" asked Miss Kate.

"The Rio Grande." Jon hated lying to her, but he could not divulge his true destination to an enemy civilian. "Why?"

"Just wanted to know where you be. I might need to redeem that favor one day."

Not only did Jonathan Shelby the military man respect Kate Pearson, but the civilian man inside him accepted her as an equal. She was hard when she needed to be, yet, he could tell, there was something missing in her life. And that was a *real* man.

Shelby tipped his hat, nodded his head, and stepped boldly toward the swinging doors. The crowd had slowly dispersed from the saloon, disappointed that nothing more had come of the white man—Black man standoff.

Jon turned left and headed to the livery. He flipped another coin to Cinque for caring good fashion for his horse, and he and Easel set out slowly toward LaDonna's Place.

For a change, it seemed to Jon like he was back in the army again because surrounding the town was a skeleton crew of Union soldiers in bivouac. He was lucky this day was done. Soon he could be himself, soon he could rest . . . in peace. This had been one long and powerfully tiring day.

As he headed down the darkened street, Jon suddenly felt lonely and in need of a friendly face to lay his red-shot eyes upon. The blackening horizon, with streaks of purple blues and peaking reds, appeared to go on forever. The wind had risen to almost ten miles per hour. Late evening had arrived in the land of Texas, and Jon was prey to its power.

He thought again of Dan'l Walton. They had always cherished the times when they had made camp to bed down for the night. Their talks beside the fire before dinner were worth more to Jon than he had ever imagined. Now he had no one with whom to share his thoughts. Even though he was part of the Union Army controlling the town, Jon felt cut off. White folks were all the same when it came to keeping colored folks informed. "A dumb nigger is the best kind of nigger," he'd heard some old farm owner say back in Tennessee before he'd joined up.

From the end of Main Street, Jon saw in the nighttime distance the place where his immediate journey would end. "Looks like LaDonna's is a mighty big place, Easel, boy. Must have a whole bunch of rooms."

An elegant sign that could not go unseen read:

LADONNA'S PLACE

EATS   SPIRITS   ROOMS

——— Your Fancy ———

Undoubtedly the most posh joint for the Negro establishment in Red River County, LaDonna's Place was an old wooden structure. The planks and thick boards, once pale brown, unseasoned, and new, were now an ugly, dirty, rain-washed gray. The funhouse sported a veranda that sheltered the first floor, and the ten rooms inside provided ample space for the goings-on.

Jon tied the fairly rested Easel to the hitching post. From out of nowhere a boy appeared and silently led the horse to the stable behind the brothel.

Jon Shelby didn't know what to expect once inside La-Donna's Place. Food and sleep were what he needed most; a bath could come later. Jon had never before seen the inside of such a place of business, and he hoped he could get his more mundane needs seen to here. The Union man was met with calls of greeting almost immediately upon entering the blue wallpapered front room that was deco-

88

rated with soft-looking sofas on which reclined several soft young women. Suddenly a powerful voice filled the room and made everyone jump to attention, and when he looked quickly from the desk back to the lounge, everyone was gone, vanished. That voice, smooth, sensuous, and commanding, could melt a churn full of fresh butter or stop a charging bull in his tracks.

A woman, quite large and quite healthy, beckoned to Jon from behind the desk where she was proceeding to make preparations for the Black stranger to sign in for the night.

LaDonna possessed one of the prettiest faces Jonathan Shelby had ever seen on a fat colored woman. Her small, shining eyes were adorned with makeup—just the right amount—and her hair was long and piled atop her head. Her nose was cute and extremely flat, and when she spoke, all within range of her voice knew that immediate order was apropos.

"Miss LaDonna?" asked Shelby, tipping his hat.

"So you's the new niggra soldier in town, huh?" LaDonna said, boldly looking the colored man up and down. She liked what she saw, and that was good for Jon Shelby. Having a woman like LaDonna as an ally never did hurt none, and in Clarksville, Texas, it might mean the difference between life and death.

"Shelby's the name, ma'am. Sergeant Jonathan Frederick Shelby. U.S. Army. Kate Pearson told me to see you about some victuals and a room for the night."

"You'll learn fast," said LaDonna.

"Learn what, ma'am?" Jon asked.

"Where'd you come from, calling white folks by their first name?"

"Kate called me Jon. Reckon I can call her Kate," said Shelby.

"That all you want? Some victuals and a room?" LaDonna said, adjusting the book for him to sign in.

An ebony man dressed in Union blue sure looked good to a Black woman stuck dead in the middle of the Confederacy during the Civil War. She handed him the pen and watched to see if he hesitated. LaDonna had learned that if a man hesitated when signing his name, it was proof that he was lying. Once people decide to tell the truth, they usually don't hesitate in telling it, she mused. The same went for writing the truth, LaDonna had decided.

"They told me you had on Yankee duds, and I called them liars," she said. Jon smiled, and she continued, thinking what a fine young man he was, from good stock. "So you's the colored fella who brung in them bank robbin' killers?"

"Reckon so," said Jon, looking the place over.

"Them outlaws really the ones who killed the district sheriff's gal?"

"Saw them with my own eyes," he said, nodding.

"Do tell!" said LaDonna.

"I do!" Before she could ask, he added, "And yes, she was expectin'."

"You one a' them emancipated Northern nigras?"

"I ain't from no North, Miss LaDonna. I'm from Tennessee."

"Used to know a fella from Tennessee. Shot up ten white men afore they hanged him. Woulda hanged him twice if he'd a' had two necks. Least he died with a smile on his face. I saw to that!"

Jon Shelby had relaxed, since he'd set foot in LaDonna's. He enjoyed his brief talk with the Black madam; it was a pleasure speaking to someone not out to see him dead. From the kitchen came the tantalizing aromas of pork-cooked turnip greens, white fried corn of the hickory cane variety, egg and plain cornbread, biscuits, and, of course, chitlins and succulent blackberry pie.

In Jon's mind, LaDonna was a lady. Her presence offered safety in a maternal sort of way. He figured he might never really understand the feeling, but it sure felt good at the moment.

"I hate to rush you, ma'am . . . uh, Miss LaDonna, but . . ."

"Drop that 'Miss' stuff, Sergeant. My friends call me LaDonna. Get it?"

"How about that room? I'm plumb tuckered out."

"This ain't no place for no tuckered-out colored gunslinger." LaDonna laughed.

"I ain't no gunslinger," said Shelby. "I . . ."

But Jon lost his train of thought when he glanced toward the winding stairway and saw there the prettiest sight he'd seen since he and Dan'l rode through Shreveport. It was a young woman dressed like an angel, in a vermilion-red, low-cut dress, and her face was more beautiful than a fresh-opened morning glory.

The young woman smiled, turned, shook her shapely body, and walked back up the stairs. LaDonna's face lit up. "You like Zena, huh? She'll be back down directly," said the big Black woman.

"A helping of them victuals I smell is what I'd like, ma'am." Jon's mind had drifted away again, his senses now teased by the good smell of home-style cooking.

"Zena Beale's her name," said LaDonna, trying to bring her customer's mind back to bigger business.

"How much do I owe you?"

"All taken care of. You must have made a *big* impression on Miss Kate."

"I pay my own way, ma'am—if you don't mind."

"Two bits for the night. Take up the rest with Zee."

Jon reached inside his vest pocket, pulled out the fee plus a generous tip, and laid it on the desk top. He tipped his hat and headed toward the stairs.

"You have a seat in the lounge, soldier. Supper'll be out soon."

"Make that double helpings of everything," said Jon.

"Your fancy . . . and next time you come in here, you'll remove your hat," LaDonna scolded, a grin threatening to bleed through her exaggerated frown.

Jon smiled and promptly removed his hat. He did know better, since most honorable women had the same rule like his mother did back in Tennessee. He had been away from home and peace for so long fighting the war, he had forgotten such amenities. Back home, my mother would have knocked my hat off if I wore it inside the house, he thought to himself.

"Next time I'll knock it off, soldier or not," said LaDonna, slamming closed the big, thick book of patrons and looking up to finish her thought, as if reading his mind. "Jes' to make you feel at home!"

Chapter

Twelve

Jon walked through the vestibule and down the five steps into the sunken living room area of LaDonna's Place. Carefree sounds permeated the entire floor—sounds the soldier had not heard for such a long time: men and women having fun. The heady aroma of mixed perfumes and ladies' powder made him feel like he was in a different world.

The new surroundings caused Jon to suddenly remember a voodoo woman named Nasha he had met back in Shreveport. She was a tall, well-to-do Negro woman. "Creole," she had told him. In her sleep she would shout, *"Papa Legba, ouvri barrie pou nous passer,"* so loudly that he heard her ravings all the way out in the barn where he and Dan'l had bedded down for the few nights they were in the Louisiana parish.

He knew the words were French, but he didn't know what they meant. She had the "power of evil," Shelby felt, and he had told her so. "'Tain't natural, 'tain't natural," he said the day he left town. He had known before colored folks who dealt with magic and the like, and too often it had backfired and the spells they had cast on others came back to haunt them three times over.

For all of her black magic, though, Nasha was one of the best cooks he had ever known. And at that moment his guts growled and he realized his hunger had returned.

The first thing Jon noticed when he walked inside La-Donna's lounge room was the high ceiling, nearly twenty feet or more. All of the candles resting within their holders on the sparkling chandelier were lit, and the soft light made Jon feel good.

The blue-and-gold wallpaper on three of the walls looked new. The fourth wall, bisected by the entrance, was painted a blue-gray color. The paintings on all the walls were fine and all lively-colored. The furniture was old, but clean; at least the spreads covering the hulks underneath were clean. The rugs were worn, too, but well kept.

The room was empty now, all of the couples having left and headed upstairs. Jon supposed by the aroma of chitlins and turnip greens in the air that victuals would soon be served. Tense with hunger and expectation, he missed Zena Beale when she first walked into the room. When he did finally see her, he stood up like a gentleman and didn't move a muscle until the young woman moved herself. She was beautiful and awfully young-looking. She seemed embarrassed, looking away from him as if searching for a way out of the room. She walked slowly toward the soldier, and soon they were eye to eye.

"Well, well, well. Jon Shelby, Union man. How ya be? I'm Zena Beale. Folks call me Zee."

"How-da-do, Miss Zena. I—" Jon's words were cut short.

"You don't have to call me 'Miss.' I ain't no white lady. I'm jes' here to"—she paused nervously—"pleasure you," she continued, running one of the lines she was instructed to say when she'd been hired on by LaDonna several days ago.

"You look more like a Zena to me than a Zee," said Jon. "Don't mind if I call you that, do ya?"

"Don't make me no never mind. You gon' be here long, cowboy?" she asked.

"I ain't no cowboy," said Jon.

But for a moment, talking to the lovely young woman, Shelby had forgotten all about the war, the dead men, and the streams of blood that ran across the battlefield into the nearest body of water when it rained. For a split second he didn't think about the struggle for freedom, or about a reason to keep moving on. For once, the words of Frederick Douglass didn't echo through his brain, and even Dan'l Walton's name wasn't on the tip of his tongue.

Jon Shelby and Zena Beale sat down on the plush, gold-patterned love seat. They were quiet and polite in their shyness. Zena rubbed her hands together, which were moist with perspiration. Jon gave the room a second look-see, as if he were planning to put money into the place. And just when he decided to speak again, another young woman strode into the room.

"Supper is ready for you, Sergeant Shelby," she announced as she walked over and took him by the arm. "Come this way, soldier man."

The woman, whom Jon had never formally met, led him through two large rooms and into the dining room, where only three place settings were laid out. Zena trailed behind Jon and the woman. She didn't like anyone interfering with her "company," but she had yet to learn what to do about it. After all, she had just been there a few days, trying so hard to learn what to do when a customer came in.

The meal at LaDonna's made Jon feel special, and when he took the final bite of blackberry pie, he knew that a bath and bed were next in line. He had enjoyed the small talk with the women; it was a shame Zena had left the table so soon, but LaDonna had hurried into the dining room and insisted that Zee leave and get herself "ready."

Jon wiped his mouth on the finely sewn linen napkin, and before he could ask where his room was, LaDonna let go with a shower of words, her large frame twisting as she smiled and finished her say. "Up the stairs, to the right, down the hallway, four doors. Room five."

"Ma'am?"

"You said you wanted a room, didn't ya, man?"

Jon stood up and adjusted his belt, which was heavy with the tools of war. "Number five it is."

"And now you listen to this. They'll be no rowdiness, breaking up the furniture and the glass in them windows. You break it, you own it . . . after payin' for it, that is. And if you rough up that gal, I got two shotguns and a Henry. She gets hurt, you get hurt. Understood?"

"Understood," said Jon with a serious nod.

Upstairs Jon counted the doors as he drew near to number five. He knocked once, then twice. The door eased open.

Zena Beale stood proudly in front of the Black man, her breasts straining from the top of her long, red, satiny dress like lava from a volcano. Her lips were crimson red, and she had that lovely medium-brown skin only a Black man could really appreciate. Her coy smile told him she was as pleased as he was that their acquaintance had taken place.

"I hope you get your eyes full," she said, a delightful Southern drawl easing between her lips.

"They's full, ma'am." Jon smiled. "They's full!"

The young Negro woman looked the handsome young soldier up and down for the second time. Though truly attracted to Jon, she still seemed oddly nervous, as if she were inviting a man to her room for the first time. "You gon' come all the way in—or stay half a' the way out, soldier? Lot warmer inside, if ya know what I mean."

The large room was adorned with old furniture that must have been around since Negroes were brought over on slaveships to the devil's land. The room was longer than it was wide, a suite, no doubt, made especially for high-paying guests.

The curtains were of the finest, heavy velvet brocade, a golden background with raised green paisley print designs. Jon was pleased to the hilt.

The windows faced the front of the building, looking over the ample porch. The curtains were drawn back, admitting the sounds of the Texas night. Jon stared past Zena Beale's French rolled hair and saw mostly inky dark through the windowpanes. Several bright stars stood out over the Texas range, lighting the night for his fellow Union soldiers in bivouac around the city of Clarksville.

Even at night, Jon knew the prairie spoke of desolation and barrenness, the dust and sand and wind making life worth damn near nothing. But for tonight he was safe from the elements. Tomorrow he'd go on to complete his mission. General Williams was counting on his success, and so were the colored folks of Clarksville, though most of them would never know it. If he let the general down, he let himself down, but most important of all, he would have let all Black folks down. If one darkie was a quitter, thought Shelby, them yaps think all darkies are quitters. And that was wrong, dead wrong.

But from the look of one Miss Zena Beale of Clarksville, Texas, she had only one mission on her mind.

"My, my, my," she said. "Miss LaDonna was right."

"Right about what?" asked Jon.

"Oh, never you mind, soldier. Jes' girl talk, that's all. Where you from, big man?"

"Tennessee. A place called Cabin Town, not too far from Nashville."

"All the fellas from Tennessee tall, strong, and tolerable like you?" asked Zena.

"Don't rightly know. I never had time to observe no hard-ankles. My mind was usually on other things."

"What kinda things, soldier?"

"The war, I 'spect."

Zena Beale commenced to talking up a storm as she helped Jon off with his duds. "You gon' be here long or jes' passin' through?"

"Leavin' round sunup, no later than high noon, for sure. By order of your Marshal Richards."

"Shoot somebody, did ya, Jonny?" Zena inquired.

"Nope . . . well, not exactly. Ain't nobody ever called me Jonny before."

Zena's hands trembled as she fumbled in unbuttoning his dusty blue shirt. The young woman dropped to her knees in front of him and slid between his legs to yank off his brand-new army boots. Dust from his pants legs flew all over her hands and up her tiny little nose, and she sneezed. "When's the last time you had a bath?" she asked with conviction, turning up her nose.

"Don't recall such things, ma'am. Couple of days ago in a creek outside of Mt. Pleasant, I reckon."

"At least you don't stink like a lot of folks do," she said, frowning and grinning at the same time.

By the time she got off his shirt and boots, Jon's eyelids had grown heavy. While the young woman stood up and laid his clothes across a chair, he fell fast asleep.

Zena's body went limp. She turned back the covers and helped the dusty soldier crawl inside. Soon Jon Shelby was out like the nighttime sun over Texas, and she was relieved her secret was spared, at least while the man was asleep. How could she tell him when he awoke, and what would he tell Miss LaDonna? This was her last chance to prove she could handle her job, or else she'd have to find another line of work. If Zena lost this job, she'd have to go back to her father's house to work the fields again. She had thought that when her folks bought their freedom down in Huntsville near the Trinity River, their slavery days were over, but she had learned the truth after overhearing her master tell his wife that the darkies would still really be slaves under the guise of freedom. But as long as there was one more Beale still under that master's reins, Zena could never be free. As long as her brother, Santee, was a slave, she had to find a way to buy his freedom.

A few minutes later, when a knock came at the door, Jon woke with a start. He reached for his pistol, the same Colt's Navy he had taken from a dead Rebel. His finger was snug against the trigger as he slid it under the covers. Zena jumped up and ran to the door. It was a boy and a girl, carrying two buckets apiece full of steaming hot water for Jon's much needed bath.

Chapter

Thirteen

"You really think Marshal What's-his-face is weak-minded enough to fall for it, Wooly?" asked Manny James.

"Shore as I'm standin' in this here jail, Manny," replied Wooly.

"Go ahead. Ask him. I bet he says no to your blamed idea."

"Well then, boy, put yo' money where yo' mouth is," Wooly snapped. He laughed wide and loud. The filth between his teeth was caked over with fermented food and had turned green.

It took only a second for Ace Wiggins to take the hint. "Fifty-dollar gold piece says he ain't that dumb."

"You ain't got fifty dollars to your name."

"Damn you, Wooly. Since Jake and Hank and them new fellows are six feet under, that means a quarter of that loot is *mine*. And I aims to git it."

Wooly Samples had been thinking for some time what it would be like to have fifty, maybe a hundred thousand dollars in his pocket. And the grungy hombre from El Paso wondered too how the war was going, if it would end before he could make it farther east to become a hero and win a medal for bravery. He could still be rich and still be a hero out there in freedom land, 1865. When the white killer came out of his reverie, he remembered that *he* was the boss of his gang. After all, it was *he* who had masterminded all of the robberies his gang had pulled off with success. Robbing that stagecoach had been Hank Parsons's idea, but he was dead, too.

And again it was *he*, Wooly Samples, who had actually schemed the plans that worked. Why should he, the man with the ideas and the brains to engineer such great plans, share the booty? He had often said to himself, Shucks, a man only gits one chance to make it big. And dang-nabbit, when it's my time, I plans to take it all or I ain't fit to carry the Samples name.

It was settled. When the time came, Wooly, usually a master of timing, would see that Manny James and Ace Wiggins somehow fell by the wayside: a tragic accident, like a bullet through the gut maybe, or being pushed off a bluff with their hands and feet tied. And Wooly Samples would be richer than a general's daughter. He'd hold the winning hand, all of it, in the end.

Wooly laughed to himself when he heard footsteps. It was Marshal Richards coming to bring in the evening meal.

"Time to have a bite, boys. Now y'awl stand back from them doors, ya hear? Don't wanna have to call old man Wixey this time a' night to fix up a death box for no low-down killers. Understand?"

"You's jes' the man I wanted to see, Marshal Richards," said a scheming Samples.

"Ain't got no time for none of your bullshit, outlaw. Spill it out fast, I'm on my way home to fetch me a bite and get some shut-eye," said the marshal.

Wooly was undeterred. "This town seems like it's a might small for a big man like you to run. I mean, seein' you ridin' up to us on the outskirts a' town, I'd a sworn you's a big-town lawman. You see, they's right about me and the boys stealin' that loot. In fact, we got damned near a hundred thousand dollars in gold pieces and other riches of considerable value jes' a-waitin' in several safe places. And if the right time, right situation, and lest we not forget, the right man came along, why, I could be talked into partin' with a percentage of the take."

"You can't bribe me, Samples. I'm goin' home."

"Wait. Wait...now wait, Marshal. How does five thousand dollars sound to ya?" offered Wooly.

"Ain't interested," Marshal Richards replied, his ears visibly widening for the next offer that would come from the imprisoned outlaw. Richards took another step toward the door that led into the front room of the jailhouse. Samples, feeling a bit desperate, yelled out, "Wait now, dammit! Ten thousand in gold. How 'bout it, Marshal? Game?"

Marshal Cotton Richards turned his back again and continued toward the door to leave the cell room. He seemed to be walking in slow motion. He could do a lot with that money. Get away from Clarksville, for one thing. Move to San Francisco. Start a detective agency, like Allan Pinkerton did back in Chicago town in the early fifties. He could see the lights flashing now, reflecting off on San Francisco Bay:

COTTON RICHARDS NATIONAL DETECTIVE
AGENCY:
— We Aims To Please —

Sure, he could do it. If they called Pinkerton "the Eye" after he'd solved several baffling cases, they'd surely dub Richards something catchy, like "Keeper of the Peace."

That case of the missing chickens the other day had baffled everybody in town, except him. Through telltale evidence like several handfuls of feathers and lots of blood, Cotton had correctly named a gray fox as the culprit.

It was a confirmed fact that this Samples fellow could be had. Any Southern man who would let a Union soldier, let alone a Negro, catch him in the act of doing wrong and bring him to justice didn't have his noggin screwed on straight. Show him the fifty thousand dollars, Richard thought, and with some fancy shooting he would take all of the money for himself. These men were wanted in several territories, so he could legitimately kill them, say there was no money, and leave for California.

Cotton looked through the hole cut in the door leading to the front office and out through the glass window. He saw a bunch of clouds covering the moon as it began to rise higher into the sky. Full moon meant people acted crazy. And maybe that's what he was doing. But if actin' crazy meant a chance at a hundred thousand big ones or more, he was as crazy as a grizzly she-bear in heat.

"Hold on, Marshal, now. Don't run outta here without hearing my final offer," said Wooly. The marshal kept on walking, opened the door, and prepared to step through it.

"All right, Richards," shouted Wooly. "Twenty thousand if you break us outta here!"

Cotton Richards stopped and said, "Another thirty thousand . . . and you boys might see the sun rise tomorrow mornin'."

The impact of the statement hit Samples like a backhanded slap to the jaw. If he was going to kill Manny and Ace, why not save a bullet for the marshal? He could promise him anything to get out of this musty jail, and then he could do whatever he wanted. "You got yo'self a deal, Marshal!"

Cotton Richards drew up a brief IOU, and Wooly had to sign it. Then he took the key and set the hombres free. It was as useless to tie Wooly Samples to a contract as it was to leave a longtail weasel napping in a henhouse.

"Now you got to lay low, Samples. Townsfolk know you's locked up here, but other than those of us here, and that Negro soldier, they don't know what you look like. We got to do all of this pretty fast, and then we can get outta town, get that money, and all go our separate ways."

"Couldn't have planned it better myself, Marshal," said Samples, that sneaky grin spread across his mouth. "Smart man like you's hard to find!"

When Marshal Richards went back up front, Drew Murdock and three of his boys were waiting. Murdock was pacing the floor.

"I been waitin' fer you damned near ten minutes. What you doin' wid them prisoners, reading 'em lullabies?"

"You know, Murdock, as much time as you spend in this jail complainin', you might as well rent out a cell," said Richards with a shake of his head.

"Knock it off, Cotton. I want you to arrest that Negra feller that got me thrown outta Kate's place."

"What'd he do? Catch you cheatin' again?"

"Made light a' me in front a' Kate, he did," puffed Drew.

Dexter Simmons, one of Murdock's sometimey friends, laughed as he spoke. "Yeah, Cotton, you oughta seen Drew's face! It looked like a cherry in a basket a' eggs!"

"Shut up, Dexter. I owe you a punch in the nose as it is. Don't you rile me any further. I'm waitin', Richards. You the law in this here town, and I'm a law-abiding citizen. I lost two hundred dollars. I want that Black bastard arrested and my money back!"

"Make up your mind, 'law-abidin' citizen, which one you want: the two hundred or that boy arrested?"

"Both!" said Drew.

Wooly Samples walked through the door with Ace and Manny. "We overheard your conversation, sir. The name's

Wooly Samples," he said to Drew Murdock. "These here's my boys, Ace Wiggins and Manny James. Seems we's lookin' fer the same man, exceptin' I want him dead. Maybe we can work together. We'll need a few good men, and we'll hang him higher 'n a coot-a-brown."

"Ain't gon' be no illegal hangin's in this town, Drew— not while I'm the local law," said Cotton Richards.

Dexter Simmons yelled out, "Don't need to be legal in Texas to hang a nigger . . . especially when white folks's doin' the hangin'.'."

"Law." Murdock laughed. "You jes' as crooked as a snake on a log. Hadn't been for me talkin' to them Union men when they came to town, you'd still be a line-ridin' ranch hand out on the Triple-B Ranch, sloppin' pigs and pickin' up cow dung chips to stay warm on the range at night. Don't you speak no law to me, Cotton. I say the word for Hamilton to call in that loan, and your marshalin' days are over."

It was like a cold slap in the face. Cotton Richards knew Drew Murdock was telling the truth. He had been a no-account hog slopper, breaking in wild horses for a nickel a head when Drew Murdock took a liking to him. He was embarrassed that all of the other men within hearing distance knew his business. He had to back down and let Clarksville history take its course.

Murdock turned and looked at the stranger with the dark brown hat on. "Drew Murdock, Mr. Samples. It's a pleasure to know you, I'm sure. I don't rightly know about hooking up with your kind, mister, but if you're half the man you's talkin' to be,"—Murdock cut his eye toward Richards—"then we may hire *you* as our next marshal, when the time comes."

Drew turned to one of his boys, Cecil Jackson. "Cec, round up the rest of the boys, tell 'em to meet us at the Chelsea. Make it snappy. We gon' lynch us a Black boy at high moon!"

"Tonight?" Cec asked.

"Tonight!" said Drew.

Chapter

Fourteen

The children retrieved bucket after bucket of hot water, and each time they entered Zena's room, they poured the steaming-hot fluid into the large bathtub, whose legs were shaped like animal paws. Zena tested it with her hand from time to time until it was just right to soak a tired man's bones.

The beautiful Black woman tossed the children a coin apiece. They both bit their pieces to make sure they were real, legal tender, and then Zena ushered them out the door. As she pulled Jon out of bed and pushed him into the tub, Jon fussed, not used to such treatment from a woman.

"I ain't never took no bath before with a lady in the room," he protested.

"You's takin' one now, soldier," she said.

Zena unrolled a soft cotton washcloth, Northern-mill made. A large hunk of white lye soap was nestled inside. She herself had never actually watched a man take a bath in his birthday suit, but it appeared that she would see one right now. "Got anything to drink over there, Miss Zena?" asked Jon, lying back and feeling finer than a pea in a pod.

"Whiskey, if you please," said Zena Beale.

"Don't mind if I have a drink, do ya?"

"It's over on the dresser," she said.

"I'd be much obliged iff'n you'd hand it to me, ma'am."

"You's in the tub with no clothes on. I ain't never seen no man . . ." Zena began softly, almost giving her secret away. "Ah, I . . . you ain't my masser, and I ain't no slave!"

"Reckon I'll get it myself, then," he said. And in one motion Jon stepped out of the tub and grabbed the towel hanging off the washstand. When Zena Beale saw him walking naked as a bird across the floor, dripping soapy water everywhere, she rushed to cover her eyes. Jon thought that it was a real peculiar reaction for a woman in Zena's profession.

"You's a strange woman, Zena," said Jon.

"What you mean?" she said as he walked back over to the tub and got inside again. "You back in the tub?" she asked, her eyes still covered.

"Yup!" said Jon. The young woman slowly peeked through her fingers and relaxed when she saw the man; he had the bottle turned upside down, drinking to his heart's content.

"You's drinkin' that whiskey mighty fast," said Zena. "You'll get drunker'n a snake in a barrel of beer."

"What you doin' in a place like this, woman?" Jon asked.

"Don't rightly know what you mean," said Zena, thrusting out her chin.

"This ain't your kind of place."

Zena thought fast, thinking that if Shelby got drunk, he would fall asleep like her father always did when he drank too much rye. That would put him to sleep until morning light, and maybe if she was lucky, she could get paid and Miss LaDonna would never know the truth.

"Tell me about Tennessee," she said.

"Ain't nothing to tell. One big battlefield, that's all."

"You really fight in the war, or did you steal that pretty blue uniform?"

"I fought, Miss Zena. Shore did. I wish I could say I hadn't, but I have."

"I ain't never seen no colored soldier afore, Jonny."

"Most folks ain't," said Jon. "You want to know about the war? Tell you what, you tell me what you know about the war, and then I'll know what to tell you myself."

"Well, white folks down here say the North and the South is a-fightin' because the North wants to take all the slaves up north and the South wants to keep them here. And if the South wins, then Black folks'll be better off workin' for their same old slavemasters than the slavemasters up north."

"White folks told you wrong, Zena," Jon said, swigging on the bottle again. By now he was feeling the heat from the rotgut bubbling in his belly. His head got light, and suddenly he recalled what he had meant to say to the young woman before she'd led him to talk about the war. He spoke now as if he were still sober.

"Tryin' to change the subject on me, huh, gal? I think I got you figured out," he said.

"That whiskey tellin' on you, child," she said.

Suddenly Jon jumped up from the tub, splashed over to the woman, and yanked her into the area of the tub. They were as wet as minnows in a pond. He pulled her inside, smack dab into the cooling water. She was glad she had pulled her dress off because it was borrowed from Miss LaDonna. The robe she had on could be dried before dawn. But she was in the tub with a strange, undressed Union man!

"Well, since you *decided* to keep me company," said Jon, "I'll tell you all about back east."

Zena Beale was supposed to entertain the young, handsome man and earn her board and keep, but here he was doing the talking and *she* was being entertained. She listened to Jon Shelby talk and decided he must be white with Black skin. No Negro ever said so many exciting but frightening things about a world she had never known. Somehow she began to relax in the tub, and after she removed her robe, she got real cozy. Jon Shelby was a fascinating man.

"Whew, Miss Zena, my jaw dun plumb got tired of talkin' bout fightin' Southern white men," Jon said with a yawn.

"You never did tell me how it felt to kill men you ain't never met before," she said.

"No soldier worth his salt ever talks about killing on the front. Reckon it's an unwritten code, Zena. Some things too intolerable to jaw about."

Jon held the woman close to him. Relaxed and cozy now, Zena Beale jumped out of the tub. After making Jon promise not to look, she removed the rest of her woman clothes, and he convinced her to scrub him down. After a

105

bout of heavy silence, Zena started to talk, and she told Jon Shelby the honest-to-God truth.

"I feel so easy with you, Jonny," she said. "I jes' wish I could tell you what nobody else knows. At least nobody here in Clarksville."

"I got a feeling I know what you's about to say," said the soldier. "But I ain't *too* good at guessing what's on a woman's mind."

"You gots to promise you won't tell Miss LaDonna that we ain't done nothing. Iff'n you do, she'll let me go, and I'm a long ways from home, and without a job and no money, I'd be in an awful fix."

"You a runaway slave or sumpin'?"

"I ain't no slave. My family's free," said Zena defiantly.

"Well, say what you gots to say. I ain't got all night. Got a hard day ahead, hard day riding west."

"Don't rush me, man. You got me confused. Talkin' 'bout Atlanta and Tennessee and that Lincoln man runnin' the North. I don't know how I'm going to make it, Jonny." Zena started to cry. "My brother's depending on me. Ain't nothing turning out right. Nothing."

Jon sensed a troubled woman was about to admit the reason for her actions. Her body had already been freed; now she was on her way to freeing her spirit. And that, thought Shelby, was real progress.

"You've never been with a man before, have you?" he asked quietly.

"I can't keep it inside," said Zena. "I just don't know how to tell you."

"Say it, gal. I'm listening."

"I've only been here since last week. And I meant to make the most money in the shortest time. I need the money bad, Jonny. If I don't save him, he'll die, I just know he will. He's always been sickly ever since he's born. That old master'll beat him to death with that whip. He don't work 'cause he's too sick."

"Who is he?" asked Jon.

"My ten-year-old brother," Zena said.

Now the soldier understood. Zena's brother was within the cauldron of slavery's brew, and she had set out to find a way to save his life. Money was the only way to get a white man's attention in 1865—in this new world of kill and take.

"Master Wicklow Capshaw said Santee would have to be the last to be freed because he's younger and stronger and can work more years." Zena bowed her head, tearful but not yet crying. "I've got to get the nine hundred dollars to buy his freedom, Jonny—or else . . . or else, he'll die without ever having a chance to live. I left home to make enough money to buy his freedom. That old master only pays us fifty cents a day. That ain't no way to make enough to buy his free papers. Miss LaDonna's was the only decent job I could get.

"You know how important it is for Black folks to have a job. If as freed men we can't work and earn our keep, we die. When Miss LaDonna told me how much I could make every day, if I worked hard, I thought I could have the money to buy Santee's freedom before winter sets in."

"Nine hundred dollars is a lot of money, Zena," said Jon, thinking about a means to help this beautiful young woman. "Don't you fret none, now, gal. Where there's a will, there's always a way!"

The Union soldier sobered a bit and realized that if Zena Beale never found a way to rescue her brother, words of hope would never ring true to her again. There *must* be a way to help her. He recalled one white man saying to him that about the only valuable thing white men really had was white women, and the same applied to Negro men. All they really got was Negro women. And they was worth fighting for, even to the death.

Jon dried Zena's eyes and they sloshed around inside the tub. Zena smiled and hugged Shelby like she meant it. She fished around inside the tub for the washcloth, and when she found it she washed the parts of Jon's body visible above the water line. He flinched when she obliged his fancy below the soapy suds.

"Whatchya doin' in these here parts, anyways?" said Zena.

"I came to see you, ma'am."

"Stop shuckin', Jonny," Zena said, blushing. "Be serious now."

"Business," he said.

"You can tell me, I ain't gon' tell nobody," purred Zena,

107

her voice smooth and slick like her pretty brown skin.

Ordinarily he would have kept his mouth shut, but with Zena it was different; *she* was different. Never had Jon felt so good with a woman, except Manama, but that was an entirely different kind of feeling—nothing that deserved comparin' to Zena Beale. Deep down inside, he hoped to see her smile from the heart; if he had more time in Clarksville, he could help her reach her goal. But he was leaving in a few short hours. His mission came first, even before his personal feelings.

"I'm a Union scout. Got important information to deliver to Red River Station. Information too considerable to trust over them telegraph wires."

"You's an important man, then," said the woman.

"Nope. Just doin' what I can for our people. South's gon' change, honey. No way the Rebels can win—they ain't got no money, let alone arms and ammunition. Most of our forces double theirs. The Rebels that didn't freeze to death during the winter got so frostbit, they had to cut their toes and legs off just to keep from gettin' blood poisoning. White men think they's God, but can't no man run and fight without legs and toes.

"Got hundreds of them in prison camps. Colored men's the ones who have to see to their every whim." Jon paused and shook his head. "It's a shame. Even when a white man's a prisoner of war, Negroes still pretty much got to obey their every word. Ain't fair, Zena. Hot-damn, just ain't fair!

"The war's changed everything. Lots of high-livin' peckerwoods done already gone bust. North ain't buyin' no more goods, the white man's bank accounts down here's dwindlin' mighty fast. Some of them shootin' themselves in the head, can't take being poor like colored folk. Farms that used to yield cotton and peanuts by the acre ain't doin' nothing but wasting away, soaked in white man's blood, nigger blood, too."

"What's gon' happen after the war, Jonny?" Zena said, hoping and praying that this night wouldn't be the last they spent together.

Zena Beale liked the man she was with, and she figured the more they saw each other, the more they could grow close—if it was meant to be. She had never been around anyone colored from so far away from Texas. Her world was expanding if only a taste, and it was a pleasant addition to an otherwise drab and painful existence.

"Can't rightly say," said Jon. "One thing I do know is that the Black man's got a long way to go 'fore he can truly be free. Lincoln's talkin' 'bout sending colored folks back to Africa or maybe even to South America somewheres."

"I ain't never even thought 'bout goin' to no Africa, let alone south of Texasland. You gon' let them send you away?"

"Nope," said Jon.

"Whatcha gon' do, then?" Zena asked, more confused than ever before. She thought white folks were fighting to make Negroes free to go north, but after listening to this Negro sergeant talk with all of his experience and worldly ways, she figured there was a lot she didn't know.

"I been dreamin' about a place. A place where there ain't no prejudice, where the colored man can carve his own notches without the credit goin' elsewhere. A place I call . . . and don't you laugh now . . . a place I call Paradise Run. It's been in my mind a long time, darlin'." Jon grabbed the lovely African woman by the arms and looked into her eyes. "Ain't *nothin'* in this here world gonna stop me, Zena . . . nothin' short of death!"

"That's a nice name, Jon. This Paradise Run place, is it in Texas?" she asked.

"Don't know, shore don't think so, iff'n the rest of Texas is as rowdy as Clarksville. But I do know that whenever I see the place, I'll know it. Then whatever name it's got, I'll change it to Paradise Run. It'll be my town, and other good folk of all colors can live there, too—as long as they ain't the hating kind. That's the way it's gonna be, Zena. I'm determined."

Zena thought about Jon's earlier words, about the will to see Santee free, about Negroes being sent back to Africa, and since she believed his every word, she was scared. "How they gon' send us 'back' to Africa, Jon? Seems to me, that if you's gon' send somebody 'back' someplace, they'd a' had to been there before. Our folk ain't never been outta Texas, ain't no way they could go to Africa! This is the only place they know—and anyways, I don't even know which way Africa is, really I don't." Tears rose in Zena's eyes, and she turned her head away from the Black man in near despair.

"I know it don't make no sense," said Jon, gently turning Zena's head toward him, looking deep into her pretty eyes. They were gray when he'd first met her in the lounge, but now they were a pale brown color and had the intensity of a deadly serious woman.

Zena Beale was quiet as they both towel-dried themselves. She looked out of the window at the full moon hanging high in the East, and she dreamed the wildest dream.

When she looked back at Jon, her eyes were gray again. He pulled her close, and between then and the hour of midnight, Jon Shelby and Zena Beale relaxed in loving togetherness. The new day approached, and they were pleased that hope had been found within the dark Texas night.

Sergeant Jonathan Frederick Shelby of Cabin Town, Tennessee, and Miss Zena Beale of Clarksville, Texas, were in the midst of a deepening friendship. Time grew still, the cares of a trying day were swept away. Relaxing completely, they fell asleep in each other's arms. Nothing in this world could come between them, nothing could disturb their peace. . . .

Chapter

Fifteen

Jon Shelby and Zena Beale had drowsed peacefully on the soft, clean, cotton-filled mattress; after their melee in the tub, they no longer were shriveled up like natural-born bloodhounds. Then, all of a sudden Zena woke, screaming her head off, in the middle of a nightmare. It seemed so real, the young woman could have sworn that she was drowning in Olsen's pond—the swimming hole she'd played in when the Capshaws owned her family down in Huntsville, on the Trinity River.

"Wake up, honey. Zena . . . wake up," Jon said in as soothing a tone as he could muster with his deep voice, being a bit woozy himself. He was still dazed and bleary-eyed from the brief snooze, but it didn't take much of Zena's shrill screeching to sober him up.

After the nap, the young, soft-skinned woman seemed changed somehow—even softer and more lovely.

She was breathing hard as Jon rubbed her head, smoothing back her jet-black, hot-bone-pressed hair. "Ain't no danger, honey," he crooned as he held her naked body close to him. "I won't let nobody touch a hair on this pretty little head a' yours."

Over in the heart of Clarksville on Main Street, the townsfolk walked proudly down their peaceful street, confident their safety was under the careful watch of Marshal Cotton Richards and those who "ran" the municipality. They strolled through the fine evening later than usual, men and women holding hands, the music of the Lazy Day Saloon filling the void between laughing chorus girls and men yelling for more rotgut and sour mash while they shuffled the cards.

As Wooly Samples, Drew Murdock, and the boys got ready to leave the Clarksville jail, the door burst open. It was Tavares, the Mexican who sat in the jail every night to watch over the prisoners until Marshal Richards or Deputy Fats arrived in the morning. He was a short, stocky man, with a body that looked stronger than a mule's. His skin was tanned from taking in lots of sun all day. He had two pistols strapped to his side and a sequined blue shirt that looked brand new.

"Who the hell are you?" asked Wooly with a sneer.

"Buenos tardes, señor," Tavares said, smiling as if he had been told a joke.

"Buenos what? That's a hell of a name for a man," snorted Wooly.

"That ain't his name, Samples," Drew said. "He's Tavares, the local Mexican. Been in town ever since I can remember. He just watches over the prisoners at night. He don't speak no English. Them words and several more is all he knows, I reckon." Wooly pulled out a wad of chewing tobacco, broke off a piece, stuck it in his jaw, and chewed several times to make it sit the right way.

"How you gon' have a jail tender who can't speak white English?" he asked.

"Hell," said Murdock. "Any man works as cheap as this here greaser don't *need* to speak the language. We'd have to pay him fair wages if he's a white man. He'd git even more if he understood white folk talk!"

Now that made sense to Wooly Samples, who finally decided to drop the subject of English and Mexicans, for the moment. "Tell him to either stay, leave, or git out of the way," he said, dropping the last cartridge into his Colt and spinning the chamber. He checked it to make sure no bullet was under the hammer. It wasn't.

Little Effie McGraw was some distance up Main Street from the commotion that was coming her way, but she was the first to catch a glimpse of the lynching party. It was getting late in Clarksville town. Usually, most folks went to bed with the chickens, but a few stayed up a lot longer on comfortable nights to enjoy themselves.

It was the first time Effie's pa, Emory, the man who ran the local land office, had let her take a stroll in a boy's company without a chaperone. The lucky cuss was Sammy Whitfield. "Family's got good blood," Emory had said just the other day. "Yup," his wife, Annie, replied. "Ought to make strong young-uns, too, Pa."

Emory looked up and said, "Young-uns! Darnit, Annie Mae. This here's their first goin' out. Now you got them having young-uns. Don't you think that's a little pre-a-ma-ture, Ma?"

"You's right," said Annie Mae. "Reckon I was ridin' the high hoss a bit."

Annie Mae was looking out of the second-story window of their flat above the land office they'd run ever since their contrary draft horse had thrown Emory and put an end to his farming days. His son, Cullum, had headed east back in 1862 to fight the Yankees, so there had been no one left to tend the farm. When Annie Mae saw the mob coming up Main Street, she let out a yell for Pa McGraw.

"Pa! Pa! Sumpin's goin' on down the street yonder. Wonder what it is?"

Emory didn't give a hoot; all he wanted to do was smoke his corncob pipe and nod off over too much tonic—at least that's what he told Annie Mae it was. She would have died had she known it was corn liquor, the best and strongest in the land, that he had poured into his elixir bottle while Annie Mae was cooking and cleaning, chores forced upon her when the Negroes they'd hired out escaped to Northern Freedom. Annie Mae had helped the Negroes get free, but she never told Pa Emory.

Up the street, Effie McGraw held her breath, not knowing what to think of the commotion heading their way.

"Look, Sammy. What's happenin' yonder? Some ruckus, you s'pose?"

"I don't see nuthin', Effie," Sammy Whitfield replied.

"Down the street," said Effie. "Looks like a fire."

Sammy refocused his wide blue eyes on the distant happenings. That was when he saw them, and he knew something was up. "Ain't no fire, Effie. If it is, it's a-comin' this-a-way."

"Reckon I oughta go on home and tell Pa. He'd be a might upset iff'n I knew danger's a-comin' and didn't fetch him."

"No cause to do all a' that, Effie," said Sammy. "Whatever it is, if it keeps up that pace, it'll be here faster'n a bird can catch a worm."

The hanging party got louder as they drew nearer to the Chelsea Hotel, where the boys had been told to meet. They talked louder than normal, probably due to hearing Wooly Samples yell at the top of his lungs that it was time to kill a nigger. Most of the fellows figured that talking loud made a man tough. When they thought of the silence of Lonesome Hill Cemetery, where no one ever spoke a word, they yelled even louder.

"Y'awl c'mon, now," said Drew Murdock. "I's aimin' ta get my two hundred dollars back afore none of it's left!"

"What we gon' do to him, Wooly?" Ace asked.

"Gonna hang that nigger, boy," said Wooly. "But before he hangs, we gon' teach him a history lesson."

"What's history got ta do with hangin' a darkie, Wooly?" asked Manny.

"Gon' teach him that no Yankee nigger can bring white men to jail to hang without payin'."

"But . . ."

"Will you shut up, Manny! A man can't think with you yappin' all the dang time!"

Business at Stevens's Livery had been unusually brisk for the middle of the week, and Cinque Kele had hung around late to help take care of the volume of horses that needed tending to. Both Zeke and Savage Stevens had left for the night, and Cinque was about to close up shop. He still had a few more chores to do before he headed home to supper and some sleep, and he busied himself with the task at hand.

The brightly lit torches were the first sign that a lynch mob was on its way to a hanging. The group grew louder and more radical as gambler Drew Murdock and outlaw

114

Wooly Samples led the way up Main. Most of the men didn't know where they were headed, or what they would do when they got there, but it didn't matter as long as they were with the boys.

What sealed the validity of the raid was Hamilton Featherstone running out of his midtown flat and joining the gang. Nobody'd talk to him, though; they were too busy wondering who would get killed besides the colored fellow. Some wondered if vengeance was worth all the fuss. Still, most men figured, it didn't matter how many white men got done away with as long as the nigger died in the process. They could always even up the score later on, by killing even more darkies.

"Look, Drew, if you don't tell me what's goin' on, I swear that that loan you asked for don't stand a she-dog's chance in hell of gettin' approved," said Hamilton Featherstone. "You know me all too well."

"Dammit, man, can't you see we's gon' kick that Negra's black ass and stick a noose around his neck—after we get my two hundred dollars back, of course."

"You mean, *my* two hundred dollars," said the fat banker man. "*You*'s the one who stole it away with yore cheatin'."

"I won that money from your fair and square, Hamilton!" Drew said.

"Now, Drew, I been pretty white with you ever since you came into town lookin' for a spread. You was so broke, why, a mosquito could've flown all the money you had from here to New York City without a breather," said Hamilton. "Ain't no need to get violent with that colored fella. Maybe we can talk it out with that boy. I reckon all Ne-grows ain't as dumb as you think, else they'd all be dead."

By then the mob had arrived in front of the Chelsea Hotel. Their torches smoked, and the flames flickered like the devil had come back from hell. The noise and the lights woke up all of Clarksville city proper. People scurried to the doors and windows, curtains were pulled back, spectacles were donned. They all knew there would be another man to bury tomorrow morning. Most didn't care if he was Black or white.

Some of the children sneaked out of bed to watch the commotion. Even Little Petey Freeman, Jr., saw the mess.

He also heard Wooly Samples when he yelled out the first orders.

"I'm gon' take some men inside and surround his room," Wooly said. "Then we'll give you the signal to call that son-of-a-bitchin' nigger outside."

"You boys be careful, don't want to hurt LaDonna's Place. Y'awl know Kate...uh, Miss Kate and that fat nigger gal that runs the place is in cahoots," said Drew. "We so much as put a scratch on that building and our goose is cooked with Miss Kate."

"*Your* goose, you mean," said someone in the crowd. There were a few snickers, but then no more, and the men got quiet all of a sudden.

"Who the hell's Miss Kate?" Wooly yelled.

"It ain't important now, Samples. Just don't tear up the place no more'n ya have to," said the banker. "She built that place with my money."

"Let's go, boys," Murdock said, frowning. "We gon' do some hangin' at LaDonna's."

High above Main Street and the primitive alleyways of Clarksville, a large barn owl hung in flight, its white, heart-shaped face and body emitting the aura of a ghost in pursuit of the night. The large and haunting head of the nocturnal beast calmly observed the citizenry in its frenzied action. This denizen of the dark, instinctive, cool, and sure, had killed every day—but only to survive. Never because of color.

As the men closed in on LaDonna's Place, the owl snatched its prey: a hispid cotton rat that had just filled its belly with the eggs of several sleeping chickens. And as the rodent was devoured within the body of the owl, Jon Shelby, unaware, stood to die of man's need to destroy with a vengeance all that he refused to understand.

The building's top floors were lit up like a lighthouse on the shores of the Atlantic. Twenty-five, maybe thirty men made up the invading group, including the boys with slingshots and rocks and a vaquero named Angel de la Guarda Tavares, who, though he appeared not too smart, was a hell of a lot smarter than the white men gave him credit for.

Wooly and his men burst through the doors of La-

Donna's Place, pushed LaDonna down, and kicked her in the side. They destroyed whatever they put their hands on as they made their way to the stairs. The young colored boy who cared for the animals of the men who frequented the brothel had tipped Wooly off as to Jon's whereabouts within the bawdy house. He had given out the information for a measly two bits. Now the Black soldier fighting for the boy's freedom stood the chance of losing his life.

"Give 'em the signal when I give the word—and not before," said Wooly to Ace Wiggins.

"What's the signal?" Ace said.

"Just pass the word that we's ready on this end, dummy."

"You don't have to get mean, Wooly."

Wooly barked, "Shut up, hot-dammit. I'll give the word myself!"

Drew Murdock swallowed deep, and sweat popped up on his forehead like welts from a slaveowner's whip. He looked around and was relieved that there was ample support to catch one man. Mobbing a helpless Negro had always been fun and would surely amuse them now.

"Hey, boy," yelled Murdock. "Shelby! Jon Shelby! We knows you's in there, boy. Come on out and bring my two hundred dollars wid ya." And right on cue, first one rock and then a whole slew of rocks were fired in succession. Several hit the window of the room in which Shelby and Zena were sleeping. The little boys of the "slingshot brigade" had taken over the fight. They knew that what they were doing was fun, but they didn't know that someone would be hurt. If they had, some would have stopped immediately, scared of getting into trouble.

Inside the second-story room above the high veranda, Jon and Zena woke up again with a start. Zena screamed at the sound of glass breaking and the sight of debris flying about the room. "What's happening, Jonny?"

"Some fool's breaking out the windows...." A stray piece of glass nicked Zena on the head, and a trickle of blood ran down her left temple.

"C'mon, gal. Let's get out of this here bed, we's in direct range of them windows. Get your clothes on fast. We gotta find out what these white folks is up to."

Jon jumped from the bed and, sheltering Zena, pushed

her aside. She grabbed her dress and struggled to get into it. He eased over to the side of the window as the glass continued to break. He saw the rocks flying through the window and knew that something wasn't quite right. Grown men after a nigger wouldn't use rocks, they'd use bullets and shoot to kill. He grabbed his breeches and hopped around the large room on one foot, the rocks continuing to fly slingshot-style from below.

"Dammit, boys," snapped Drew. "Y'awl's tearin' up the place."

Outside room number five, Wooly Samples and his men were poised, ready to rush the room.

"Now!" said Wooly as he and his men broke open the door, ran into the room, and commenced shooting at the walls.

Down on the street, Drew Murdock had finally calmed the boys down, when he heard the gunfire inside the whorehouse.

"What the hell is that Samples shootin' at! We got enough men to take him without shootin' irons!"

The Colt in his hand, Shelby fired off a shot at Samples, missing his head by inches. He dropped behind the divanette and fired several more rounds at the intruders.

Wooly grabbed Zena, who had foolishly tried to run from one side of the room to the other to get out of the way. "We got your whore, boy. You want me dead, you got to shoot her first." He thrust Zena in front of his body as a shield. Samples smelled her perfume and made the mistake of squeezing her soft, firm breasts. "You's a purty little thing, ain't ya, even though you is a nigger gal. I might be back, honey, fer some bed talk—when I finish killin' your boyfriend." Zena screamed loudly into Wooly's ear.

Drew Murdock and Hamilton Featherstone panicked at not knowing what all the ruckus was upstairs in the darkie nest.

"Samples! *Samples!*" yelled Drew.

In room number five, Wooly was in control. "Throw them guns out, boy," he said, "or she gets it!"

Not wanting to take any chances with Zena's life, Sergeant Shelby tossed his Colt out on the floor. Wooly laughed like a bull in a pasture full of heifers. Shelby held his hands high, but it was too much for him to take when

118

Samples stuck his slimy, spit-covered hand under Zena Beale's pretty dress and felt her private parts.

Out of instinct, Shelby lunged forward as Zena jerked loose from the outlaw's hold. The Black man kicked the gun from Samples's hand, then ran toward the door, knocking Ace Wiggins into Manny James, who fell into the other men. They tumbled out of the door, and several in the back fell down the stairs, breaking bone after bone.

"Idiots!" snapped Wooly. "Shoot that nigger. Shoot him dead, you fools!"

Shelby slammed the door with Wooly stuck outside. Samples rammed his shoulder against it, forcing it open again before Jon could flip the latch. Samples fell forward. He saw the gun on the floor and crawled over to the firearm. He had almost reached it when Zena stepped on his hand. Samples yanked his arm free from under her light body weight. He grabbed the gun, and with the other hand, he held Zena's wrist.

Zena thought fast. She sank her teeth into his dirty flesh. Wooly hollered and was off balance for the moment. Jon pounced on him, pulling Zena from Wooly's grasp. He punched Samples in the face, and the men grabbed at each other, fighting furiously for possession of the gun still in Wooly's hand. Samples delivered a left hook to Shelby's eye, and he was caught plumb off guard. But a right to Samples's jaw almost caused the gun to fly from his hand. The two men struggled until the gun was out of sight, hidden between their bodies. Then a bullet dislodged from the barrel, making an awful lot of noise.

Smoke billowed from between the two men's bodies. Zena screamed and fainted. Someone grunted, and the room was instantly silent. The whole damned town stood still. It didn't matter if the Yankee nigger got shot to death, but if it was the white man who was dead, that nigger, Jon Shelby, would hang before morning light.

Chapter

Sixteen

"Them damned fools still shootin' up LaDonna's Place," Drew Murdock said out loud. To himself he mumbled, "Now, Kate ain't never gon' speak to me again."

"Why you so gall-danged worried about a nigger whorehouse?" yelled someone in the back of the crowd.

"Who said that?" asked Drew Murdock. No one spoke up, afraid of what the man might do with his gun.

"Somebody git up there and see what the hell's goin' on," Drew ordered sharply. "It's too quiet. Bad things come when things is quiet!"

Upstairs, a war was under way. As the smoke plumed inside Zena Beale's room, Jon was overwhelmed by the same feeling of weariness he had had on the battlefield at Vicksburg in 1863, when the fourteen-month siege ended with General Grant in victory. The War Between the States had raged for so long and so many men had been lost; it was hard to forget all of the death he had seen. He wished somehow he could close his eyes and never hear a wounded man cry out that his legs were missing or that his arm no longer hung from his body. That "hot-damned war," as he often called it, was no longer back east; it was here, within the room, beyond escape.

The persistent silence had sunk into the bones of the three inside the room. The door to Zena's room creaked, opening very slowly.

One of Murdock's men, Albert Potter, fell through the entrance, deader than "yestiddy's hay," as Shelby's father would have said. Shelby and Samples were breathless, each thinking that he could have been dead instead of Albert Potter.

When Shelby saw Zena sprawled out on the floor, he forgot about getting away and ran to her at once. He turned to Samples with a rage in his eye and said, "If she's hurt, white man, you better kill me now, 'cause I'm gonna see that you die a thousand deaths. Go ahead, pull that trigger you son of a bitch. Go ahead. . . ." Jon hounded Samples, who stood there paralyzed with a gun in his hand.

Now Shelby knew that Samples was a coward—at least, when it came to killing. He couldn't believe he had just challenged death with a gun in the hand of a fool, and even more remarkable to him was that he had come out ahead this time.

Jon Shelby had had a revelation; never before had he been so outraged as he was at the moment. He had felt that the only way to contain his anger was death—his death— and that scared the wits out of him. Denmark Vesey had apparently felt the same way when he'd organized several hundred slaves to rebellion. Death can sometimes seem the only way to get what you want so desperately, and at that fleeting moment Jon Shelby had chosen to die instead of seeing his people torn apart one by one, instead of living with the pain of Zena's death. But that was a fool's way of thinking, for only living men could change the world, while courageous dead men rotted away.

Zena moaned in her delirium. The Union soldier scout picked up her limp and fragile frame in his arms, as behind him he heard the cocking of no less than half a dozen pistols and several rifles. He knew what he faced.

After Jon laid Zena on the bed and determined she had only fainted, he glanced toward the window and knew there was but one way out.

Zena came alive. She looked at Jon Shelby. Her face was shielded from view of Samples and the others gathered behind him, and Jon kissed her on the mouth to keep her from speaking. Then he hugged her and whispered in her ear, "My saddlebags are under your mattress; keep them for me until I come back. Nod if you understand." She nodded, and he continued, "Don't give them to no one, Zena. If I don't come back, give them to the Yankee commander, ya hear?" She nodded again.

Jon pretended to reach for a pan of water and a cloth to lay across Zena's forehead . . . and in a flash, he flung the water-filled washpan at the men behind him, specifically at Wooly Samples. He dove through the shattered window, landing on top of the forward veranda. The soldier had never bargained on jumping out of windows in his fight against the Rebels, but after all, he was still fighting the South, even this far west in a hell-hole known as Texas.

Down below on the street, the mob was tense with the quiet that was suddenly filled with a Black man on the run.

"Lookee thar," cried one citizen, pointing.

Everybody looked up and saw the man sprawled out on top of the LaDonna's porch top.

"Shelby, you can't get away, boy. Not with my money, you can't," Drew Murdock said.

"*My* money," added Hamilton Featherstone.

Drew Murdock pulled his pistol, and Hamilton Featherstone cringed, thinking he was about to be shot by one of his alleged friends. Instead, Drew fired into the air. Some of the boys fired rocks up at the soldier, which was foolish. The rocks just rolled back down onto the mob standing below.

"Give up, Shelby," Murdock yelled. "You don't stand a chance."

"What you want with me?" yelled the Black man from on top of the veranda.

"My two hundred in gold. Every penny of that money belongs to me," Drew said.

"And me," said the banker man.

"I only got the fifty you stole from me in your cheatin' ways, Murdock," Jon said. "Take it up with Miss Kate. She's got the rest of your kitty in her bosom."

"Now you leave Kate's bosom outta this," said Murdock. "I mean—"

Someone yelled, "Go get 'em, Drew!" The crowd hub-bubbed, and the joke was over.

Wooly and Ace had their heads stuck out of the window of Zena Beale's room. "Let me shoot him, Murdock."

"No. Don't," Drew yelled. "You might put a bullet in my money. Bank don't like its legal tender peppered with bullet holes."

"Damn right," said Featherstone.

Shelby's feet began to slip on the slick, cold roof and

before he could get a fresh grip, he slipped and fell the twenty feet or so to the ground. It was the bodies of several men down below that broke his fall and kept him from being hurt something awful. The remaining men gathered around the Black man and kicked him in every way that they could.

"Wait for me, you fools," Wooly called out from the window in Zena's room. "Don't kill him 'til I git there. I want the last lick myself!"

Wooly ran out of Zena Beale's room, forgetting she was lying on the big bed. While Samples's gang headed outside to Main Street, she ran to the window to see what she could do to help her Jonny. Her first instinct was to run from the room, and then she remembered what Jon had whispered in her ear. She checked under the mattress to see if his saddlebags were still there, and they were. She would guard them with her life, even if the soldier never returned.

Zena carefully perused the vacant hallway. The desperadoes were gone. She grabbed the bags and took them to LaDonna. Once she explained the story, LaDonna hid the bags away where not even God could find them if He tried. Jon's victory was their victory, too.

Downstairs on the street, Jon Shelby got the beating of his life.

"Let's hang us a nigger, boys," yelled someone in the crowd.

"Yeah," said Wooly Samples, who had Jon by the shirt, punching him like he was a one-hundred-pound sack of seed. "That's what you get, nigger, for bringin' me to jail."

There was a roar of agreement as several men continued to whip the snot out of the Black Union soldier. Jon tried to gather his strength, but the top of his head was throbbing with pain. Someone jammed his fist into the spot where the bowl of his hat should have been but wasn't; blood poured into his face, and he couldn't hear all of a sudden. A salty hot goo filled his mouth. One of the punches had cut his lip on the inside.

"We gon' kill him," moaned Hamilton Featherstone, who stood back and tried to figure out what to do. He was, first of all, worried about what Kate Pearson would think about the way they had broken up the room at LaDonna's, and then he was concerned that he would never get a chance to lay with her again. "Y'awl better stop, boys. We gon' have a killing on our hands directly, and I don't want no parts of it."

"Shut up, banker man," said Drew Murdock. "This nigger's got to be taught not to make a white man look like a fool in front of a white woman."

Jon's nose was bashed in, and he could barely breathe. His jaw wasn't broken—not yet—but it sure as hell felt like it. He was still being kicked and punched and kneed by the angry mob when Zena Beale ran upon the scene. But there was nothing she could do but watch the bloody carnage. She sorely wished Miss Kate were around, but she was busy making hay with a "customer."

By the time someone yelled, "Hang that nigger," Jon Shelby was drenched with blood and sweat. He looked like a dead man on the bloody field of battle. All that the Tennessee-born grandson of a man brought in shackles from Africa's Goré Island could think of now was his dream that might never come true. His time with Zena flashed before his eyes as another man struck a boot in his chest.

Jon's middle caved in. He felt hotter than he ever had under the most brutal sun. His side burned like a fire was raging inside his body.

"Stop it! You're killing him!" Zena cried. Two white men who held her back made sure she got some of the punishment, too.

"Shut up, you loud-mouthed nigger gal, afore I ram the butt of this here Allen inside your middle line," snarled one of the ruffians.

"Don't kill him! Don't!" Zena could not stop her screams.

Cinque Kele heard the commotion in the distance, but he figured it was just a bunch of drunken fools making fun like they often did, especially when restless cowboys had drunk one bottle too many.

Young Kele continued his work in the back of the livery, hoping that by the time he completed his chores the white man's games would be over. He knew that with drunk white men on the prowl, if he walked outside and tried to go home, just the mere presence of his Black face would cause even more of a row.

Nights like these, thought Cinque, was what made life

so miserable for both slaves and free Black folks in Clarksville. Whenever white men got drunk in town, they often raided the local darkies and did some hanging or torched several colored men's homes. He hoped one day he and his family could escape this kind of senseless violence.

By the time blood started to pour from Shelby's mouth and the lateral scar above his left eye, he felt like he'd been dragged a mile or two, maybe more, by a stubborn old mule that refused to let up the run. Something flashed in his eyes, but he didn't know what it was. A photographer had taken a picture of the scene. Jon Shelby was the star of the show.

Shelby's teeth were loose, his back was sore, sharp pains struck his head. He knew he was in a generally hopeless situation. He heard a familiar voice and somehow, through the torture, knew they were the words of a fool. Why he hadn't passed out, he didn't know; maybe the blood clotted within his ear had stopped some of the blows from filtering in. Maybe I'm dying, he thought in his frenzy. If this is the end, let it be, Lord, he prayed. Let it be!

Zena Beale had been dragged back into LaDonna's Place, where a cowboy punched her in the mouth and she was out like a light. LaDonna ran to her side.

Back outside, Wooly Samples, who had been too busy beating Shelby to even talk, finally said, "Let's fire up that hangin' tree, boys! And lynch that black-ass nigger 'til he's dead!"

Jon Shelby felt his feet being tied up with a lasso, and then the rope was hitched to a horse. The men slapped the animal on the butt, a big draft horse damn near eighteen hands high. The horse took off, dragging Shelby feet first toward the gallows. The men roared their approval and ran along behind the animal, yelling and screaming. Some of them held whiskey bottles in their hands, drinking themselves silly as they headed toward the gallows to take Jon Shelby's life.

Jon heard the crazed voice rise out of the din once more, then a muffled array of loud voices that got softer and softer.

"Where's that varmint that made me look like an idiot in front a' my Kate? Hot-dammit. I'm o' keel the dirty nigger dawg," said Tandy, who staggered up to Jon after the horse had stopped pulling the Black man along the street. He pulled his pistol from his scabbard. "That's it fer you, boy. You won't mess with another white woman's place a' bidness. I'm a-sending ya to ya Maker, boy. Someplace you ain't never been." He laughed, his eyes almost closed from drinking another half bottle of rotgut. "Good-bye, nigger," he sang. "See you in hell!"

As Tandy squeezed the trigger, several men untied Jon and dragged him up onto the hanging tree and stuck his neck in a rope. There were so many torches lighting up the sky that from a ways down the road a lone rider thought something huge was on fire.

The rider had headed into town to get a drink and pass away some time while he thought about his dilemma. He had trouble sleeping these days. As a future cattle rancher, he was plagued with cattle and horses being stolen, and every last one of his scouts had been killed out on the trail. He had been told long ago that the best scouts were Indians and Blacks, but there were no Indians around that he could trust, and none of the Blacks around Clarksville knew anything about scouting.

Without a good scout who could negotiate his way with hostile Indians or whoever else stood in his way, he might as well give up his dream . . . and that was something he would never do.

If he could find a good man for the job, he would hire him on the spot. Trouble was, no Indian or Negro scouts ever passed through Clarksville.

The lone rider raced as fast as he could toward the cluster of torches and saw that some poor colored fellow was about to get hung. And he didn't like that one bit. If a man was guilty of a crime, let him get his day in court. He had a special reason for wanting to see justice prevail, a secret he held within his heart.

"All right, boys! Hang that nigger!" Wooly ordered.

"Gotta git my money first," yelled Featherstone.

"Shut up, Hamilton," Drew Murdock said. "You can git what's left of the money after I git mine."

"All right, boys, let's do it," said a voice in the crowd.

And at that instant, the crack of a Henry rifle echoed from the nearby darkness. The crackle in the night came from the barrel of the lone rider's gun. From atop his fine bay he yelled to the folks to stop what they were doing or be shot.

"What's going on here?" yelled the rider. His name was Devers, Montana Devers, a Civil War hero from Fort Fisher and a local landowner soon to be a cattle baron.

"Nigger stole our money," Drew Murdock said.

"And we's a-hanging him 'til he's dead," said Wooly.

"Not until he's tried in a court of law," replied Montana Devers.

"That's what I say," Hamilton Featherstone agreed.

"Negras don't git no day in court, Devers. Ain't you learned that yet?" sneered Murdock.

Devers fired his Henry into the air again. He jumped from his horse, and the crowd parted as he walked through to the hanging platform, then up the steps to get a good look at the Black man about to be hung.

"So, he stole your money, huh? What'd he do, outcheat you, Murdock, in a game of poker?"

"You callin' me a cheat, Devers?"

"Reckon I am," said Devers.

"Why, you . . ." Murdock reached for his Allen revolver, but before he could pull the weapon, Devers had him covered with the Henry.

"Hold it right there, Murdock," Devers said, removing the noose from around Jon's neck with his free hand.

Jipson Tandy stumbled up and fired his old rickety pistol. The wild shot hit the *O* in O'Riley's seed store. The weapon flew apart at the seams, and Tandy jerked his hand back. The smoking pieces fell into the dirt.

Devers pulled his pistol and fired a shot near Tandy's feet. "Anybody else want to try somethin'? Do it now. My trigger finger's itchin' for a good target." Tandy was scared and hung his head to avoid Devers's glare.

The crowd didn't move until Devers holstered his gun. He kept the Henry in his hand. The men and several brave women crowded around the hanging tree like flies at dinnertime.

"This ain't none a' yore business now, Devers. This man stole my property and's guilty of several other things. Due to be hanged," said Drew Murdock. "We's lynchin' him up directly."

"Where's that no good marshal a' this town? Hidin' out, no doubt, in one a' them hotel rooms with some whore," challenged Devers. "Anyhow, ain't gon' be no lynchin' tonight 'til this man's had a fair trial, by law!"

The crowd parted as someone with evident authority walked through. It was Marshal Richards, ready to lay down the law. "You want me, Devers?"

"This man almost got killed. Where were you..." Devers paused before he said in a disrespectful tone, "Marshal?"

"Reckon 'tain't none a' your business. But I'm here now. So it might be wise for you all to go on home." He turned to the crowd, seeing Effie McGraw and Buck Whitfield's boy, Sammy, as he spoke.

"All right, break it up, folks, and go on home. Fun and excitement's over now. I'll handle it from here. Go on home now," said Cotton.

"What about him?" Devers said.

"What *about* him?" said Richards.

"You ain't jes' gon' let him lay here half-dead, are ya?"

"Hadn't thought much about it, Devers," Richards said.

"I suggest you do some thinkin' for a change," said Devers.

"I suggest you go to hell, cattleman."

"You know, Richards," Devers said, "I never did like you one bit. You're high on my list of things to feed my pigs."

"How high?" challenged the marshal.

"Number one!"

"Looks like my days are numbered," Richards drawled.

"Reckon so!" said Devers evenly.

"You as good with that gun as they say you are?" asked the marshal.

"Better!"

Chapter

Seventeen

Montana Devers never backed away from a good fight, especially if he thought he could win it. But that wasn't on his mind at the moment. He hated to see a man mobbed and beaten. He had been a victim of rabble-rousers several years ago himself. Just ain't fair, his second mind kept telling him.

Cinque Kele had finally completed his chores at the livery. He walked out of the front doors of the establishment and saw the rowdy scene at LaDonna's from the distance. He ran over to the ruckus as fast as he could. Montana Devers stood up, alone now with the bleeding hulk of Jonathan Shelby. He saw the young Black child standing there, and he called out, motioning for Cinque to head his way.

"What happened to the sergeant?" yelled the boy, beginning to cry, upset that his newly found hero was hurt and maybe dying.

"Got a wagon in that livery, son?" said Devers.

"Yessir, but I can't take it out without Mr. Savage sayin' I can."

"Don't you worry 'bout that none," Montana said. "I'll take care of that tomorrow. Now go git that wagon, we's takin' this man to my spread."

"He ain't dead, is he?" asked Cinque nervously.

"If you don't hurry up and get that wagon so we can patch him up, he will be," Montana Devers said. "Now git, boy. The faster we get outta town, the better. Them heathens may be back, and I don't plan to be around when they do."

And with those words came what Devers hoped would be another ally. Devers didn't hate Blacks, never did. He

129

didn't like them any more than he liked the next white man. But there were times when he couldn't stand to see the abuse Negroes got. He had sworn to himself the time he got beat up in Indian territory by rampant, self-made rangers that he would never see it happen again to any man . . . and that included Blacks, too.

He had always known that one day he would sort the Negro issue all out and take a side. Now he realized that that day had already come. He had sided with a Negro against some ornery whites. No more was Montana Devers a neutral man. Maybe he was a "nigger lover," as some called it.

Cinque ran back to the livery and hitched up the wagon out back. He closed up the shop again, and headed over to Montana Devers. They were preparing to lift Shelby into the back of the wagon when they heard someone yell from over near LaDonna's. Two people in a buggy were racing their way as fast as a Texas tornado.

"Whoa," coaxed the driver of the canopied buggy. "Whoa mule, whoa." It was LaDonna at the reins, Zena Beale beside her.

"What are you doing to him now? All you white men just alike! Gang a man and then come back to rob his pockets," cried Zena.

"He ain't robbin' him, Miss Zena," Cinque said. "This is Montana Devers. He saved Sergeant Shelby from gettin' hung." Jon managed to hear the word *Montana* before, mercifully, he passed out.

"That's right, ma'am," said Devers. "The boy's tellin' the truth. Now if you want this man to live, we better git him loaded onto this here flat. We's takin' him out to my place. He's gon' need some patchin' up."

"Wherever he goes, I'm going, too," said Zena, turning toward Miss LaDonna. "I'm sorry, Miss LaDonna. I jes' ain't cut out for your kind a' work. I reckon I'm jes' a failure, that's all, but I can't let Jonny out of my sight. I jes' had to tell you the truth. I won't come back again."

LaDonna looked Zena Beale straight in the eye and saw the mirror image of her younger self. She remembered long ago, many, many years ago, when she had been in a similar situation. The only difference was that she had taken the other road and become what she was today. She had

130

taken that wrong road, but she would help Zena Beale go the right way.

"Go on, gal," she said. "Don't worry 'bout 'pologizin' to me. And you better come back when that man's all well. I may have another job for you yet." Zena hugged La-Donna and they parted, still friends.

Zena Beale, Montana Devers, and Cinque Kele loaded Jon Shelby's mangled body into the wagon. It was getting real close to the bewitching hour.

"You sit tight and hang on, Sarge. We'll get you fixed right up," whispered Cinque.

In the depths of Shelby's mind, he could hear the word *Sarge*. "Dan'l, Dan'l," he murmured in his delirium as Cinque yanked rein and they headed off. Montana Devers led the way to his spread, the Circle D Ranch. Jon's head was cradled in Zena's lap like he was a baby. She spoke softly as she gently rubbed his swollen face. "Calm down, Jonny. We's takin' care of you." They drove out of sight of the town, into the blanket of darkness.

The March sun rose brightly in Texasland. The warmth emitted by the bright red ball of fiery light slowly eased into the soil. The "pew, pew" call of a purple martin bounced about in the morning stillness, and the winged, white-vested bird flew across the yard of Montana Devers's house on the Circle D Ranch in the middle of Devers's Hollow.

Jon Shelby had survived the rickety, bouncing wagon ride, Zena Beale by his side. He had been unconscious all night, and for a time he mumbled incoherently. Zena answered every word that the feverish soldier muttered. She felt somehow that she owed him something, what exactly it was she had yet to figure out. And she had yet to understand why Montana Devers had saved a colored man's life when he didn't have to. She closed her weary eyes. Some things she might never comprehend.

Zena figured that Devers had his own personal reasons, and she also realized again that all white folks weren't bad. In fact, Zena had almost concluded that most white folks were really good people, and that only a handful were mean, nasty, and angry at the world; but that was one handful too many.

Devers had told her to tell Jon that he owed him a favor when he was well, but Zena hadn't told him yet. He also told Cinque the same thing, to make sure the Black man got the word. Zena reckoned it would be a long time before Jonny was ready to think about debts owed and such.

The next day folks filled the new sidewalks of Clarksville, one of the few acts of beautification the town had ever seen. Another day had sprung, and there were lots of chores to do. The whites were busy making money, and the Blacks were helping them make it.

When the rooster crowed each morning out behind Zeke and Savage Stevens's livery, most Clarksvillians got up and were about like nobody's business. Drew Murdock, Cotton Richards, Hamilton Featherstone, and the rest of the gang had agreed to meet at the jail early to decide what to do about Montana Devers and the Negro, whom they hoped had died.

And although Wooly, Ace, and Manny had camped out of town away from the jail just in case the district law came by without prior warning, they were into town early, ready to cause more trouble.

They had been free for a day now, and the district sheriff hadn't yet been wired that he was needed in the town. Wooly had convinced Richards not to telegraph that his gang had killed the lawman's expectant daughter-in-law. Therefore, the district sheriff had no reason to rush to town.

It was nothing unusual for news to travel slowly when white men wanted it that way. Samples also knew that the district sheriff or the district judge—one or the other or both—would soon hear the news no matter what and come a-running to Clarksville with a badge, a gun, and the law in their favor.

But by that time he would be long gone, the desperado suspected. If he had been as smart as he professed to be, he would have left town as soon as Richards had let him out of jail. But Samples's mind was set to get revenge on a nigger. Jon Shelby must die for destroying his image, and he *would* kill him or his name wasn't Horace Lee.

The three cutthroats were back in town now, Ace and Manny waiting outside the lockup while Wooly Samples went inside to scream and yell at Richards, who was waiting comfortably for the other men to arrive.

"Dammit, Richards! You son of a b—you's 'bout as dumb as a man can be!"

"Wait a minute, Samples," said Cotton Richards. "I ain't know'd you long enough for you to curse me like that. I'm the law in these here parts, and I deserves respect. You rile me, you know what'll happen."

"Who says?" demanded Wooly.

"*I* says," Richards said.

"Some law," Wooly huffed, but he backed down.

"I could throw you behind bars for that. I's a mind to," said the marshal.

"You try it, and I'll sic that Devers fella on you," Wooly said.

"I ain't a-scared a' no ex–Confederate cowboy, even if he is a war he-row," said Cotton. "He ain't got no medal, and as far as I'm concerned he's just another tenderfoot, like you."

"You big enough to back up them words, cowboy?"

"Half of me is bigger than two of you, Samples. I want one thing from you, and when I gits it, I'm gone."

"You better come through," Samples warned.

"We still got a deal," said Cotton.

"We's still dealing all right," Wooly said. "So you stop rebuttin' me, Richards."

Drew Murdock heard the argument outside the door, and he stepped through as Wooly tried to grab Richards by the throat. Murdock broke up the fight, then scolded the two.

"Now you boys suppose to be working together, am I right?" said Drew. "Now we gotta git that boy from the Devers fella so we can git that money. Then we'll get Devers."

"It's your darn fault. You beat him up to a pulp, and you didn't even go in his pockets to get what we went after in the first place!"

"I searched every pocket that boy had, and not a sign of the money," said Murdock. "I tell you—"

The door flew open, and Hamilton Featherstone stood there in a new suit, as bold as the sun at night. "Got good news, boys," said the fat man. "Half our work done been done."

"What are you talkin' 'bout, Hamilton?" Drew said testily.

"Pete Freeman's boy says he overheard two of Devers's men talkin', sayin' Devers was leavin' the ranch, goin' away for several days. I figure that's the time to go and grab that boy, get our money, and let that colored gal patch him up—or what's left of him."

"Patch him up, my ass," said Wooly. "Gon' kill that boy with my own two hands if he ain't already dead."

"Don't care what you do after we get our money," Drew said. "Then you can kill him twice if you want to."

Cinque Kele had visited Devers's ranch every day for the past four days, and he fretted at times, since Jon Shelby had not regained consciousness, at least not while he was around. Jon had talked off and on to Zena Beale as she bathed his wounds and swollen parts with poultices soaked with liniment and herbs, namely myrrh, wood sage, and slippery elm, to keep the swelling down to a minimum.

Jon had told Zena about Tennessee, Louisiana, and some other places he had heard of but had never seen or set foot or eyes upon. She, in turn, told him all about herself and how she'd have to go back home without the money to free Santee. She also told him about her only boyfriend and how he disappeared without a trace.

"His name was Geffen Slaughter, and he was only fifteen at the time. I hear him calling my name sometimes," said Zena. "It's so hard when you know he's alive."

"I hope you find him one day," Jon said.

"Don't think I will. White folks found some bones down near the river, said that must have been that Slaughter boy. Iff'n they'd a' let me seen him, I'da known right off if it was him."

"I lost a friend, too," said Jon, reminiscing.

"Was she pretty?"

"No, 'he' wasn't pretty. He was my partner, Dan'l Walton. But unlike you, I know where old Dan'l is. I buried him six feet under just...ahh, some time ago...don't rightly recall how long it's been."

"Was he a sergeant jes' like you, Jonny?"

"A private, he was," said Jon, and they both were silent. Time passed, and the two said nothing. Thoughts of yesterday were fading away—today and tomorrow crept into their minds.

"When you get well, what you gon' do, Jonny?"

"I's headed west," said Jon. "You still got my saddlebags, ain't you?"

"They's safe," Zena said. "In Miss LaDonna's safe place."

Zena Beale and Jonathan Shelby got to know each other well during his convalescence. Once Jon got out of bed while no one was in his room and tried to walk outside to get some fresh air. But he was still too weak, and he fell. Zena scolded him for trying to kill himself. One of his wounds had burst open, and she had a hell of a time stopping the bleeding.

Once they talked about the Spanish slaveship the *Amistad*, and how thirty-eight slaves led by an African prince had seized a ship off the United States coast. But before Jon could finish the story, he had fallen off into one of his usual naps, which he needed for a speedy recovery. Zena knew he would finish later and smiled. She knew he was getting better, stronger by the hour, but in the distance she heard the rumble of the mighty thunder and grew cold at the sound. The rains had come off and on in recent weeks, and they appeared to be on their way again. The awful sound of the thunder filled Zena with an unnameable fear.

Zena was also puzzled that Montana Devers had left them alone in the room and had not once come in to visit. She wondered why the Chinese cook served them as if they were white folks. Maybe the times are changing, thought Zena Beale. "It always gets worse before it gets better," her uncle Collie had said. "When the burden is too much to bear, child, then you know the sun gon' soon shine." Maybe uncle Collie Beale was right. It was a distant, hopeful maybe. . . .

The sound of horses' hooves broke the silence of her dream, and Zena Beale jumped up from her bed and ran to the window to see a lone horseman tying rein. Tang Chow knocked on the door to the bedroom almost immediately. Cinque Kele ran in, soaked with rain. He screamed his words with fear:

135

"Some men comin'!"

"What you sayin', boy?"

"Mr. Tandy's comin' to shoot Sergeant Shelby! I heard 'em, I heard 'em. They's comin' soon!"

Zena fetched Tang Chow and asked for Devers. The Chinaman said he was gone to the far end of the hollow.

"When's he comin' back?" she asked.

"Don't know," said Tang Chow. "He be back soon, he say."

Zena was a fast thinker, which gave her an advantage in bad situations. Most men, colored and uncolored, thought women were slow, incapable of speedy decision making, and that therefore God had made man to keep her on time. Not Zena Beale. She stayed on her toes. She knew what to do . . . and she did it.

"Cinque, can we take the sergeant to your pappy's place?"

"You ain't said nothin' we can't handle, Miss Zena. My sister, Safiya, will sure take care of him."

She turned to Tang Chow. "We're leaving, Tang. You understand."

"I understand. I help you," said the Chinaman.

Zena shook Jon gently. He awoke in a daze. His wounds were sore, and he wished at times that he had died. But he *hadn't* died; he had lived to see another sunrise, and he vowed to reach his destination—Red River Station, Texas.

Within minutes Zena Beale and Cinque Kele headed out through the woodsy, rain-soaked area. They would get Jon Shelby to safety at the Keles' house. The drunken Jipson Tandy or gambler Drew Murdock or outlaw Wooly Samples could cause a lot of problems, and Zena refused to stand by and let this good man be harmed any further.

They arrived at the Keles' spread in record time for a flatbed wagon. The Keles were free people. Their former master lived just up the road. Their freedom had come as a gift, and they took it for a job well done. They were nestled within the most beautiful green meadow in the land.

The crackle sound of metal on gritty wet Texas soil was a signal that someone was coming up the road to the plot of land owned and deeded in the name of Kele. And it didn't take long before the wagon arrived at the door. The voice that rang out belonged to Cinque's sister, Safiya Kele.

"A wagon's coming up the road, Pappy," Safiya said to her father, the elderly and proud Thaddeus Kele.

"Must be old man Crosson bringin' those kids back from that hayride. Remind me, Sister"—that's what Thaddeus Kele called his only daughter sometimes—"to give Crosson a mess of them turnip greens and some tomatoes that just come in. Can't let our next-door neighbor miss out on some good eatin'."

Thaddeus Kele was a jet-black old man with a head full of white hair. The skin covering his forehead and all the way down to his neck was smooth with a reddish tinge, and he wore an old straw hat that had long since seen its best days. He was about five feet seven and a little bent over at the waist—a remnant from his days as a slave. He wore heavy cotton coveralls that had never really fit even when they were new.

Now, as the old Black Texan looked around the walls of the newly-built log cabin, his chest swelled with pride at having gained a functional keepsake for his children before he passed away. His white slaveowner had had a change of heart about the practice of slavery and had let his family go when Safiya was a baby and Cinque just a dream. He had prayed for his freedom for quite some time, and now he was a firm believer in miracles, a God-fearing man who thanked the Lord for setting him and his own free from the whip. He had defied the odds, defied what most deemed impossible.

At seventy years, Thaddeus was usually as spry and chipper as a candle fly at a barbecue. But in recent days his spirit had dwindled; a melancholy mood filled a part of every day and most of every night. So many of his fellow Negroes were still on plantations, working an hour before dawn until the moon shone through at night. How to get them free, old Thaddeus didn't know, but he knew the white man's war had something to do with Black folks' freedom. The details he had yet to figure out.

Chapter

Eighteen

"Wagon train comin' up the road," Safiya yelled a second time, her hearing far better than most folks because of her "disability."

"Pappy! Safiya! Pappy!" called Cinque as he jumped off the rig to help Sergeant Shelby out of the back of the wagon.

"What you got, Cinque!" Pappy Thaddeus asked, coming toward the boy.

"Jon Shelby," said the boy. "The sarge, Pappy—the fella I told you about that got beat up by a hundred white men in town the other day. He's a real sergeant in the Union Army. We bringing him from the Circle D."

Thaddeus Kele looked at the injured man under the soaking-wet blanket.

"Who you, gal?" he said, looking straight at Zena Beale.

"Zena Beale, sir," said Zena.

"Howdy, gal. Don't jes' sit there," said the old man. "This man's damned near dead. Get him inside. Safiya, got a sick man here, you know what to do."

Safiya Kele was a devastatingly beautiful young girl of fifteen who was destined to grow up breaking the hearts of men who would lust for the love in her heart. From her Texas accent to the tips of her supple fingers, she was perfect—except for that lone imperfection that made her special.

The girl made her way to the soot-coated cast-iron kettle that straddled a slow-burning, dry-wood fire in the front of the yard. The light from the Texan sun made notice of its presence, but the sparkles of its silver threads meant little to Safiya Kele, except for the warmth that she knew so well. The steps she took were steps etched in her memory.

She found the bucket used to carry the water, and by the time the young Black woman made it back inside the four-room cabin, Thaddeus and Cinque had placed Shelby on the feather-stuffed mattress.

"Y'awl move away now. This is woman's work. I'll take care of him," said Safiya.

"He's barely breathin', Safiya. I'll get the liniment and some rags to soak up the blood," Cinque said.

"Leave us alone now. Sick folk need clean, fresh air to breathe. Now go on. Get out," said Safiya. "I'll call you when I need you."

"I reckon you won't be needin' me, either," Zena said softly, hoping the young girl would ask her to stay.

"I understand what you're doin'," said Safiya, taking a wet compress soaked in goldenseal herb from a washpan. "Go on, Miss Zena, I'll take good care of him. You will be back, won't you?"

"I'll be back as soon as I can. He's been sick for darn near a week. Didn't do no good to get him wet. Day before yesterday I thought he'd be up and around, now he looks like he can barely hold on.

"Good-bye, Jonny," Zena said. She looked at Cinque Kele. "Thanks, Cinque. You let me know what the talk is about town when you hear it." Cinque nodded his head as Zena left the room, and soon the sound of horses' hooves on the packed rain-wet Texas soil faded in the distance.

The rain continued to fall throughout the night, and Jon Shelby's fever raged on until dawn. It was the start of his sixth day that he was finally out of danger. The capable hands of Safiya Kele had pulled him through.

Safiya's mammy and pappy were saddled with guilt from her birth. They felt they were to blame for Safiya's dilemma—and they never forgave themselves. But Safiya wasn't angry; she just hoped that one day she would be able to overcome her problem, which wasn't such a problem to her at all. An operation up north might make her whole. There was a fifty-fifty chance of success. That hopeful fact, coupled with the thousand-dollar hospital fee, brought tears to Pappy Thaddeus's eyes. Ain't no way I can afford to pay money like that for such an operation on my child, Pappy Thaddeus often complained to himself. A man'd have to be rich or white to afford that kind of money.

The light brown-skinned girl's hair was thick and coarse, and a widow's peak divided her face. It was a wonderful face, so bold and so round. Safiya's hands searched the outline of Jon's face as he lay on the bed. She knew the size of his eyes, nose, and ears. She knew every curve on the upper part of his body as well, where most of the bruises were. She paid special attention to the man's physical features, and she would have known him anywhere, just by touching him.

The recovering U.S. Army soldier scout had been hampered by night sweats and fever, and the sight of first light was foggy and obscure. When Safiya's image focused in his brain, he knew he had to be alive.

"Don't try to talk," were her comforting words to him when he first awoke from his long sleep. "You must rest. You don't have to be hungry, Sergeant Shelby, to take some of this broth. It will help mend your bones and bring you back to health."

"Who are you?" asked the soldier.

"Safiya. Cinque's sister. And you are Sergeant Jonathan Frederick Shelby of the U.S. Army. How do you feel?"

"Like some ribs are missing," Jon said.

"Don't try to move," said the young Kele woman. "Just lie still and I will make you feel better."

"Wait . . ." Shelby began.

The young woman patted his hand, then rose from her chair beside the bed and left the room. She had a strange look in her eyes, a dreamy, far-off look. But Shelby figured it was his illness making him see the world in a haze. Still, he reckoned now that the worst had passed; nothing ever kept a Tennessean down for long.

Jon's attention was drawn toward the door of the room again as an old man came through it and shuffled toward the bed.

"I'm glad you're doin' better, Sergeant. I'm Thaddeus Kele; Cinque's my youngest. You were near dead when they brought you here last Thursday. Safiya's done a good job, though. She's my onlyiest girl." The old Black man

140

looked feeble, but just for an instant. "Yup. She done real good."

"Thank you for taking me in, Mr. Kele," said Jon. "I'm much obliged. You can call me Jon."

"Safiya says what you'll need is a good meal in a few days," Thaddeus said.

"How did I get here?"

"Said some fool white man's after your hide. That gal, what's her name . . ."

"Zena," said Jon.

"That's her," said Pappy Thaddeus Kele. "She and my boy here brung you in during the rainstorm. You was bleedin' pretty awful. You been here, I reckon, for almost a week."

"I've got to go," said Jon, feeling a sense of duty welling up through his weakness.

"Ain't no way, Sergeant. You need at least another several days to come around to normal. You'd be a fool if you leave any sooner."

"Can't wait that long. Got to get to Red River Station," said Jon.

"You leave now, you'll arrive there in a casket," Pappy Kele said firmly.

Jon tentatively moved his body, and although it was painful, he knew it was just the soreness that always stayed around after the wound had for the most part healed. He cringed a little at the pain within the hollow of his chest, but he had work to do. He would leave bright and early in the morning.

Two weeks had passed already since he'd first come to Clarksville, and in that time spring had arrived. The weather would get even warmer and the winds agreeably softer. Yes, tomorrow was another day, the day he would leave the Keles.

But something more bothered him. Zena Beale still had not returned with his saddlebags and folio that she had hidden at LaDonna's Place. Something might have gone wrong. Jon prayed for her safety and hoped she would return with his gear. Only then could he head out to Red River Station, never to come this way again.

* * *

Zena's moving Jon Shelby from Montana Devers's Circle D Ranch to the home of Thaddeus Kele had only been a precaution against Jipson Tandy's drunken rage. On his way out of the Lazy Day Saloon, Jipson had picked up a bottle of that special expensive bourbon sitting in Kate's room, and it tasted so good he forgot all about trying to kill a blue-clad nigger several miles away. That's why nothing ever came of Tandy's run to kill Jon Shelby. There had never really been much of a threat there; everyone in town knew that. But Black folk couldn't afford the luxury of indifference.

Wooly Samples and his gang decided to pull one more job before they left Clarksville's territory. At first Cotton Richards was against it. He was ready to get his money and get out of town. He knew he'd be in big trouble if the district judge or the district marshal came to Clarksville. Aiding and abetting fugitives from the law was just asking for trouble . . . but extra cash could go a long, long way. He decided to wait for the robbery Samples planned to pull off, and then he'd leave.

A shipment of gold was coming from Tucson, and Wooly had known about it for some time. Since he had hung around and waited to kill Jon Shelby, he figured why not wait another three days and take the shipment, kill off Manny James, Ace Wiggins—and Cotton Richards if he got nasty—then head back home to El Paso, where he and his folks could be richer'n a river bottom's dirt. The gold would come through next Sunday, and the district sheriff and the district judge were still nowhere in sight.

Cinque returned home for lunch with a message for Sergeant Shelby from Zena Beale. As he prepared to grab the latch to Shelby's room and enter, he overheard his pappy Thaddeus telling the sergeant that if he had to leave tomorrow, he needed a good meal tonight. His pappy finished his words just as the youngster walked into the room.

"Good food'll help make up for all the blood you lost. We ain't got no fancy food, Sergeant, some chitlins, fried hickory cane corn, smoked salt-back, and some turnip greens with enough pot liquor for seconds and thirds, if you like. I make the best egg bread this side of Clarksville, though. We'll be pleased to have you. See you at supper, Sergeant."

Cinque walked into the room, which smelled like a tub of herbs. His pappy rubbed the young boy on the head, but Cinque rushed past to tell the sergeant the news.

"Miss Zena says the white men took your saddlebags from Miss LaDonna's Place. They tore up the place somethin' awful!"

"Zena all right?" asked Jon worriedly.

"She's on the trail 'tween here and town when that Samples fella, Drew Murdock, and several others busted in the place and stole your saddlebags."

"LaDonna?" Jon said.

"Ain't nobody hurt, Sergeant. Zena said she's sorry at what happened."

"My bags—did she say where they took the bags?"

"Jailhouse, I reckon. The marshal was with the gang when they raided Miss LaDonna's. Said something about the place being operated illeg . . . illeg . . ."

"Illegally," said Jon.

"Yeah, Sergeant. That's what they said," Cinque said, nodding.

"How does a twelve-year-old boy learn so much, Cinque?" said Jon, laughing and for a moment forgetting about his pain.

"I listen a lot, sir. Pappy says you don't learn nothin' by talking, you learn by listenin'. So that's what I do. Listen to what everybody's saying. White folks say anythin' 'round a little Black boy, thinking he's too dumb to know what they's saying. But I ain't so dumb, that's how I learns what I knows."

Jon and Cinque shook hands, and the boy left to take on some victuals. Then he'd be on his way back to work. Jon used the quiet now to plan his next move. He would rest during the afternoon, walk around some to gain his strength, then he would eat, get a good night's sleep, and in the morning head back to Clarksville to get his saddlebags. After what Cinque had told him about the raid on LaDonna's, he knew the marshal was on the take.

Later that day Jon instructed Cinque to tell Zena about his plans to retrieve his saddlebags tomorrow sometime and to meet him at LaDonna's.

That night, at the Keles' supper table, the Keles and Shelby had a meal that made the sergeant feel at home.

Safiya and Cinque were quiet while the menfolk got acquainted even further. Pappy Thaddeus Kele hated to see Jon leave, but he could tell the man had willed himself much healthier in just a few hours.

"Haven't had a supper like this'n since the night before I left Shreveport. That peach cobbler, Safiya, set me a-fire. Always was my favorite." Jon laughingly patted his stomach.

"Yup, Sergeant, for a fifteen-year-old gal, Sister makes it just like her mammy Rashida did," Thaddeus said. "She's the spittin' image of her, too. Young Cinque never saw his mammy, except as a baby. And he really didn't see her then, since his eyes were closed for several days. He's seen some pictures, though. I still remember her. Young and so, so beautiful. She was the pride of my life. Still is."

"I'm sorry," said Jon.

"Destiny. That's all it is, Sergeant. Even Black folk have destiny. Rashida made me promise to teach these chillen how to read, write, and count. I did my part." Thaddeus cleared his throat. "What about you? Where ya headed?"

"Got business in Red River Station. Official military business."

"I done heard most of the bad news about the war. White folks say the South done won. I's kinda hopin' you had some good news for a change."

"You heard lies, Pappy Thaddeus," said the sergeant. "Northern army's winning, last I heard. If the U.S. Army loses, the sun won't rise tomorrow morning. Don't know when or where, but General Grant gon' lead Union blue to victory, only a matter of time, the way I see it."

"Sounds good, boy," Thaddeus said.

"You heard about Fort Pillow in April of last year?"

"White folks don't tell us nothin', ain't never heard of no such place."

"Three hundred of us Negroes were gunned down 'bout year ago at Fort Pillow, Tennessee. The bad part was that they were surrendering at the time to General Forest. Even after that, most white folks don't think the Black man is brave enough to fight. Sometimes there's no figuring them."

"My oldest boy, Antonio, been thinkin' 'bout joining up when he gets back from Missouri."

"War'll be over by then, I say," said Jon. "'Less'n he gets back pretty soon."

"How'd you join up, Sergeant?"

"Saw a notice from the War Department saying they's looking for colored men to join up. So I headed to Louisiana and signed up with the Corps D'Afrique of General Nathaniel P. Banks. During a bivouac, I met a self-appointed general named Williams. We hit it off, and here I am today, a scout for the Army of the United States."

"Still set on leavin' tomorry morning?"

"Yessir, sure am," said Jon.

Safiya looked up, startled and alarmed that Shelby would be leaving so soon. She had grown accustomed to his being there with her. How could he leave so soon, before he could tell her more about the world outside of Texas? At fifteen years old she was a woman by every standard in the book; she had grown hot and restless when Jon had touched her in his delirium, and she liked what she felt inside.

"You're not well enough, Jonathan. I mean, your wounds could stand some more healing," said Safiya Kele.

He liked the way she said "Jonathan." "Got no choice, Safiya. I've lost precious time as it is." Jon turned to Pappy Thaddeus. "Your other son. Where is he?"

"Antonio?" said Thaddeus. "Why, he's gone to St. Joe to see about a doctor for Safiya."

"Doctor?" Jon said. "The child's perfectly healthy."

"Healthy? You haven't noticed, have you, Sergeant? Safiya's blind. You really didn't know?" Thaddeus wondered.

Jon shook his head. "She seems . . . so . . . so normal."

"I *am* normal!" Safiya cried. "Just because I can't see don't mean I'm different. One of these days I'll be able to see. I been prayin' every night that the good Lord will bless me with sight."

"You keep on prayin, gal," said Sergeant Shelby, sorry that he had offended the young woman who had saved his life. "Don't you ever give up hoping, ya hear?"

Jon, Safiya, Pappy Thaddeus, and Cinque finished din-

145

ner, and the men went outside. Pappy smoked his pipe, and Jon rolled a smoke. Thaddeus took a swig from his jug of corn liquor and reluctantly let the sergeant take a drink. Still, Pappy got several more swallows than the soldier did, and both men felt good. It didn't take much for Jon's weaker body to feel the juice.

"A sick and healing man can't have too much good corn," said Pappy Thaddeus Kele. He enjoyed Jon's company. It was good for men of color to relax and jaw together on occasion, as long as that occasion didn't come too often. There was always work to be done.

"You got some boy in that Cinque, Pappy Thaddeus," said Jon. "He's gon' grow up to be a leader."

"Hope so, Sergeant. Sometimes I think he's too smart to be in this kind of sit'ation. A school up north might be better fer him."

"Don't you worry none, sir. A smart Negro will find a way to be free, and make the best of hisself. He'll also find a way to get the education he needs. If I could do it, Cinque certainly could."

When the buzz from the corn liquor died down and their heads started to swim, they said good night and headed for their beds. What the two grown men didn't know was that young Cinque had listened to their talk and was almost bursting with excitement. When they went inside to sleep, Cinque lay down and fell asleep clutching a wooden knife in a new leather sheath. It was an early birthday gift, carved by his pappy. In three short days he'd turn thirteen years old.

Inside the kitchen whipping up another dish, Safiya had listened intently as pappy told Shelby more about the operation needed to repair her sight. She ran into her room and cried in silence. If only she could *see*, maybe Sergeant Shelby would come back when the war was over.

Each night since he had been at her home, Safiya had checked on Jon to make sure he was resting well. Now, on this last night, she did the same, walking into his room quietly. She assumed he was asleep.

"Safiya," Jon whispered, startling her. He watched her now, watched her every move. It was hard to talk to her. He was afraid of hurting her feelings again. She was the woman who had nursed him back to health. He owed his life in part to Zena Beale, in part to Safiya Kele and her family. The healing soldier paid close attention to her lips when they parted to speak her peace.

"I didn't mean to snap at you at supper," said Safiya.

Jon watched her move around the room. There was nothing she couldn't find in a hurry. It was times like these that made him thankful for the things he took for granted. "*I* shouldn't have spoke out of turn," he said softly.

"I hope that one day you'll come back to us." Safiya was surprised at her own boldness.

Jon clutched her hand. Safiya smiled and left his room. She fell asleep that night dreaming of better days to come, dreaming of the things she had learned from a man named Sergeant Shelby.

Chapter

Nineteen

The crow of the rooster darted lonely through the dew forest, its echo christening the morning with life renewed and fair. A thirteen-lined ground squirrel stuck its head out from behind a tree and yanked it back in a hurry, scared of the raucous heralding.

The smoky smell of the early wood fire meant that another day had arrived. The cabin was alive with the sounds of life and the sounds of peaceful resolve. The elder Kele had long been up and about, and now he and Shelby said their words of good-bye.

"Stop by when you come back from River Station. I'm sure Safiya'd be tickled to mix up one of them peach cobblers for ya. . . ."

"I already did, Pappy," said the young woman. She had baked the cobbler the night before while her pappy and Jon were busy drinking. Now she handed it to him, then hugged him close. Her plea was short and unexpected as she whispered in his ear.

"I will one day see you with my own eyes, Jonathan. Please come back. I want to make sure you got well and to see if I done good."

Safiya placed an African charm in his hand, whispered some words, smiled, then stepped away. "*Gris-gris*, Sergeant Jonathan Shelby. For good luck." And then they heard the noise. . . .

A bunch of animals' hooves raced through the trees, and the light of torches in the half dark of the morning came bursting into view. Cinque was the first to holler.

"Sergeant! Look yonder! Toward the gristmill, over by the creek."

"Y'awl get inside," said Jon. "Some fools attackin' us."

Jon grabbed Safiya and shuttled her over behind him. She was frightened at not being able to see what was going on. He looked over behind him; luckily the horses had been unhobbled, saddled, and were ready to go.

"I'll get my gun," Thaddeus said.

"Cinque! I want you to take Safiya inside the house. Take the horses and make them lay down, you know how?"

"Is that an order, sir?" said Cinque.

"That's an order, soldier," Jon said, humoring the boy. "Make the horses lay down back to back and put Safiya between them, just in case a stray bullet ricochets off one a' them walls. And you stay in there with her."

"But, Sergeant! I can't be no soldier by hidin' out with the girls and horses," Cinque argued.

"A good soldier takes orders," Jon said. "Now move it, soldier."

"Yessir, Sergeant!" said the boy.

Thaddeus returned with his rifle. "This ain't your fight, Jonathan," he said. "These bigots ain't got nothing against you."

"Them yaps got somethin' against my skin, Pappy. That makes your fight my fight, too!" The soldier cocked his rifle.

A bullet flew past Thaddeus Kele's head. Jon grabbed the old man and they fell behind the wagon. Safiya and Cinque lay down on the dirt floor of the cabin.

Cinque saw his pappy's Colt hanging on the wall on a ten-penny nail, and he knew how to use it well. He crawled over to the bed, eased up on the soft cotton ticking, and yanked the weapon down.

Cinque checked the chamber. Empty. He found several boxes of bullets, loaded up the gun, and peeked out the crack in the door. He told Safiya to stay down. The blind girl grabbed for air as Cinque ran through the door. "Stay down," the boy yelled. "It'll be all right. Sergeant Shelby won't let nobody be hurt." He crawled out of the door and over to the wagon where Jon and Pappy Kele were holed up. Only twelve years old, he was ready to take a stand to defend his own.

"Git back in that house, boy," Thaddeus hissed.

"Two guns ain't enough to hold off them Rebels. I'm aimin' to shoot me a few, too."

Before Thaddeus Kele could explain to his youngest boy that fighting was for men, Cinque let off a shot that hit one bigot right in the gut. Surprised, Thaddeus looked at Jon, and Jon looked back at Thaddeus. The old man's chest puffed up with pride. "That's my boy!"

"You better tell your boy to git down 'fore one a' them forty-fours makes him lay down."

A loud, dispiriting yell echoed from the woods deep inside the bush. Three horsemen appeared, ready to finish off the game they'd begun during the night when they'd burned the home of white man Aston Bingham, who was rumored to give shelter to runaway slaves.

Wielding bloody, grounded hatchets, the raiders swung their arms above their heads in random fashion. In 1865, it was typical for wild, renegade former Confederate soldiers and present-day no-accounts to rape, pillage, and loot all those within their sight. It was all in a day's normal doings, and that was the only reason these marauders were attacking the Kele clan.

These disorganized men were attackers from the lower twenty-third, debased, conniving dogs that should have been snuffed out long ago.

Grayling Tatum led Natty, his son, and Travis Dickey on a romp through the Keles' well-tended homestead garden, making mulch of the corn stalks and crowder peas. They came at full speed toward the two armed men and the boy.

"Gon' git us more a' them darkies, Travis," yelled Grayling Tatum. A two-day-old speckled beard coated most of his wide, hog-like face, half hidden under a blue bandanna tied across his nose and mouth. Travis Dickey's sweat reeked of snuff and yeast and cheap one-step barley from Sip Spurling's backyard distillery.

"This one's mine, Pa!" Natty spoke with a mug full of slobber, dripping from a mouthful of inch-long teeth that had been rotten and jagged ever since they grew in.

"They don't know who we are, anywhos," said the handsome Hobby Wyatt as he rode up to join his three

150

buddies. "Don't make me no never mind what you do, Natty boy!"

Hidden behind the wagon, Jon, Thaddeus, and Cinque were trying to hold off the attacking varmints.

"C'mon," whispered Shelby. "We better lead them away from the house. They'll think ain't nobody there and follow us into the bush."

"I ain't leavin' my gal alone," Thaddeus hissed.

"We ain't leavin' her, Thaddeus. We'll keep an eye on the cabin from over there. After what she's done for me, I'd die before I let something happen to Safiya."

"I ain't leavin'!"

"Trust me, man." Jon grabbed Thaddeus by the shoulders and stared into his deep-set eyes. "I'm on your side. Trust me."

The two colored men and the boy ran toward a sturdy oak tree across the way. Their ammunition was low, but there was hope, always hope. Their heavily booted feet carried them deep into the grove of cottonwood trees and sycamores. They ran fast, through the thornbushes, the briars pricked the skin on his face. They were lost in the bush, but not for long.

A sweeping sound swished past Jon's head in an awful hurry; it was Travis Dickey's hatchet. Shelby shifted direction, grabbing Cinque by the shoulders. Close behind them, a weed oak stump caught Dickey's mount's front right hoof, and he tumbled and fell on his other hatchet. Dickey's chest was exposed, and gobs of blood pumped from his heart into the Texas soil. His bigoting days were over!

From their angle, neither Grayling nor Natty could see their dead companion's condition. Just then, through the garden, came more horses bearing men with no good intentions. "It would take all of their heads to produce one good brain, and then you'd be lacking for some," Tatum's father, Homer, had said the day he died of consumption back in 1863. Others had agreed that his words were true. "This Secret Order white man's business," Homer said with his last breath, "is surely a waste of time, I reckon." The Secret Order was a group of men who would attack innocent people unlike themselves. They would even kill white folks they didn't particularly like.

The outlaws' support team had arrived, and the desperadoes clearly had the upper hand. Jon shook his head, peeved to the hilt. "Ain't fair," he said amid the fright. "All a' them against two men and a boy."

Some of the men were brandishing burning poles. They dashed toward the three dark heads they saw trying to hide in the distance.

"Hang that nigger, nigger boy, too," one of the marauders yelled in a deep Texan accent.

"Surround 'em! Do I have ta tell ya everything?" cried Grayling Tatum to his boy.

"Can't get away now, boy!" another marauder cried jubilantly.

The army man raged from within. He pulled his Colt and fired, hitting home with the first four pellets he let go. A bullet bounced off the tree behind his head. He looked down to make sure little Cinque was safe. He was.

More shots riddled the forest, and suddenly a puff of smoke and a *whump* sound spewed from Shelby's left. Thaddeus Kele lunged backward. The old man had been hit by a large-caliber slug. Cinque clutched his pappy and screamed. "Pappy, Pappy! Don't you die!"

"Shut up, Cinque . . . they can't rightly see us through this thick green. Don't give us away completely."

Jon tore Pappy Thaddeus's shirt away from the wound. He cringed at the hole and thought of Dan'l Walton. The soldier tried to fire his weapon, but his pistol was empty, and when he felt around his belt for some extra rounds, he remembered that Safiya had removed the gun and bullets from his belt, put them in an old piece of cowhide, and laid them outside the door. She didn't like guns, and without lead a gun was useless—as his was now.

"Damn," said Shelby. "Looks like that's it."

"We got to do something for Pappy," Cinque cried. "He's bleedin' awful bad."

"We will, boy," said Jon. "We will."

A shot of hot lead hit the heel of Shelby's boot, then another ricocheted near his head. Thaddeus Kele moaned, hurting bad. A shotgun blast kicked up dirt in the soldier's eyes, blinding him for the moment. Shelby rubbed clear his eyes and pulled the Colt's Navy from inside the belt of the bloody Thaddeus Kele. He fired again, and more men fell, dead as dry flies in December snow.

Click. Click. The Navy said "empty" to Shelby. "That's all she wrote, Cinque," Jon said. "We gotta run."

"Ain't no place to run," cried Cinque. "We's surrounded!"

Chapter

Twenty

Out of the denser forest came a tall, hooded figure, perched proudly upon the back of the largest black stallion Jon Shelby had seen to date. The horseman wore several layers of buffalo skins in three brown tiers wrapped in deliberate overlap. Two pistols hung crisscross fashion inside a midriff belt, two Remington new model Army forty-fours, ready to kill. The mother-of-pearl grips displaying the classic emblem were shiny and new, and they appeared, to Jon, to hold those animal skins in place.

A thin, sienna-colored hood made from the skin of a whitetail deer covered the head of the rider, though its front stood open for visibility's sake. The red light inside the hood near the mouth, Shelby assumed, was produced by the coals of a large cigar. The fire looked like a small sun cradled within a dark little universe.

Suddenly guns blazed from atop the mount—first a Spencer seven-shot breechloader, then a Joslyn that refused to misfire a single time.

"Damn! He's a good shot," Jon said to Pappy Kele. "Hasn't missed a bigot yet."

Circling closer to Jon, Cinque, and the bleeding Pappy Kele, the lone gunman tossed Shelby a Spencer and an Allen revolver, both fully loaded. By the time Shelby got off two or three rounds, the ground was covered with dead or dying invaders. They were now only splotches of blood and jellied flesh, on their dark way to meeting their Maker.

The few remaining attackers sped through the hollow, and the rumble of steel-bottomed hooves sounded as they faded into the early morning mist. The foray was finally over, and Jon and Cinque shook hands. Pappy Kele smiled through piercing fettles of pain, proud of the courage within the heart of his youngest son. A fine man he would be someday.

The mounted warrior turned and faced the sergeant and his party, seemingly displeased with the folks that his surprise appearance and fancy shooting had managed to save. The outsider's words were direct, unminced in phrase and in speed.

"You can get up now. I'm not here to hurt you. Seems like a body who saved your life deserves a thanks or two."

"We're mighty obliged to ya, sir. I'm Sergeant Jonathan Frederick Shelby. This here's Cinque Kele and his pappy, Thaddeus—" Jon's words were cut short when the mounted rider flipped back the hood of the cloak. Jon's mouth dropped open when the Black face came into the light.

"Lavinia T. Gurley's the name. Folks call me Vinia. Now git this straight. I ain't no sir!"

"He's . . . a . . . she!" gasped Cinque.

"Sorry, Miss Gurley. Didn't know you's a she."

"I shoulda shot you two first! Y'awl act like you ain't never seen a woman before. Your mammy was a woman, wasn't she?"

"No . . . I mean, I just thought. I . . ." Shelby stuttered, then laughed and slapped his thigh with his hand. "The way you handled them shootin' irons, I thought you were one a' them bounty hunters or somethin'."

The plainswoman turned her head toward the field of dead and dying men. The expression on her face never changed, nor did she crack a smile. The texture of the forest softened at once, and only the moaning of the injured men broke a robin's happy song nearby. The rattle of death was on its way to claim another kill, but the sun continued to rise.

"How bad's he hit?" asked Vinia, looking at Pappy Kele.

Jon shook his head. "Pretty bad. He gon' need a doctor, I reckon."

"Ain't no doctors out here. That your cabin over yonder?"

"Mine," whispered old man Pappy Kele, grimacing in his torment.

155

"Let's get him in it and see what we can do to stop that bleedin'," Lavinia T. Gurley said.

"I never expected my life to be saved by a woman," Shelby said as they entered the cabin. Vinia rolled her eyes at Jon in such a way that made him embarrassed. He hadn't meant any harm, but he still felt like a fool. That was one thing he would never say to a woman again, and certainly not to Miss Lavinia T. Gurley. First Zena, then Safiya, and now Vinia! Yes, sir, he would think carefully before he spoke again!

This dark-skinned Vinia *could* have passed for a man, and that was pure fact. She kept the same hard, fearless expression about her face at all times. Shelby scanned Vinia from head to toe and concluded that beneath the flat, puffy nose, the light bronze eyes, and the grim expression was a real compassionate person. A ray of sun snaked between the trees and through the windows, reflecting off the early morning fog. Yes, Lavinia T. Gurley was a real human being after all—and she was Black and strong, and that was good.

Pappy Kele hurt badly while Jon and Vinia cut the slug from his body. The whiskey Vinia gave him helped to make the pain go down easier. She bragged about how many bullets she had removed from men both good and bad. "Part of my job is to keep the prisoner alive when I'm bounty huntin', less'n the law says I still get paid if he's dead. Dead man's too much trouble, though. Have to rush him to the outpost where my connections is awaitin' and grab the bounty before maggots start eatin' him up. Of course, that don't apply to the old man, since he ain't the one I was looking for at the moment in the first place."

It was a painful ordeal when the knife scraped the surface of the left clavicle, and that was when Vinia realized the bullet had entered Kele's upper arm and lodged near the shoulder blade. The pressure from Vinia's digging into Pappy's chest made him wish God would either end his pain or death would end his life. But Pappy Kele was a strong-willed man who had often endured pain as a child when the crack and slap of the white man's whip melted the tender skin on his back. That bottle of sour mash he'd guzzled before Vinia's knife pierced his flesh made a bad situation nearly tolerable. And when it was over he felt warm, and he pretended to sleep. His life was fulfilled, and he felt peaceful inside, yet he didn't know what it all meant. And when his eyelids truly grew tired and his body gave way, he dreamed of his new friends, the sergeant and Vinia, and was thankful for the having of his life.

While Safiya sat by her father's side, Jon contemplated the situation. Because of all the emotional turmoil he'd endured during the past week, vivid pictures of his past life rushed before his eyes. He saw the smile of his mother, Hallie, and he felt for a moment like a little boy, content to be held and rocked when the sadnesses of childhood overcame him. But this image was rapidly and cruelly replaced by a picture of Dan'l Walton, dying under the hot Texas sun. Jon's mouth set in a grim line, and he got ready to hit the trail with renewed vigor.

A few minutes later Vinia knocked on the door to his room and entered. "We got to hurry. There'll be a posse nosin' around here soon." She turned to Cinque, who had come in behind her. "Got any shovels, boy?"

"I'm not no boy," Cinque said defiantly, still flushed with pride after his first killing. "I'm a small man that ain't growed up yet."

"You'd better answer me, boy, or I'll turn yours ears inside out."

"They's outside in the smokehouse," Cinque answered, his lips stuck out to the limit.

"There's no time to dig them fools' graves, Vinia," said Jon.

"Peckerwoods be stinkin' before nightfall in this heat," she replied, pulling out a Wanted poster. She kept it well hidden from all other eyes as she took a look at it, then she rolled the paper up again and began loading her weapons. The poster was identical to the one Jon had seen at the Clarksville jail but he didn't know it.

"We've got to do *something*," said Sergeant Shelby.

"I'm glad we ain't too close to town," said Vinia. "We can git a head start if we think fast."

Looming in the minds of both Vinia and the sergeant was the problem of leaving several dead white men strewn across a Black man's field not three hundred yards from his brand-new cabin.

The Kele family would be defenseless against angry

whites, thought Vinia. They would beat the old man to a pulp, then, as her father used to say, "hang him on general principle." Cinque might have a chance, after playing houseboy to some heathen slaveowner, Jon reflected. What would happen to Safiya? Lovely, fine Safiya. He shuddered with anger at the thought of white men pawing and having their way with the young woman, and he vowed to save them, no matter how long it took.

"I'll take care of those bodies," said Thaddeus, who had staggered to the door of Shelby's room. Jon and Cinque helped him to a chair. He swallowed deeply and wheezed several times. Then, looking older than before, he told Cinque what to do. "You know how to get to Richard Talley's spread, Cinque?" Cinque nodded. "Go. Tell him we got some dead white men over here."

"What good'll that do?" asked the sergeant.

Thaddeus Kele cringed, the hole in his arm and shoulder throbbing with ripples of pain. Fresh hot blood soaked through the bandage. Clearly the old man should have stayed in bed. "Talley's white," he said. "He helps us in times like these. Talley's a good man, he'll explain that the dead men were trespassing on his land. We'll move them —he'll do the rest." Thaddeus stopped to catch his breath. "You two best be goin'. We've been through this before, I reckon we'll survive this time."

"But—"

"Ain't no buts, Sergeant," Thaddeus said firmly. "Y'awl get goin', ya hear? I didn't get to be this old not knowing what I'm a-doing!"

Both Jon and Lavinia T. Gurley felt their stomachs rumble. They didn't like leaving their kind alone to face the unknown. Reluctantly, however, they agreed to go their ways.

Jon kissed Safiya like she should be kissed every day. He told her to keep believing that one day she would gain her eyesight, and she made him promise to return and celebrate that day.

Sergeant Shelby squinted his eyes, grinning at the old man's will to live. He tipped his hat and winked at Safiya. She couldn't see his expression, but he was sure that somehow she got the complete message.

Shelby and Vinia slowly led their horses from the yard and said their good-byes.

"A bounty hunter. Never would have thought. What if I said I didn't believe you?" said Jon to the woman.

"Believe what?"

"That you're a bounty hunter."

"Don't make no never mind to me. The truth is always harder to believe than a lie. Tell you about it someday, if I live," said Vinia.

"Who you after, Lavinia T. Gurley?" Jon asked.

"None a' your business, nosy nigga!"

"You close?"

"I'll know pretty soon, I s'pose."

"What's the *T* stand for in your name?"

"Tough," said Vinia. She pulled the hood over her head and was off.

Sergeant Shelby rode south, down a small hill toward Clarksville. When he looked back, he saw Vinia headed the other way. Safiya stood by the cabin, waving high and proud. Cinque, on horseback, saluted, then dipped below the hill within the pasture. Jon had only known them for a few days, but they seemed like family. They were good people who had made him feel like one of their own. And suddenly he remembered young Cinque Kele's words. "That Devers fella said you owe him a favor for saving your life."

The hot breeze suddenly turned cold and seemed to slap Sergeant Shelby in the face. "Two spirits just passed ya, boy," Grandpap Navius had said when it happened to him long ago. "Also means you'll pass this way again. Happens ever' time. Sho' nuff does!"

It was Jon Shelby's borrowed Colt's Navy that surprised the varmint sneaking up behind Montana Devers's back. "Best damned shootin' cowboy this side a' the Rio Grande," folks had said about Jon down in New Orleans one time.

Montana Devers was a blond-haired, blue-eyed cowboy who said he was on his way to the Chisholm Trail to pick up another small fortune cutting a deal with one of the big trail bosses from a big city up North. He had decided to take a brief vacation and come back to Texas over a new and different route. Instead of heading back to his ranch, he would seek out the company of the opposite sex in Clarksville. He had a pocket full of money and a three-day-old beard, and he was ready to kick up his heels.

"Much obliged, cowboy, for savin' my hide. I'm Montana," he said.

"I ain't no cowboy," Shelby said, extending his hand for a shake.

"That's it? Montana? Only one name?"

"That's all," said Montana. "For now."

"Reckon that's your right," Shelby said, not wanting to probe too far into another man's business. That was one code of the West he would never break. He had used such a covering name game himself. "Jonathan Shelby. Glad to be of assistance. If you're all right, guess I'll be on my way."

"No cause to run," said Montana, knowing this was the man whose life he had saved weeks ago. "Got a bottle here. Ain't city liquor, but it'll shore set the record straight. Least you can do is to have a swig. I ain't meanin' ta keep ya from your bidness. You can drink and run, if you like. Never did like drinkin' alone when folks in hollerin' distance."

"Don't mind if I do. Good stuff . . . still nearby?"

"Naw. Left over from Indian territory. All I got left is this here bottle. Best corn liquor I's had since I left from back East."

"I'm headed to Clarksville. In a bit of a hurry. You headed that way, I'd be happy to have some company."

"Don't mind if I do. I've a hankerin' to visit some of them whores they got there—all of 'em fine and sassy."

Shelby smiled as they pulled rein. He thought of Zena Beale, not wanting to consider her a whore, which is what she was pretending to be at the time when they met. Jon thought Montana was a bit harsh when he used the word *whore*, but since he didn't know Zena Beale and didn't know what she meant to Jon, he reckoned the cowboy meant no direct ill will.

Shelby and Montana hadn't needed to talk too long before feeling good. There was something they liked about each other. Of course, liking a man who just saved your life wasn't too awful hard. That happened sometimes between menfolk, just like that certain attraction between man and woman—even if one was Black and the other one white.

After a while they stopped to catch a breather and get a swig of nature's nectar at the Rocky Bowl Spring. It was good water—the kind of drink that made a man honest. Montana reached inside his saddlebag and pulled out a scroll that he unrolled as he walked over to his Black "partner."

"You the man on this here Wanted poster?" he asked.

"Yup. That's me."

"Says here you tore up LaDonna's Place, raped a colored gal, cheated one Hamilton Featherstone and Drew Murdock out of their ante, then made a public spectacle when you jumped out of a window and caused a ruckus off Main Street. A thousand-dollar reward."

"A thousand dollars!" said Jon out loud. To himself he thought how strange white men were to pay out a whole slew of money just to get back fifty dollars from a darkie who was cheated out of the money in the first place.

"You do all them things?" asked Montana, eyeing him closely, wondering if Jon's hide had been worth saving after all.

"Not a one," Jon said.

"You could be lyin'," Montana tested. He decided to keep up his charade of being a stranger to the man whose life he had saved. A man like Montana could never be *too* careful.

"Could be . . . but I ain't."

"Whether you guilty or innocent, I 'spect if it was me, why, I'd be headed the other way," Montana said.

"But I ain't you, friend."

"Sounds like they got a noose'd just fit your neck to a *T*."

"I'm scared to death," said Jon with a little laugh.

Shelby explained what had happened in Clarksville, being careful to let his new friend know what kind of place they were headed for.

"They gon' arrest you as soon as we get to town," said Montana.

"Man's a fool," Shelby quipped, "to let hisself get hung for saving himself. I reckon they'd like to lock me up—

161

make an example of me. But they got to catch me first."

"What you gonna do?"

"Goin' ta find my saddlebag and my guns and ride as fast as this horse will carry me—in the opposite direction."

"I ain't one to be nosy, but why's this saddlebag so durn important? If you's a Union man, then you can get another satchel at the trading post." Montana pressed. He needed a true bead on Jon if this soldier was gon' to be his man.

"Not with what I lost in it."

"I'm gon' be bold and ask you what's in it."

"Important keepsake." He cut his eyes toward Montana. "My family photograph . . . the only one I got," he lied. True, he did like this Montana fella, but there was no way of telling who he really was. Sometimes telling the truth to a stranger was a waste of time and strategy, and this could be one of those times. "It's my only link with the folks back east. A man's kinfolk is mighty important. They done took away everything Black folks got by splitting up and selling off families like they's cattle. But they can't take away my folks. They'll always be mine—even when I'm dead!"

"Say no more. I hear what you're saying. But I still think you's crazy for goin' back to town."

"You don't have to go. Been by myself this long, reckon another day or two won't matter none."

The beginning of the run toward Clarksville was fast and carefree. It was the first time in over a week that Shelby got a chance to really breathe. He and Montana were silent of tongue but not of mind. The sun beat down upon them as they rode, each now absorbed in his own thoughts.

Suddenly Montana spotted the group of horsemen, a couple of dozen riders in a big hurry. Men traveling that fast in such heat were either idiots or after somebody for doing wrong, or possibly both. And according to the town up ahead, Jon Shelby'd done plenty wrong.

"Posse up ahead. Kicking up an awful lot of dust, travelin' mighty fast."

"Could be, could not be," said Shelby.

"We veer off the road now, Shelby, they's shore to want

to know why. More'n likely they'll hunt us down and ask why."

"Let's get ready," said Jon, loading his Colt.

"Can't take no chances," Montana said.

"Here's what we's a gonna do, friend. . . ."

"Howdy, stranger," Montana called to the first white rider, a medium-size man with a red nose from heavy drinking and sharp, intelligent eyes.

"I ain't no stranger. *You*'s the stranger. I'm Hoot Farrell, leader of this here coterie."

Montana Devers didn't rightly know what a "coterie" was, but he reckoned it had something to do with the mangy group of no-'counts riding up behind Farrell in a cloud of dust.

"My name's Montana. Pleased to be knowin' you. This here's my bounty. I'm returnin' this here runaway slave to his rightful owner."

"Mighty healthy-lookin' nigger. We can save you a lot of trouble. Why, we'd be happier'n a frog in a swamp to take him off your hands, then you can be on your way directly."

"Owner be mighty peeved if his nigger gits his feathers ruffled," said Montana. "You know how some Irishmen is 'bout their property, I'm sure, Mr. Farrell, sir."

"Here's the rope, Daddy Hoot." A snaggletooth, red-neck boy rode up by the older man. He was sitting uneasily on an Appaloosa that refused to stand still. In fact, when the boy got close to Hoot, the horse failed to stop. It kept right on going. Everybody laughed and sniggered, including Shelby.

Hoot Farrell glared over at Jon, pissed. One of the other rednecks, Cecil Simpkins, said, "That boy's got some gall, laughing at a white man in front of white men."

"I ain't laughin', Mr. Hoot. I's jes' joinin' in the fun, dat's awl," Jon answered in his best slave patter. And although his hands were tied with lash cord, he could feel the weight of the straight edge that was hidden up his sleeve. Knowing he was only playacting and could free himself at any time helped his boldness come to life.

"Makin' light of my boy don't set too well with me,"

said Hoot. The snaggletooth, redneck kid was his; Hootie "Junior" Farrell looked like his father had won him in a sideshow. Papa Hoot pulled out his pistol and led Shelby's horse over to a nearby tree. "It's lynchin' time, boys. Come and git 'em." Montana complained as one of the outlaws held him at gunpoint, but forgot to fake his guns.

All the men—two dozen men or more—roared in agreement. It was time for another hanging, the grand finale, where Shelby's army stripes had no power. Some of the horsemen were only boys, soon to witness their first hanging. They didn't know what to expect, and a few just knew inside that something was awry.

Wrath Stevens and Call Strickland were only sixteen years old apiece when they shot their first squirrel. Today, they would graduate into manhood. Soon they'd be hanging darkies all by themselves. That's what being a member of the Border Patrol was all about, they reckoned, killing darkies just because they were dark. But as excited as they were, still, the injustice of the whole thing touched and confused them.

"This ain't right," said Wrath quietly.

"You betta' shut up, fo' the rest of 'em hear you," Call whispered.

"You know it, too," said Wrath.

"You don't know what I know."

"That boy don't look like the hangin' kind to me none."

"You been drinkin' that brandy 'gin, ain't ya?" whispered Call. "Wish you'da give me some."

"I'm scared."

"Ain't nothin' to be scared of. Hell, we's the one's got the noose and the guns." Call's face relaxed.

"Killin' don't always solve the problem, Call. You kin watch an innocent man git hung if you want to," Wrath said disgustedly. "But I don't have to."

Montana looked at Jon, thinking as hard as he could on how to stop this affair. But before he could speak, Shelby spoke up in his own defense, buying time to work the loosely tied lash cord from around his wrists and at the same time keep the mob from seeing what he was up to.

"You ain't gon' let 'em hang me, is ya, Montana? I mean, it ain't fair!"

"Life ain't fair to nobody, boy," said Hoot Farrell. "You

164

might as well get used to dyin'. The way I hear it, a man only gets used to dyin' once. And by the time he learns his lesson, he ain't around to practice what he done learnt."

"Will you stop all that yappin'?" Cecil Simpkins said, moving his calico up beside Hoot. "You gon' hang this boy—or talk him to death? Whatever you plannin', get on with it, man, or hand the noose over to me. I got no qualms 'bout hangin' a felon."

"What you mean?" asked Hoot.

"He's wanted," Cecil said, showing the Wanted Poster with Jon's picture on it. Now Hoot had a real reason to hang Shelby, thanks to Cecil Simpkins. The event would commence.

"So you's a Union man, huh? Better call out loud, blue-coat! Ain't nothin' gon' save you now."

The rope was around Shelby's neck faster than a clock hits the hour. The varmints in Hoot Farrell's Border Patrol gathered around. Their pistols were still holstered, and that was a blessing, since there was only one way out. Both Jon and Montana knew that by the time they got their six-shooters out and cocked, precious seconds would tick by, time enough to surprise the gang of reprobates with a bolt of gunfire and running anger.

"Halt!" said Montana. The men grew quiet, and Montana thought fast at what to say. "I'm glad you boys come along and knocked some sense into me. I agree we should hang him high."

Shelby frowned. He couldn't get his hands loose. He rolled his eyes toward his companion. He really didn't know this "Montana" cowboy. Had he snapped? His liberal talk back there when he was getting his life saved, was it whitewash? If that was the case, his mind had told him right—he should never trust a white man for any reason. It could be too late now. He still couldn't get his hands loose.

"A man deserves a final wish. Grant him that," said Montana, "and the nigger'll shore enuf be a goner."

"Mighty white a' ya, Montana," replied Hoot Farrell, who motioned for the man with the gun pointed at Montana to put it back in his holster. He did. He turned to Shelby, one eye squinted. "Got a last wish, boy? Iff'n ya do, speak up now"—he laughed—"or the rope'll see that you forever hold your peace!"

"You don't mind, sir, I'd like to sing a song," said Shelby, "song my dear old pappy learned me back in Tennessee, when I's jes' a pickaninny. Please, sir. It's my dyin' wish."

Hoot Farrell took off his hat and wiped his brow. "I like you, boy. You talk more shit than a widow's mama." Farrell cut his eye toward Montana, who hunched his shoulders, then turned back to Jon. "Song's your dyin' wish, huh?"

"Yessir, it is," Jon replied as Montana moved around right front.

"Go ahead, then, commence. We's got some patrolling to do over in Fenton's Hollow. Git singin', boy, 'fore I loose my patience."

Shelby had the men ready for some jumping-up-and-down dancing music, and they were shocked with the song that he chose:

> I know a man,
> Man named Blue.
> He got a dawg:
> Look jes' like you.
>
> Lazy dawg,
> Lazy Blue:
> Got dang dawg
> Look jes' like you!
>
> If I wasn't dyin'
> Here's what I'd do:
> Go git me a dawg
> That look jes' like you!

"He's makin' fun of ya, Pa," cried Hootie Junior.

"You shut up, boy. I know it . . . I know it," Hoot Senior snapped. His manhood was on the line. Farrell fired his Henry into the air, and the men roared as Cecil Simpkins tightened the noose around Shelby's Adam's apple until it hurt. Hoot Farrell's blood pressure rose, and he yelled the final order loud and clear.

"Hang 'nat smart-ass nigger, hang 'em high! Hang 'em 'til he's deader'n a bear in a trap! Yeeee, haaah!!"

Chapter

Twenty-one

"Now!" mouthed Montana, winking at Shelby. The Black man yanked his hands again, but the lash cord wouldn't let go. "Shit," Shelby mumbled, twisting his wrists. The braided cord burned into his veins, and a clear, bloody-pink fluid stained the rope.

The noose tightened around Jon's neck. He had always wondered why a hanging man never screamed out as death closed in, and now he knew the answer. The twine of the rope played no single favors. The sound of death was silent.

The white men's horses reared up, their Appaloosas nervous with the shouting and hollering. Jon tried to ignore the violent voices surrounding him. The rope was working itself loose, but it was too slow, so Jon decided to use his added protection; the razor-sharp, straight-edged blade up his sleeve finally slipped down the way it was supposed to and with a slash and a snap, the leather was cut. His hands were free to save his life again.

The rope around his neck bit deep into his tender skin. He felt the bite of the rough-hewn hemp, and according to the direction in which he turned his neck, he saw stars of reds or greens, the signal that death was calling. With every last bit of nerve, the Union soldier grabbed the noose with his large hands and, in what seemed like an eternity, worked it open and yanked it over his head. He had cheated death one more time.

Hoot Farrell and his men were caught off guard, and while some of the fools froze in their saddles, others were thrown to the ground by their contrary mounts. They watched in awe while the brown-skinned soldier and the blue-eyed white man made their escape.

Montana tossed two six-shooters toward Shelby, who caught one by the handle while the other one flew in slow motion through the air. The second pistol firmly in his hand, Shelby aimed without thinking and pulled both triggers almost at the same time. Hoot Farrell's boy, Hootie Junior, was the first to get it in the belly. A bullet bounded off the horn of Shelby's Texas saddle. Montana scrambled and fired off his Colt and emptied both of his pistols into the crowd of do-wrong slave hunters. Several of them fell, wounded, killed, or scared half to death. None of that mattered to Shelby or Montana, as long as they were out of the way.

If cowardice in the heat of battle had been an honor, Hoot Farrell's men would have been decorated with top honors. The zealous Border Patrollers who managed to stay a-mount ran as soon as the first few shots were fired. Of course their running didn't make sense, since they could easily have sent one white man and a darkie to their Maker. But these were lesser men, doomed to represent the lower twenty-third, men who would rather live, talk loud, and be cowards than die bravely at the hands of a traitor and a Yankee nigger.

Sergeant Jonathan Frederick Shelby, U.S. Army scout, and Montana Devers—whom Jon still believed to be just another local cowboy and former trail boss—ran as fast as their mounts would carry them. Jon knew that he owed a "Mr. Devers" a favor for having saved his life back in Clarksville, but he knew nothing of the man's Christian name. And this blond cowboy had made no mention of a prior acquaintance when they'd met earlier that day, so there was no way for Jon to even suppose the true identity of his partner in escape.

The rays of golden sunlight beat down upon their heads as they rode, its waves of heat almost unbearable, seemingly determined to bake their noggins like bacon in a hot skillet. At first the sand and dried tumbleweeds hampered their way somewhat, but the two men had good horses that were smart enough to pick their way through.

Behind them a ways, Hoot Farrell's men had regrouped. They were riled more at the nigger-loving white man for helping a darkie escape than at the nigger for getting away. They began to give chase, shooting wild and furious. Hot lead parted the air like lightning in an April blizzard.

The Texas plain was a new frontier for Jonathan Shelby. It was Montana Devers who knew the way to cover. He yelled to Jon to head for a hollow up ahead, and when they looked each other's way they heard a rattling sound. Shelby's roan reared high as Montana caught a glimpse in the distance of a lone rider in an awful hurry, heading in the general direction of Clarksville. A bullet struck something nearby and richocheted with a *ping*, then a thud. Shelby's horse reared again, still spooked by the rattle and now the shot. The Black man was tossed up into midair. If he fell on his head, as horsemen often did, he was a goner for sure, thought Montana in the moment before Jon hit the ground.

Back in Clarksville, at LaDonna's Place, a man coaxed a boy in through the back door. It was clear the man urging the boy to enter didn't want anyone to know what was going on. The boy was about to enjoy his first time in a brothel. He was scared, and he didn't know what to do.

Everything had been set up between the older man and LaDonna, although the large Black woman didn't like it much 'cause the boy was as skittish as a new-broke colt. The whorehouse owner sent him right upstairs to room number five, Zena Beale's room. The young woman had been instructed what to do. It was to be Zena's last time in the room with a stranger. She had been given another job by LaDonna, managing the place when LaDonna was "indisposed."

"I ain't never kept cump'ny with no gal like you berfore," said young Winfield Nixon, who was about to have his first "closed-door session" with a woman. He lay on one side of the bed, fully clothed, while Zena, in her white lace dress and petticoats, looking like an angel in hell, kept inching farther away from the cowpoke every time his hand drew near.

"I know what ya mean, stranger," she answered, cringing whenever they touched. She knew she didn't have to do anything with the boy, just keep him pacified until another "lady" was available.

"Well, I reckon it's about time fer us to . . . ah, well . . ."

"Don't tell me this is your fist time?" she asked.

"Yup. Pa said it was 'bout time I had me a woman. He said I could practice on a colored gal, so's I can get ready for a white woman," Winny explained, taking another swig out of a bottle of the cheapest whiskey.

"You drink a lot?"

"No, ma'am," said Winny, proud of himself. "Shucks, this here's my first bottle ever."

The liquor immediately made the seventeen-year-old cuss foolishly bold, and without a warning he lunged at Zena, kissing her as if it were his dying wish.

"Stop, fool," Zena yelled, slapping the boy across the face. He backed up and frowned like he was going to cry. "That ain't the way you treat a woman. You's s'pose to be gentle."

"Well, you's a colored gal, ain't ya? Pa said you can treat colored folks any kinda way."

"Yore 'pa' was wrong. You don't treat me any kinda way, you hear me, boy?" Zena said through gritted teeth.

"Well, you's s'pose ta kiss back, ain't ya?"

"No, I'm s'pose to slap you like I did," said Zena sarcastically, not thinking the boy would take her seriously.

"That ain't what Pa said, Ma'am. Why. . ." He swigged again and was now determined to get what he came for. But since it was his first time, he didn't exactly know *what* he had come for—and if he didn't get it, he wouldn't have known what he hadn't got. "Fergit bein' gentle," he snapped. "I's payin' my hard-earned money fer a good time, ain't never heard nothing 'bout bein' gentle." He moved up and squeezed Zena Beale from behind.

She was thinking about Jonathan Shelby, tears running down her naturally reddish cheeks. It was when Winny fondled her left breast that she knew it was time to end the bullcrap. She screamed and jumped out of his arms. "Get out! I can't stand you touchin' me, man! Get *out*!"

"Wait just a gall-danged minute now. I ain't a-gonna hurt ya. I ain't even got outta my breeches yet," Winny moaned, nervously trying to pull his last leg from within his trousers.

"And you ain't. I don't want no part of you," Zena yelled, picking up the boy's gunbelt and tossing it at him.

"Calm down now, ma'am. Ain't no cause to git all riled. I only—"

"Git, boy, 'fore I throw you out!"

Zena Beale hit Winfield Nixon with first one boot, then the other. She pounded him with the porcelain-covered washpan, briny water and all, that was sitting on the washstand.

It wasn't Winny that Zena hated, but what he stood for, and she was determined to stay a respectable woman. As she pushed the Nixon boy toward the door, she picked up his pissy-dirty pants along with his six-shooter and forced him out of the room. After she had slammed the door, he heard something break against the inside. The coal-oil lamp that luckily was unlit had exploded against the door. He remembered he had left his bottle of liquor inside, but then he heard a second wet crash up against the door and knew his rotgut was a goner.

Everybody upstairs, downstairs, and even outside on "LaDonna Street" heard the commotion. LaDonna figured it was a rowdy cowboy tearing up the place, and she would have none of that, not at her expense. She grabbed her pistols from behind the bar, ran upstairs, and saw Winfield Nixon standing scared in his underwear and yelling cuss words at Zena Beale, who should have been stalling the man and taking his money instead of kicking him out of her room.

"What's all the ruckus, Winny?" asked LaDonna, her pistols pointing at his middle.

"It waddn't none a' me, Miss LaDonna. That blamed Negra...ah, colored...uh, gal done gone plumb loco, I tell ya."

"If you hurt that girl, I'm fillin' you full a' lead, then if there's anything left of ya, I'll give it to ya pa or to the funeral man—whichever claims you first. Now git out," LaDonna growled with fire in her eyes.

"But Miss LaDonna—"

"Out!"

"But she got my money, Miss LaDonna. And she didn't give me nuthin'—nuthin' a-tall!"

"All right, boy. You just wait," said LaDonna, knocking on Zena's door. "Open up, Zee. It's me."

The door swung open, and Zena looked at Miss La-

Donna, her tears flowing like the falls at Boggy River when it rained. Then she saw Winny standing in a less-than-presentable fashion. "You—get away from me! Get *away*!"

"He says you got his money," LaDonna said.

Zena reached in between her lovely round breasts, pulled a wad of Confederate notes from her cleavage, and threw it at the boy. He dropped to the floor and crawled around, picking up each bill.

LaDonna watched him scampering around and shook her head. "You best be goin' boy. Seems you done enough here already."

"But I wants me a gal," said Winny. His eyes were red, and he had lint all over his black, stringy-straight hair. "One that ain't wild and crazy like this-un."

Zena raised her hands and started toward the white boy, but LaDonna jumped in between them. Winny Nixon sobered up real fast and ran downstairs in his long johns, the rest of his clothes in his arms. The hims and hers "keeping time" behind closed doors had come out to watch the tussling and anger at Zena Beale's doors. The few other folks inside LaDonna's Place laughed and yelled jokes and innuendos to the young man; old Happy McClusky was still downstairs, too woozy from last night's drunk to make the fun.

LaDonna yelled to the other girls and their customers—mostly out-of-towners moving west to cities like Colorado City, Arizona, and San Diego and Los Angeles in California. They listened and obeyed, getting back to what they were doing before the ruckus. LaDonna walked through Zena's door. "I'll talk to *you* later. Don't you go nowheres 'til you see me, got it, Missy Zena Beale? Ya hear?" she asked, her hand on her hip, the gun still cocked. "You got some talkin' to do!"

Marshal Richards reached inside the big drawer in his desk and slowly pulled a bottle of high-class sipping whiskey from its innards. He took a big swig, got up, and strutted out the door. Peering down Main Street, he suddenly thought seriously about Wooly Samples. It was a gnawing in his gut that made him fearful that whenever Samples left town, he would eventually end up at Montana

Devers's. If Samples teamed up with that alleged war hero, with all that land, Devers might just be planning an empire that wouldn't include Marshal Richards. Maybe Samples would keep all of the money once he switched partners. Richards didn't like owing the bank, and he didn't even like the man who ran it. Fat folks ain't worth shit, he thought bitterly. All they do is sweat and eat and take up space. He would get that money and head to northern California. He would make it there—sure he would.

But first things first, he convinced himself. It was time to do some courting, and the woman he had in mind was only a few yards away at the Lazy Day Saloon. The day was young yet, he would hit the Circle D Ranch as soon as he could verify the facts. If Devers was who he thought he was, then some changes would have to be made soon. But first, he'd get himself some pleasure.

Montana aimed his Colt at Sergeant Jonathan Shelby, and before Jon could move, the white man fired. Sand and dirt flew up in his face, and for a moment he thought he was a goner. When Shelby opened his eyes and saw the bloody coils of the sidewinder rattler lying on top of his chest—the snake's head had been blown clean off—he knew why Montana had fired.

"Thank you, pardner," Shelby said, regaining his composure. "I reckon you got one comin'."

"Reckon so," said Montana.

"We'd better get the hell out of here," Jon said. "Them fools gaining on us mighty fast."

In two shakes of a bobcat's tail, Shelby had grabbed his roan, mounted, and the two men sped off. Hoot Farrell's gang was already too close for comfort.

"Looks like we got company up ahead," said Montana.

"Hope they ain't part of the same group."

"Can't be. Nobody could run that fast and get help. Anyway, we's the one that needs help, not them bigots."

"They's surely seen us now. Nothing we can do 'ceptin' talk our way out of a mess."

"What if they ain't friendly listeners?" Montana said.

"We fill 'em full of lead—or try to, anyway. After all I've been through, no way I'm gon' be taken alive. Anyhows, I've got a mission. General's countin' on me. I ain't never been stopped before from completing a job, don't plan to be now, neither!"

Four tall-in-the-saddle horsemen ran fast toward Shelby and Montana. The dust kicked up by their mounts filled a small section of the Texas horizon. They were traveling mighty fast, too fast to be on casual business.

Shelby and Montana looked at each other and decided to veer left. Being sandwiched in between their enemies wasn't too smart. Hoot Farrell's gang had closed in in a hurry, their bullets singing past the two men's ears like mosquitoes on a river bottom night. When the other group commenced to firing back, Shelby realized they were in a crossfire.

"Got any suggestions, friend?" yelled Montana, who was lagging behind. His dappled gray had gone suddenly lame.

"Ain't but one thing we can do," Shelby returned with a tinge of foreboding. "Our only chance to live is to reach them trees over yonder."

"I swear, the next time I get ambushed," puffed Montana, "I think I'll just give up, to keep from meeting up with a stranger like you. Seems like I been in trouble ever since I met you. You musta done something wrong. Be best I go my separate way!"

"If you don't stop yappin' and do some ridin', won't *be* no next time, friend!"

In town, Lawman Cotton Richards held his head high when he stepped out of the Clarksville Town Jail. He straightened his gunbelt, pulled his breeches up off his flat behind, clutched his badge, and spit-shined it with slobber on his shirtsleeve.

The War Between the States continued to rage over the horizon, but he, Marshal Richards, was the local authority behind the Union occupation. He felt good about being alive in 1865, he felt good about the way things sized up. He might have to kill Wooly Samples on the road to San Francisco. But he was the law. The Wanted poster said the man was "WANTED, DEAD OR ALIVE." Killing a lady-killer was as easy as pie, like punching old Tandy in the mouth.

Cotton tipped his hat to the ladies and bid a good day to

174

the hard-ankles; he would stop by the bank on his way back to his office and discuss the latest events with Hamilton Featherstone. Since Drew Murdock's stagecoach wasn't due until later in the day, he'd spread the good news about his potentially able-bodied posse and their successful exploits under his astute supervision. Of course, Cotton's posse had yet to go into action. Drew Murdock had had to go out of town on urgent, secret business. He had gone to place some orders for some new suits and have a talk with his old friend the district judge. Step one of his plan had worked, and step two would be a cinch.

Marshal Cotton Richards arrived at the swinging doors of the Lazy Day Saloon just in time to see Miss Kate's bosom shaking like butter fresh from the churn as she walked down the long stairs from the second-story bedrooms. He had been upstairs many times, and Miss Kate's company was incomparable. He was as humble as a dog with its tail between its legs whenever Miss Kate was around, and today was no different.

"Howdy, Kate," said the suddenly suave Cotton Richards, marshal, the current authority when the Yankees weren't around. "You're mighty pretty this time of day."

"That's awfully nice of you to say, Cotton. What can I do for you?"

"Well, Kate, I got some good news, and dependin' on how you's dispositioned, some bad news. Best to take the bad news first, I reckon," Cotton said, fumbling with his hat in his hands. "Since the good news might change the way you feel about the bad. Bein' as to how I heard you took up for that fella the other night, I figured you'd want to know. That colored fella, Shelby, got hisself killed by a posse I sent to apprehend him."

"You had him gunned down!" said Kate, her eyes tearing at what the no-'count lawman had done.

"Nope," said the lawman. "I told them to bring him in alive, if they could. But since they've been gone so long, I reckon they couldn't, so they shot or hung him, whichever one was apropos at the time."

"I'm sorry to hear that," said Kate, looking out of the door and thinking of Zena. She would have to tell her directly, if she could muster the nerve—and she could.

"Now, about the good news, Kate," said Cotton Richards, pulling at his hat again and looking at the floor like a little boy asking for a tea cake before suppertime. "You see, I been thinkin' . . ."

Kate had turned away, obviously thinking about other things. But at Richards's words, she turned back again. Cowboys and soldiers never think too much, and that's good, she told herself. But when a lawman like Richards starts thinking, something must be up. . . . One day he'd say something worthwhile; whether today was the day, she didn't know. Then she realized that Richards had propositioned her. No, today wasn't the day. Kate declined to answer, urging the Clarksville marshal not to get his hopes up too high that she would go west with him.

Kate Pearson was wary about breaking the news of Jon's death to Zena. If she were a lesser woman, she would have gone to her room and had a stiff drink. But she was bigger than that. Kate Pearson was the richest woman in town, and that alone made her stand mighty tall.

Chapter

Twenty-two

"Jon Shelby's dead, Zee—posse kilt him, outside a' town." Kate Pearson spoke to Zena Beale while LaDonna stood silently by the bed. After getting to know Zena, LaDonna felt close to the pretty young woman. She was glad the youngster had come into her life. Zena was lively and scheming, but she was loyal to her cause. LaDonna would see that she got what she needed to free her brother, Santee, but not now. It would have to be later.

Cinque had brought the white woman's buggy around to the Lazy Day Saloon, and she had driven over to La-Donna's by herself. LaDonna and Kate had been friends for quite some time, and Kate determined that she would be Zena's friend now, too. If LaDonna liked her so much, Kate would as well.

"I'm sorry, hon. I didn't rightly know how to tell ya. I'm so sorry."

Zena stared at Kate Pearson, a woman whom, in the short time she had known her, she had grown to respect like a mother; but her words were out of place, out of order at a time when she needed to hear good news. Those whites had stolen Jon's saddlebags from LaDonna's safe place. *That* was on her mind. She was responsible, and she knew it. They were at the jailhouse and she would get them, but first she needed to talk with Jon.

"He can't be dead, Miss Kate. I lo—I mean, I can't ever think of him dead." Zena looked down and started to fret.

"I'm sorry, too, Zee. I'd hoped word would come that Jon Shelby was all right. But no word came since Cotton told me the news, so I guess the bad news stands as is."

Kate's heart was near broken over this girl's trouble.

"He *can't* be dead. He jes' can't be! I would have felt it somehow. My mama could see things in her mind when they's about to happen. I believe I can, too. Clara-voy-ance, they call it. I got to see him lyin' there for myself. You must understand, Miss Kate? You musta had feelings for a man some point in your life?"

"I know, honey. I know," Kate answered softly.

"You think I'm makin' a mistake by tryin' to help a man that's on his way out of town?"

"I don't know. All I know is that you're young enough to try—and if it is a mistake, you'll have time to pick up the pieces and begin anew. You've got my blessings, lass."

LaDonna spoke for the first time. "Go. Find Shelby. And by some miracle, I hope the marshal was wrong about Jon's dyin'. Be he alive or otherwise. You'd better wait 'til mornin', though, to travel. Gets mighty cold and danger-ous for a woman outside a' town at night."

Kate handed Zena a personal peacekeeper, a newer ver-sion of Henry Deringer's Philadelphia model, not too dif-ferent from the original miniature cast in 1825. It was the first weapon Kate had ever taken from a man the day she took over the Lazy Day. Now she made Zena take the re-volver, saying, "Don't give me no lip. Take it to protect your own. Might come in handy one day, Zee. You won't miss it 'til ya need it."

"Thank you, Miss Kate. For everything," said Zena.

Jon Shelby and Montana were delighted the men they were meeting up with in front were friends rather than the opposition. They got ready for a showdown, their second in several hours.

"My pistol's empty. I got to reload," said Shelby when he looked back and saw the second group of white men firing at the men in the lynch mob. "Slow down, man. Don't look like we got nothing to fear. At least not right now."

The men were obviously on their side. They waved as they passed, and Montana waved back. He turned around and said to Jon in white folks' slang, "Well, will ye lookee thar. Them fellers just run right past us."

"Looks like we got some friends, at least until they see one of us ain't white."

Montana spit into the whirling Texas wind to bolster his luck. Many a time the cowboy had used this trick to foster good spirits. He thought to himself, a man buys luck like a flea hunts a dawg. A little luck'll go a long way, when a man has a reason to live.

And that's exactly what the good-looking Montana had figured on doing—living. And he planned to move west as time allowed. That was his dream, his motive for fighting to survive. Of course, he would like to see New York for once, but then he'd head to the land of the sun. The hills out west, people said, were filled with peace and loving contentment, where he could make his nest and bide by the laws of the Almighty. Montana knew that his dream would come true.

"I ain't runnin' and shootin' no further," said Montana, knowing the men who had just arrived were under his employ.

"You crazy?" Shelby said.

"Yeah, I'm crazy...for tagging along with you. I's alone, even iff'n I'd a' committed a crime, they'd probably let me go as long as the crime waddn't committed in their jurisdiction. I'm a white man with certain inalienable rights you ain't got!"

"You're right," growled Jon. "Go ahead. I ain't holdin' you—scared I'll shoot you in the back or sumpin'?"

"Sumpin', I s'pose. You're too righteous for that sort of violence. Reckon that's why I like you. I'm stickin' wid ya. Don't know why." Montana looked up. "Here they come back."

The horsemen had chased off the Hoot Farrell gang. Two of the men walked their horses slowly toward the riders. The lead horse was a fine-looking roan; its silky mane glistened in the sun. The well-groomed horse was sure a prize. It was a beautiful steed, quite fine and frisky about the feet.

Jonathan Shelby had always been a sucker for a good-looking animal, and he relished the thought of raising such critters, like Harrison Dockery had done back in Christian County. Dockery's studs were the talk throughout Kentucky—but first things first, thought the Union man. He would have to stay alive first, to find his parcel of secret information and deliver it up the Red to Red River Station. He would have to do that before he could raise a vegetable stalk, let alone a fine stallion.

"Howdy, Mr.—" the man said.

Montana cut off the lead rider with a glare. "Uh . . . them men we jes' chased away do any harm?"

"No harm." Montana turned to Shelby. "My spread's just between them two ridges yonder ways apiece," he said, pointing as a smile broke across his reddened face. His mustache was a golden brown, bleached from daytime riding up in the higher elevations of Texas. "If them riders decide to return, they'll surely bring some reinforcements . . . and if they just happen to be looking for you, Shelby, why, wouldn't be much a handful of us could do to fend 'em off. Now iff'n you were looking for a hideout, some grub, and a fine cigar, you's welcome to rest a spell at my place. There's always room for one more at my table."

Shelby looked toward where the Farrell gang had turned away. The stranger was right—a decision was needed mighty fast.

"How about it, Mr. Shelby?"

"I usually like to know a man's full name who knows mine, mister," answered the Black man warily.

"Why, I'm Montana Devers, Mr. Shelby," he said, yanking rein. "I'm the one who saved your life back in town. Reckon we's even now, say!"

Montana Devers, Jon Shelby, and the men made haste in the run to the Circle D Ranch at Devers's Hollow. In a short time they arrived near the foot of green, tree-covered hills that made the men look minuscule by comparison. Shelby had heard about the mountains in Colorado and Utah, their vastness and spectacle; these Texas rocks were mere stubs compared with a real mountain range, but they were beautiful and peaceful. It was a perfect place for a man to grow a family and forget the greed of the world outside. Funny how a man thinks he's so big until he faces nature's wonders, thought Shelby. It was the same thought Montana Devers had had when he'd first laid eyes upon the land.

"Guess yous boys is safe now," Devers said. "I got a job for you, Shelby. Be my scout and general trail boss.

I'm looking to handle the largest herd of longhorns west of the Mississippi. I heard about your scoutin' abilities from the Yanks."

"Don't know whatchya mean," said Jon.

"Still keepin' up the front, huh?" Devers said. "No matter. Come, you're welcome to stay and jaw a while. Got some good corn from the local still—sippin' whiskey's the best in these parts. May not last long, iff'n the marshal gets wind of it. Stays boozed all the time, that Richards."

"Ain't got much time to be talkin' or drinkin'," said Jon.

"We got business to discuss, Shelby," Devers said.

"Reckon I still don't know whatchya mean."

Somehow his second mind told him that Devers's job offer would fall somewhere between trouble and whatever was worse. But he would hear Devers out. After all, a man only had one life to lose, and if someone saved it once, he guessed it meant twice as much if he did it a second time.

"Like my spread?" They had stopped in front of a house that was no more really than a large shack with many rooms. Nevertheless, it was a good-looking house with new pane-glass windows and new nails that set it above the mud shacks prominent farther south.

"Nice place," said Jon. "Heap a land for one man to tend, though."

"I'm a big man. Me and the boys can handle it. Got some sharecroppers interested in takin' on some of the hard work. Some hogs, chickens, cattle, and horses will fill the edges right well. My remuda ain't too bad off, as you can see."

"Can't see too much from here. Mind if I look a bit closer?" asked Shelby, polite as always, though suspicious of the man's hospitality.

"My place is your place," Devers said.

Within the Devers remuda were some of the finest wild horses Jonathan Shelby had ever seen. Some were better than others, but that was expected. A bay gelding across the way, the shiny one, would make a fine Sunday-go-to-meeting animal.

All of them were ornery, about four years, twelve to fourteen hands high. The lot was fine, an early spring bunch. Yes, Montana Devers's raids below the Mexican border had hit pay dirt. These were fine steeds to be busted down into obedient servants.

"Havin' trouble with that bay?" Jon asked, pointing out the horse.

"Yup. We been trying to calm him down damn near ten days, I reckon. He just don't seem to want to be tamed."

"I'd like a try at him," Jon said.

"My man, Harper Fellows over yonder, says he's the best at breakin' mounts," said Devers. "If he can't break him, no one can!"

"I've always been skeptical of a man who says he's the best. Seems to me he ain't good enough. I could have that bay eating outta my hand within twenty minutes, if it was worth my time."

"What'd make it worth your time?" asked Devers.

"That young Appaloosa you riding is mighty pretty. I might be willin' to help you out, if I knew he'd be mine when I won. And when I win, I'd have to know that I could leave my roan here until I come back this-a-way."

"I got a lot of faith in the bay winnin' out. You're on, cowboy."

"I ain't no cowboy," Jon said.

"Suit yourself," said Devers, shrugging.

Shelby thought about confronting Devers about his secrecy, about his having kept his name a secret, but he decided not to press the matter. Sometimes a man can be too hard on another man, even if that other man is white.

Before entering the corral, Shelby acquired the tools he needed to break the bay: a saddle, spurs, a quirt, and, of course, a bridle and scraps of hemp rope for hobbling the animal's feet.

Inside the corral, he coiled his own lariat in the proper fashion and walked slowly around the bay that was taller than usual for his breed, about sixteen hands high, he surmised. He mumbled some words neither Fellows nor Devers could make out, and the bay watched Shelby like they had once been acquainted in another life.

Shelby prepared his lariat for the fine, strong bronco. He roped its neck with ease. Slowly walking toward the bay, he whispered some precious words. Fellows squinted his best eye toward a man he didn't like at all. If he, Harper "the Breaker" Fellows, the best in the business of breaking horses, couldn't tame the wild beast, no one else certainly could. In fact, he had considered letting the bay go free, since he refused to calm down for even the shortest period of time.

The ornery horse pulled tight against the Kentucky hemp. Shelby walked closer and eventually had the bay's feet hobbled; he threw on a bridle, and the action began. The Union man stuck out the blanket on his arm. "It's all right, boy. I ain't a-gonna hurt ya. Jes' want to put this here blanket over your back so the saddle won't hurt ya none. That's it, fella. Me and you's gon' be good friends. Whoa, fella." As fast as he could he threw the covering onto its back. Soon he had the bronco saddled and had commenced to tightening the cinch.

The bay went suddenly wild and began to chase Shelby around the holding pen. And although its forefeet and one hind foot were well hobbled, Jon could tell he had his hands full. But the words the sergeant continued to speak had a soothing effect on the horse, and he rubbed its nose and whispered softly, preparing to mount.

Jon Shelby had learned long ago that at this point it was necessary to distract the bronco's attention from what he was doing. He reached for the bay's ear and twisted it til he felt and heard the gristle crack. What he did wasn't cruel. The ear would heal, like a hammer-mashed finger on a man. Jon pulled the stirrups from up on top of the saddle. He stepped up in one quick motion and was mounted, still adding pain to the horse's ear.

When he finally let go of the ear, the bay began to buck and kick as if his life were at stake. Jon yelled at the bay's first violent movement but held on to the gyrating animal for dear life. Up and down and sideways, the bay mustang bucked and swayed, almost throwing off the cowboy at the feet of Devers and Fellows.

"He can't hold on," yelled Fellows.

"Shut up," Devers said. "At least he got this far. I didn't see you saddle him up and mount."

"I coulda done it," said Fellows, who should have retired long ago. Nowadays he could only break the tamest of animals, those horses most ready for pasture.

"Coulda and *doin'* are two different things, Fellows."

"You ain't thinkin' 'bout hiring that darkie, is ya, Montana? Why, if ya is, you can ferget it. You owe me too much to let me go."

"You'll be the first to know, if I do," said Devers. "You'll still be around, no matter who I find that's better."

When the two men looked back toward the action, Jon had the bay prancing around the corral like it was right at home. He looked over at Devers and Fellows, then walked the animal their way. When he pulled rein in front of the men, he was greeted with Devers's fine words.

"So I guess you win."

"Reckon I do," said Jon.

"Harper, this is Jonathan Shelby, Sergeant. Bluecoats. Have my Appaloosa ready for Mr. Shelby whenever he says he wants it," said Devers.

"I ain't no stable boy for no—"

"You do what I said—or you're fired."

"You're tryin' my patience."

Fellows couldn't afford to leave Montana Devers's employ. The pay was the best, the working conditions superb, and the idea of starting anew with a strange ranch made him back down. But Montana Devers would never turn the old man out to pasture. He was like a father, and Devers loved him more than he loved anyone else. Fellows would always be one of the top dogs in Devers Hollow if he stayed.

Fellows decided right there and then not to let the Black man have his job. As he followed Montana Devers's order and walked the bay toward the stable, he sneered and muttered under his breath, "By God, I'll do it this time—but I shorely don't like it none!"

Harper Fellows had lost one job to a cheap-working darkie over at the Triple K Ranch down south in Houston. He had vowed then and there that it would never happen again. Jon Shelby would die sometime tonight.

Chapter

Twenty-three

Without warning, a pistol fired nearby. It was the quiet man who had just walked outside onto the Circle D ranch house veranda who had caused all the ruckus. The sound of running footsteps rounded the corner of the house, and Cappy Epson emerged, his gun drawn, ready to kill whoever had fired the shot.

"Boss, can't you stop that Chinaman from firin' off that there six-shooter ever' time he calls us to victuals!" Cappy panted. "I swear, one of these days I jes' might panic and shoot a hole in one a' them slit eyes a' his."

"You leave Tang Chow be now, Cappy," said Devers. "If you hadn't shot holes in his gong and his bell, he wouldn't a' had to fire that shooting iron a' his at victuals time. Man's got a right to have a little fun, even a Chinaman. Hell, Tang's the onlyiest cook we got. You shoot him, *you* cook, and if your cookin' ain't as good as his, you get shot. Maybe you'd be better off leavin' well enough alone."

Cappy Epson was getting old, too old, nearing sixty. Some of the hired hands spoke quietly against him among themselves. But the white-haired, bearded miser remained the best second in command any would-be cattleman would want. He had taken care of Montana ever since his pa was shot up in a bar brawl back in 1825. The two men had never been too far apart except when Devers went east for a while to fight for the Confederacy. Montana never spoke too much about the war, and Cappy thought that was strange, since most war heroes liked to talk a lot about the bravest days of their lives.

Cappy was an honest man out in western territory, where it was a whole lot less painful for a dishonest man to live. With towns full of cash, women, and cheats, Devers felt relief in knowing a virtuous man like Cappy lived among them.

"Suppertime, suppertime," Tang Chow called out in his thick Chinese accent.

"Cappy Epson, this here's Jonathan Shelby," said Devers.

"Glad to be knowin' ya. You the feller that brung in them outlaws, ain't you?"

"Yup."

"You will join me for supper," said Devers, leading Shelby into the house. "We can come to terms about the future over some steak and jawin' wine."

"Terms?"

"That proposition is still open to you." Devers cut his eye toward Cappy Epson. "I'd like to talk to Sergeant Shelby alone, if you don't mind."

"I *do*," said Cappy.

"This is a business meeting," Devers said slowly to his trusted associate, " 'tween me and the sergeant here. A private dinner." There was an unspoken threat in his simple words. Cappy left the room reluctantly.

Shelby didn't like the way Devers treated his cantankerous old friend.

"Tang Chow!" yelled Devers. "I'll call you when we're ready for victuals."

Tang Chow closed the doors and retreated into the kitchen. It was apparent from the look on his face that he, too, was tired of all the tension.

The Black soldier scanned the large dining room from corner to corner, checking first for the entrances and exits. One wall of the room was hidden by heavy, maroon-colored drapes. The wallpaper was new and buckled in places as if the finishing carpenter had been slopping hogs with one hand and wallpapering with the other. The brass spittoon near each of the six medium-backed chairs added a homey flavor. The two men sat quietly and drank their smooth sipping whiskey—the best Jon Shelby had had to date, and for a while he enjoyed every minute of the pampering. The drink went down easily, and the spreading warmth felt good to the weary soldier.

"I'm making you an offer, Shelby. I need a man to scout and help run my cattle drives up north from San Antone to Dodge City and Abilene. Damned Apache and some of the offshoot tribes caused me an awful lot of headaches the last time we ran north. A man of your experience and caliber could make a fair penny for his efforts, say sixty-five a month, including all expenses."

"How about seventy-five with expenses?" said Shelby.

"Them's trail boss wages," Devers snapped.

"Since my job would be more dangerous, it'd be worth at least a hundred."

Devers changed the subject abruptly. He'd come back to negotiating later. "I heard how you brung them white men to jail. Any man, especially a Negro, has got to have something special to pull that off in a town like Clarksville."

"I've got a job when the war's over."

"Doin' what? Shovelin' cow chips for your former slaveowner who hates your guts because you're free? You know as well as I do, Jon—if I may call you that . . ."

"Your fancy," said the Union man, listening hard with a sensible ear to the white man's proposition. Devers was right. When the war was over between the North and the South, he would still be just another Negro trying to make ends meet. Even if the North did win and all of his people were freed, the Negro would still be chattel throughout much of the alleged "free world." The job Devers offered was exactly what Jon wanted.

He had dreamed for so long of running beeves up the cattle trails north. Yet something made him hesitate. His instincts told him that there was more to this Devers fellow than met the eye. If he could hang around him, hear him talk long enough, he'd figure it out. Why was Montana Devers so set in hiring *him*? There must be hundreds of Black men who could handle the job. Still, his mind was not made up, and the gnawing in his groin told him to listen but to make no commitment. He would hold out as long as he could. After all, the South might still win in the end.

"Look, Jon. Let's talk man to man. If you're the man I think you are, and I damn well *know* you are, you also know that regardless of the color of my skin, we've got to work together.

"You may get up and walk out of this room right now—and I wouldn't blame you, 'cause I'm gonna say some things that may make you madder'n a hen stuck in molasses—but the white man has the money and the land, and the only way a Negro is going to get his share is to work for that same white man that's kept him down since them slaveships brought your folks over from Africa." Devers paused to sip his whiskey and lean closer to Shelby. He looked him in the eye. "Think your people's goin' to be free, huh? Why, even if the South does lose the war, Black folks'll still be slaves. No white man east of the Mississippi will tolerate living beside your kind. You're a smart man, figure it out."

"I may not be as smart as you think," said Shelby, knowing Devers's words were mostly true. "And anyway, what gives you the gall to think I'd take a Confederate soldier's word on what he plans to do?"

"I never told you about my warring days back east, did I, Jon?" asked the former Rebel soldier.

"You been too busy giving me choices that only lead to me working for you. What if I plan to run my own business?" Jon said.

"You have the perfect right to do what you will," said Devers. "You think I'm just another fool stealin' land from the Indians. Just ain't so. Will you hear me out—one man to another?"

"Ain't got much time," said Jon. "But every man deserves his say."

"This all took place back in January of this year," Montana began. He got up from the table, picked up his drink, and walked over to the window. As he spoke, he periodically turned to make sure Shelby was listening. "Wilmington. In North Carolina, at Fort Fisher, on the Cape Fear River, we were working Reeves Point across the river channel with the Third Division of the Twenty-third Army Corps under General Cox—all, of course, in unison with protective barrages from Rear Admiral Porter.

"One of my men got his head blown off at the neck. I was slightly wounded . . . but I managed to save all of the remaining men in my company. They put me in charge when my lieutenant was mortally wounded. Got a medal for bravery."

"Reckon you's mighty proud to be a hero," said Sergeant Shelby.

"The way I see it, we's two of a kind."

"I never heard a white man say that about a Negro."

"Never thought I would, either. Reckon times are a-changin'. I saw the way you took on that gang of Murdock's singlehandedly. Mere numbers took you out. Two men like you and half a' them men woulda been history." Devers rubbed his belly. "Ready for some victuals, Jon? I hope so, 'cause I'm hungrier'n a barracuda!" Jon nodded in agreement. Devers called out to Tang Chow, who ran from the kitchen door and bowed.

Tang Chow brought the soup. It was hot and mostly clear, with bits of tiny green leaves that looked like pieces of scallions and a film of pork grease floating on top. The way Devers ate the brew, it must be palatable, Jon decided, and he picked up his own spoon.

Jon watched Montana Devers closely. Something wasn't quite right. This man had told a simple story of bravery, but there may have been more not being said. But out of politeness, the Black sergeant refrained from questioning the white man's tale. He would watch Devers closely and then decide if he wanted to work the Circle D Ranch after his soldiering days were over.

Devers took another spoonful of the hot broth, savoring the taste. "As I was saying, if you go back east, you'll be a slave. Stay here with me, you'll be as rich as any man'll ever be—especially any colored man—"

Shelby cut Devers off before he could complete his statement. "Color ain't got nothin' to do with being rich. I always thought a rich man was a rich man. Period."

"You're right. I didn't mean to offend you." Devers looked carefully at Jon as he buttered a piece of steaming-hot cornbread with his knife. The sergeant took a sip of water as the slick-talking cattleman finished off his pitch. "I know you're working for Billy Yank. But that's okay, too."

Shelby shrugged. "Never was a secret. I'm proud to fight for a worthy cause. One day my people'll get what we deserve, and until then I'll do the best I can with what I got."

"There's no rush to make a decision. Let's finish our victuals for now. Just remember what I'm offering you...."

Devers stopped his speech when the kitchen door flew open again, the rich aroma of Texas cooking filling the dining room. Carrying the covered dishes as if they were fragile eggs, Tang Chow padded over to the table with his fresh-out-of-the-oven biscuits, savory mashed Irish potatoes, and juicy southern-fried smothered steak. He left for a moment and returned with a piping-hot bowl of thickening gravy.

A quiet tongue at the eating table was accepted courtesy in Texasland and throughout the West, although Devers broke the code for most of the meal. What surprised Montana Devers beyond a doubt was that this Negro Shelby fellow was smart enough to know such etiquette. Finally Jon broke the code of silence himself.

"I'll give your proposition some thought, Devers, but I can't promise anything," he said. "I'd like to see some of that back land, that pretty little hollow."

"The best land, the best of Texasland," said Devers. "I'll show you around. We'll get a smoke, and you can take a ride on that new roan of yours."

"Let's go," Shelby said. "Best news I've heard all day."

Montana Devers and Jonathan Shelby, two sergeants, one formerly of the Confederacy, the latter with the Union, one Johnny Reb and one Billy Yank, one white and one colored, headed out on their after-dinner venture.

The back bottom land on the Circle D Ranch was a sight to see. From the ridge of the highest hilltop to the stream that ran clear and free, it was an invaluable source for tending hundreds of cattle. This was a timber-rich part of Texas, a land that gave life to cotton, oats, and wheat, a land that fed the coyote and offered shelter to the squirrels and the bats and the rattlesnake, a paradise that man forgot in his fight to tame a land that could never be tamed.

Jonathan Shelby always felt close to the earth, and even more so in the wide-open land. Montana Devers did, too, and he was proud to own this piece of radiant beauty. They spent a long stretch out in the open, even stopping to catch a mess of fish for the table.

Devers offered Jon a room, and he decided to stay. His body was sore, and he needed to rest and get some sleep. He would catch a wink or two and then take a run into town. He would fetch his saddlebags and be on his way west. He should have been in Red River Station long ago and by now be on his way back. As he settled down to sleep, Jon thought of Dan'l Walton. He missed Dan'l, that was a fact.

Jon fell off into a doze. He slept for several hours, and that was good.

Chapter

Twenty-four

Boots and pistols in hand, Shelby cautiously sneaked out of the sleeping quarters Montana Devers had so graciously provided him for the night. Jon became even more suspicious of his host when he found a guard posted at his door. He used the window to exit the house and then proceeded on his way.

Devers's offer sounded good, but Jon refused to work for a white man if he didn't have to, especially a man who sounded almost too good to be true. The Union soldier had decided that Devers was determined to keep him around, even if it was against his will, and no man liked to be held captive, even if he had done something wrong.

When the Negro gained his freedom—and he *would* be free one day—Jon planned to farm his own land somewhere out west, where he would work for himself and only himself.

Jon eased away from the house, retrieved Easel from the remuda, and headed quietly toward Clarksville. Looking back, he failed to notice Devers's man Soble Reed on his tail. He had hoped that his absence would go unnoticed for as long as possible.

The rays of the full moon cut through the night sky like slim white swords. Agile and responsive to his master's slight tug on the reins, Easel slipped cleanly through the night like a race horse down a stretch.

Halfway to his destination, Jon spotted a light within a thicket of trees. He inched his way closer and was suddenly yanked off his steed and hit over the head. When he awoke, he discovered who his captors really were.

"Why have you come spying on us? You some white

folks' nigger tryin' to earn some points with them pecker-woods?" asked a big Black man who called himself Stan. "Huh? Tell me, Black man."

"I ain't spyin' on you," said Jon, rubbing his head. "I'm Shelby, Jon Shelby."

"You that colored fella they said jes' blew into town? You's a brave man bringin' them white folks in," said Stan. "They ain't a-gonna hang no white man brought to jail by no nigger. They probably let 'em go as soon as you turned your back. Learn your lesson, Jon Shelby—white folks stick together, like colored folks ought to."

"I ain't here to turn you in. I got business in Clarksville. I saw the light from your church through the trees. Jes' came over to see if anything was wrong."

"We's all right. Come on inside and get you a cold drink. Hear the word of the Lord, too, iff'n you's a mind to."

Inside the makeshift church were thirty-five to forty Negroes singing quietly and praying under the flickers of the low candlelight. The Negroes had struck a deal with some of the friendly local whites to use this shack for their church on Saturday nights. The crowd of Black folks looked well worked, but still strong and hoping for a future.

A man stood up in front of the crowd of equally mixed young and old folk. All of them looked up at the tall brown-skinned preacher man wearing a long black robe. The robe was lined with red satin, and the preacher was adorned to the hilt with bright gems—a baroque turquoise necklace and a bracelet to match; an aquamarine ring on one hand; a small, classy tourmaline band on the other hand. Next to him, by the fire, was an intricately carved lapis lazuli bowl. Amazed at the beauty of the setting, Jon listened intently to the preacher's words.

When the meeting was over, the crowd of Blacks stood talking among themselves. The preacher shook hands and talked about local business. Eventually he came over to Sergeant Shelby and they said their hellos.

"Sergeant, isn't it? Reverend Marion Caldwell's my name. You sure you ain't no spy?"

"I ain't no spy," said Shelby.

193

"Why have you come to us?" asked the finely robed figure.

"I was just passin' through, just like I told Stan," Jon said. The preacher nodded his head. "I knew you would come."

Jon looked around the room and noticed how shabby it was. But that didn't seem to matter; the shack served its purpose all the same. The folks were busy taking down all of the ornaments that made it look like a church, and when they were through they would go back to their homes or sneak back onto their plantations. Seldom was anyone caught. They were a cautious and close-knit group. That's how they had managed to ship several hundreds north underground, without a trace.

"If you'll excuse me, Reverend Caldwell," said Jon, looking down at the shabbiest Bible he had ever seen, "I have to get into town and back out here before dawn."

"Don't you wish to know your future?" asked the reverend, leading Jon over to the wooden altar, his skin brown and shiny with oil.

"Future?"

"I saw it in the bowl," said the reverend. Touching the tip of his index finger to the clear fluid inside its middle, he dropped a small root into the container. The fluid bubbled and smoked. Reverend Caldwell removed his finger and laid a tiny droplet onto the surface of a large mirror. The liquid spread across its shiny surface and lit up like the rays of the sun. "Ah," said Reverend Caldwell, smiling at what he saw. He began to speak in near rhyme.

Beware, unto the morrow,
Come hence in time of sorrow,
Beware, the winds of change shadow your brow,
Beware, my Black friend, Death is in the air,
All ways, all ways . . . listen to the wind. . . .
The wind will save the day.

Reverend Caldwell whispered the words in Romany, a mixture of Sanskrit and Prakrit. He had learned the language from an old book some white folks had thrown away. It was the language of the ancient gypsies, and they were good words, words of hope and of life.

"I don't know what you mean," said Shelby to the good reverend.

"You will, Black man. You will!"

"Pray for me, Reverend."

"We must pray for each other."

As Jon turned and walked away, he saw an amazing sight. Out of the woods from all directions, men walked in toward the church. They had the building surrounded so that no one could harm the congregation. Some men had clubs, and the two white men had shotguns. Shelby smiled at the thought of what good the belief in God could do, and in two wags of a doggie's tail he was in the wind, running Easel as fast as he could go. He would head to LaDonna's to talk to Zena, then fetch his saddlebags from the jail and head back to the Circle D Ranch before Devers found out he'd left.

The U.S. Army soldier looked up in the sky at the bright moon and remembered what the reverend had said:

The wind will save the day, Black man
The wind will save the day!

Chapter

Twenty-five

Clarksville, Texas, was ghostly and determined to scare off any intruders, yet the quiet it emitted when Jon Shelby arrived seemed dangerously tentative. Only a bullfrog's bellow pierced the daunting silence.

Inching his way past the outskirts of town, Jon tied up Easel in back of LaDonna's Place. There was laughter still coming from some of the rooms, though most of the clientele had sneaked home, turning the bordello into a mere hotel for the night.

The soldier eased up to the kitchen door and went in. He walked all the way through to the front of the establishment until he saw LaDonna's reflection in a mirror. When she saw him, she jumped, startled. He smiled and motioned for her to come back into the kitchen with him.

"I thought you were dead, soldier," said LaDonna.

"I'm a fast healer," Jon said. "You seen Zena?"

"She's upstairs."

"Is she . . . ah, busy?"

"Nope."

"I'd be mighty obliged if you'd fetch her for me."

LaDonna started out of the room, then turned around. "Plenty of victuals on the stove, Jon. Help yourself."

Jon found some cold fried chicken. He grabbed three wings and a drumstick and a couple of biscuits. And before he could get it all down, the kitchen door flew open and Zena ran through. She came to him like he was her long-lost son, and she hugged him and kissed him enough to choke him. The Black man enjoyed Zena's attention, but all he could think about right then was unfinished business.

"I thought Murdock and that new fella had found you and done sumpin' awful to you!" Zena cried, "I knew you weren't dead like Miss Kate said."

"What?" said Jon.

"Never mind. You're safe and that's all that matters now."

"I heard they came lookin' for me here and at Devers's spread. I'm gettin' ready to head outta town before them fools get on my tail again. I'll need my saddlebags first."

"Your bags are over at the jailhouse, I reckon, Jonny," said Zena Beale, looking pretty in a black dress that showed off her womanly curves. "They came in here and tore the place up lookin' for them. Thought they'd find the money they said you owed them. And when they didn't find no money, they took the bags anyway. I reckon maybe they's lost now."

"Well, I'm gonna find out. See you later, honey."

"You better stay mighty low. You can't take nary 'nother beatin' like they give you before. You'd die, Jonny, and I just couldn't take that," said Zena, realizing she was saying too much. Jon had started out the door. "Wait a minute! You can't leave town without saying good-bye."

"I ain't leavin' just yet," said Shelby. "I'm headin' over to the jail to get my belongings . . . and ain't nothin' gonna stop me."

"Hold on, let me get my wrap," commanded Zena.

"Wrap? For what?"

"I'm goin' wid ya," she said. "I didn't spend all that time patchin' you up to see you git torn apart agin."

"This is man's work. Wimmen only get in the way."

Zena stomped her foot—she always did that when she was mad.

"Don' you stomp your foot at *me*," Jon said.

"I'll stomp my foot anytime I please. Ain't no beat-up half-dead soldier gon' tell me what to do," she replied, fire in her eyes. Jon smiled. He liked a woman with spunk, and of all the best things Zena Beale boasted, her spunk was the one thing that couldn't be covered up with a dress. "Now you wait for me, ya hear? I'll be right back."

Jon nodded his head, but as soon as Zena left the room, he ran out the back door and over to the jail.

When Zena returned the soldier was gone, but since she

knew where he was headed, she went after him, mumbling to herself, "Miss LaDonna was right. Ain't no man worth nothin' these days. I shoulda known he'd run off without me."

Jon made his way quietly toward the Clarksville jail to retrieve his personal property. He was known in his army outfit as a silent runner. Some of the men claimed he had a ghost working for him. "Shelby's ghost," they joked sometimes, whenever he was able to pull off a spying job within enemy lines without ever being detected by the Rebels. One colored private once called him "Ghost" to his face, but Jon punched him in the nose. "Nicknames's for weak folks," he told the man lying on the ground. "And I ain't no weak man. Understand!"

Jon inched his way up to the jail and looked inside the glass-paned window. A Mexican man with a buff-colored sombrero over his face lay sprawled out on a casket-shaped pine box.

Shelby looked around him to see what he could find to hit the windowpane without breaking it. He didn't want to startle the man, since he might come up firing his pistol. Finally he decided that the best way was the direct way. He'd just go inside and ask for the vaquero's help.

He prayed the Mexican was friendly to his cause.

Shelby walked around to the front of the jail, and that's when he saw it. He lit a match for closer inspection. The poster, complete with his photograph, was a duplicate of the ones all over town.

WANTED

DEAD OR ALIVE

JONATHAN FREDERICK SHELBY
alias Sergeant Jon Shelby, U.S. Army Scout

──────── $1,000.00 ────────
Reward

SHOOT TO KILL

<< MARSHAL KILLER >>
<< IMPERSONATING AN ENEMY OFFICER >>
<< DISTURBING THE PEACE >>
<< GAMBLING >>
<< SPYING >>

ARMED AND EXTREMELY DANGEROUS

Peeved at the lies and trumped-up charges, the Black soldier scout yanked the poster off the wall. He looked inside the jailhouse window again and saw that the vaquero was still asleep. His fingers wrapped slowly around the door latch. He turned the rounded metal, attempting a quiet entrance. And then he heard a familiar click, and a sharp object lodged into the small of his back at the base of his spine. It was the barrel of a Colt revolver.

"Well, well. I've heard of breaking out of jail, but never breaking into a lockup, cowboy," said Fats Griffin, chewing on a toothpick and spitting a slap of tobacco juice from the corner of his mouth. "Now you just raise them hands nice and slow and continue on inside, so I can see who you are. I got a jail cell for you."

Within the walls of the Clarksville Town Jail, Shelby stood with his back to the deputy marshal as Angel de la Guarda Tavares stood up, fumbling with the extremely large sombrero in his hands. Jon Shelby turned around to face the man who had the legal right to shoot him in the back. He was glad it was Fats Griffin instead of Cotton Richards.

"Well, if it ain't the sergeant," said Fats. "I thought you's different from them other Blacks, but I guess you proved me wrong."

"What you mean, Deputy Marshal?"

"Breakin' into the jailhouse at this time of morning. That's a lockup offense, right, Tavares?"

"*Sí, Señor,*" said the vaquero, nodding his head nervously.

"I just came back to fetch my property."

"What property's that, sergeant?" asked Fats Griffin.

"My saddlebags. Had some mighty important papers inside. Wouldn't want to lose 'em."

"Reckon we'd better save you until tomorrow morning for the marshal. Lock 'em up, Mexican. I got some celebrating to do."

"You can't lock me up, Deputy Marshal Fats, sir," urged Shelby, his second mind urging him to sweet-talk Fats like he did Cotton Richards the day he entered town. He recalled that Fats Griffin liked him, which he hoped would add a plus to the situation. It didn't.

"Oh, yes, but I can," said Fats.

"On what charges?"

"Breaking and entering a jailhouse in the middle of the night—plus, you's a wanted man, Sergeant."

"You're lying . . . and you know it."

"It's my word agin' your'n, I s'pose," whined the deputy, "and when it comes down to weighing the words of an outsider agin the word of a law officer like me, the law is always right."

With the slamming of the door to the jail cell, Jon Shelby knew he was in real trouble. He'd be the talk of the town tomorrow when folks learned Fats Griffin had arrested a criminal Negro Yankee breaking into jail in the middle of the night. Fats mumbled a few words to Tavares, then walked out the door, making a lot of noise like he was Marshal Richards. He'd do some drinking and fetch him a whore out of bed. Little Heddy Sue Mabry with the big pretty hips and legs would do just fine.

Dreaming on his walk down Main Street, Fats saw the headline in the *Clarksville Star* newspaper:

HERO DEPUTY FATS GRIFFIN CAPTURES OUTLAW
Local Lawman Is Brave and Sure

When Cotton Richards left town or got kilt like most other marshals did, Fats would be a shoo-in for the job.

"Psst . . . psst," whispered Shelby through the iron bars. "Hey, Señor Tavares. I got words for you."

Angel de la Guarda Tavares walked heavily toward Jon's cell. He paused in front of the bars and said nothing.

"Look, I'm innocent of what they accused me of."

"*Sí.*"

"I need to find some saddlebags with top-secret information inside. I came to the jail to see if they were here."

"*Sí.*"

"You understand English, Tavares?"

"*Sí.*"

"Is that all you can say?"

"What would you have me say, señor?" said Tavares.

"I would have you see the predicament I's in. I mean . . ."

"You are trying to talk your way out of jail, Señor Shelby, are you not?" said Tavares, smiling on one side of his mouth.

"Well, if I wasn't in here . . ."

"You would bribe an officer of the law, señor?"

"I don't see no badge," said the soldier.

"This here's badge enuf fer me, señor!" said the Mexican, resting his hand on his gun.

Tavares walked out of the room, and Jon thought he'd lost all hope. What the hell would he do now? He was glad Zena hadn't come along.

Outside the Clarksville jailhouse, Zena Beale sneaked up to the corner of the building. She had one of LaDonna's girls with her, Dolores de Cruz. Dolores was a lovely, tanned-skinned Mexican woman from Monclova, on the far side of the Sabinas River. Her long, flowing, blue-black hair streamed behind her when she walked. The colored fellows loved to run their fingers through her hair, and the white men wished their women had it, too. She was a determined

201

woman who had fallen into her line of work by way of a promised love. She had arrived in Clarksville with a Mexican bandit who got himself killed. LaDonna took her in, and that was the nineteen-year-old woman's full story, up until now.

None of the other women working at LaDonna's or at the Lazy Day would have anything to do with her. She was too beautiful, they all said. Most of them thought the same thing about Zena Beale. But Dolores and Zena Beale hit it off right away.

"Thez man, he special, no?" asked Dolores, her Mexican accent so heavy that Zena sometimes had to ask her to repeat what she had said.

"Yes. He's special all right. He could be gone by now," said Zena. "I'm gon' look in the window, to see if I see him."

"It's cold out here," Dolores said.

"Oh, here, take my shawl," said Zena. "You stay here. I'm gonna look inside the window."

Zena sneaked over to the lockup's window, peeked in, and saw Angel Tavares, but no sign of Jon Shelby. He couldn't have worked that fast, Zena thought. She walked back over to Dolores. "Follow me. We gon' check another place."

Zena Beale led Dolores around to the back of the jail and whispered into the windows of several cells. From the last one she got an answer. Jon Shelby spoke up loud.

"Who's out there?"

"It's me. Zena."

"I'm locked up, Zena. You got to get help."

"I'll get you out, Jonny."

"You can't do it by yourself," he said. Silence. "Zena? Zena? Where'd you go, gal?"

The two women talked over their plan, walked up to the jail door, and knocked. Angel Tavares came to the door. Dolores acted faint, and he let the two women inside.

"She's sick, Tavares," said Zena, helping Dolores to the cot. "She needs some water. Get her some, please."

Tavares ran to get some water and returned and helped the Mexican woman. As he bent over Dolores, he looked straight into the crease of her cleavage, which was most ample. While Angel was so distracted, Zena picked up a folding shovel lying to the side, lifted the tool, and conked him over the head. As he fell he dumped the water all over Dolores.

"Tie him up, Dolores! I'm gon' let Jon outta that cell!"

"Wha . . . tie heem up? What I gon' tie heem up with? He is not my man, he is yores, señorita. I—"

"Oh, Dolores, come on. Help me, will ya!"

Dolores mumbled some Mexican cuss words and turned up her nose as Zena found the keys and went to let Jon Shelby out.

"Zena, I told you to get some help," said Shelby.

She stuck the key in the door of the cell while Jon continued to complain.

"You act like you don't want to get out," she said.

"You know I do," said the soldier.

"You lied to me. You said you were going to wait for me back at LaDonna's and you left."

"I didn't want to get you involved," Jon said.

"A lyin' man is the worst kind of man," she said. "Especially when he's lyin' to me!"

"Zena . . ."

"What was that you said a spell back, 'This is men's work. Wimmen only git in the way,' huh?" Zena held the key up in the air.

"Come on, Zena, stop messin' round! Open the door so we can git outta here afore Griffin comes back."

"But I'm just a woman, Jonny. This is *men's* work. . . ."

"Zena. Look, I'm sorry. Now git a move on, hear?"

Zena opened the door, and instead of thanking her, Jon ran past her into the front room of the jail. He burst into the room and saw Tavares all tied up with lacy material. Dolores had taken off her petticoat and bound the Mexican vaquero in knots.

"Who the hell are you?" Jon yelled.

"Who thee hell are *you*?" snapped Dolores.

"That's my friend, Dolores. Jonny Shelby, Dolores de Cruz. Dolores, Jonny Shelby."

"Oh, he's the cowboy you tol' me about, no, Zee-na?"

"I ain't no cowboy."

"Don't you all start. We got to find them saddlebags," Zena reminded them.

"You don't have to be concerned, Zena," said Shelby. "That's my worry."

"I lost 'em, I'll help find 'em," Zena replied firmly.

Angel Tavares woke up and groaned. Jon walked over

to him and grabbed him by the collar. "You seen my saddlebags? My initials were on them, 'J. S.'"

"I see them inside the desk."

Jon didn't believe him. "Tell me where."

"They are not here, señor. Montana Devers has them. That Samples fella made a deal with him," said Tavares.

"Then why didn't you say so in the first place?"

"You didn't ask me, señor," said the Mexican. "Oh, one favor, *por favor*. Don't let them know I spoke to you. They don't think I can speak and understand English. I studied at the Franciscan Mission in San Diego. They must not know."

"They won't," said Shelby. "Since I owe you one."

helby inched his way out of the jailhouse, leaving the women behind. Zena Beale called after him. "What about me?"

"Us!" said Dolores de Cruz.

"Y'awl go back to LaDonna's. I'm headin' to the Circle D," Jon said.

Zena yelled after him, louder this time. "You could at least say 'Thank you' to me and my friend!"

The call of a red wolf echoed through the Texas valley. Jon Shelby heard its cry and felt at home riding the range. These past few days had picked his temple. He longed for open spaces where nature sang its song. As he rode, he imagined the wolf in its lair: its reddish, tawny legs, snout, and ears that heard most all that moved. Of course, the sound he had just heard could have been a coyote wolf, a cross between the two. But that didn't mean nothing now. His mind turned again to what he had to do. Montana Devers had planned to hold his bags and to hold him hostage until he decided to work for the Circle D. But Devers was in for a big surprise. Jon Shelby could never be bought.

The blue mist hung low and smoky to the east, and the early sun filtered through the trees like a weary sentinel making morning inspection. Jon Shelby had arrived at the Circle D Ranch sometime before the dawn. He had a score to settle.

The smell of woodsmoke filled the room given to Shelby for the duration of his visit. Still dressed, and as tired as a fish out of water, Shelby came awake with the choking smoke. But he got out of bed without wasting any time. He was prepared to talk to Devers about the theft of his saddlebags, one of which contained an important valise.

On his way to locate his host, Jon overheard two men talking. Wooly Samples's loud, boisterous voice bled through the brief hallway. He and Montana Devers were heated in their language, Samples sounding madder than a pussycat in heat.

"I got that boy's saddlebags, Montana, from the marshal's desk like you asked. I came through, and I want what you promised."

"You'll get your pay when I say so," said Devers, "and not before."

"Don't try me, Devers. I've kilt men before, and you ain't above getting kilt yourself!"

"Killin' expectin' women is about as brave as shootin' an ant in the back," Devers snorted.

Samples stepped up to Devers and grabbed his collar. "I want my pay, cattleman, or else I'm gon' git it—personally."

"Next time you set foot on my property, Samples," returned Devers in his coolest voice, "bring a casket with you."

"I ain't plannin' on killin' you, Devers, not until I get my ducats."

"The casket ain't for *me*," replied the rancher, puffing on his brand-new cigar. "It's for you!"

To most hardworking men in and around Clarksville, Texas, morning light during the vernal equinox meant a time to prepare to plant new crops; but to men who never farmed in their lives, the dawn meant only the possibility of a new notch on their belts. It was like this for both Montana Devers and Wooly Samples. The two men had similar motives in life—to get as much as possible by any means available, honest or not.

And they weren't the only men in the Clarksville area concerned with lining their pockets in a hurry. Greed possessed the lives of many a man obsessed with material gain in life. These were men who dealt only with greenbacks from the North, the kind of money that had real value, not Confederate bills with no gold behind them. Many of them were men of withered glory, men bred in the mold of parasites; men like

Drew Murdock and the fat banker Featherstone.

"Isaac, that gall-danged telegraph machine done finally brung in some good news," said Hamilton Featherstone to the man by his side. Folks called Isaac Ramsey "Ike" for short, but the banker man liked to call him by his given name. Featherstone reached inside his pocket to make Ike's delivery worthwhile.

When Hamilton Featherstone was happy, most everybody else in town was, too. The banker tipped divinely on such occasions, and this, thought Ike Ramsey, was indeed such an occasion.

"That Devers fella's in for a big surprise. Not only did his claim fall through, but that land he's a-livin' on now is mine!" Hamilton Featherstone paused, rocking on the balls of his feet. "It pays to have connections high up in government, Issac."

"You'll have to either throw him off or kill him to get it, Mr. Featherstone," said Ike. "And he *don't* seem like the kinda bloke who cottons to having his property repossessed."

"My ace ain't been played yet. If my news don't git Devers hung, then the marshal's word will surely land him in the lockup."

"Gon' be trouble, I reckon," said Ike as another message came over the wires.

"Reckon so," said the potbellied banker. "Reckon you gonna be a might busy directly. Good day, Isaac. Good day."

Fats Griffin's brain throbbed like a bobcat was loose inside his head, scouting around for a rabbit to eat. Sometimes the best way to end a drunk was to sleep all day, but today was not a day for sleep.

It was time to head to the jail, to work, where he would break the news about catching Shelby last night. Sloshing water over his head, Griffin decided not to try and shave. He might wind up cutting his throat in the process.

When Fats staggered into the street, he saw Marshal Richards walking inside the bank. He could break the news to him there just as easily, and with the town's most powerful men inside the bank, he'd get the support he needed to oust Richards from head marshaling. Fats Griffin, Clarksville marshal. "Fearless Fats," he'd call himself.

Chapter

Twenty-six

"You'll regret it, Richards, if them eviction papers ain't on my desk by twelve noon," warned Hamilton Featherstone. Drew Murdock had arrived at the bank earlier than expected, and now he looked on with several other men. All were glad Cotton Richards was the man with his spurs against the wall.

"I ain't the district judge, Mr. Featherstone," said Richards, thinking more about the money he was due from Wooly Samples than about what he would say next.

"District judge won't be here 'til purty near middle a' the month, if then," Drew Murdock said, genuinely concerned about the welfare of Cotton Richards, for reasons he didn't quite understand. "You can't force sumpin' on a man like that, Hamilton."

"Shut up, Drew, I'll do the talkin'. You handle the rough stuff, I handle the banking business." He paused and turned again to Richards but was cut off before he could speak.

"We could call in the judge or the district sheriff, iff'n we needed to. Know what I mean, Richards?" Murdock was trying to be helpful.

"Look. I did everything y'awl said, and that includes standin' by while y'awl half kilt that Negra soldier," said Cotton Richards defensively.

"Stop wasting time! I've got the papers that gives me the lock and key on that fertile hollow that Devers is a-holdin' on to. Hell, it's mine, and I want it now. Get them papers and have them ready, *Marshal*, then we can head out to the Circle D and claim the prize." .

"Devers won't stand for it," said Richards, shaking his head.

"We'll take it even if we have to *kill* him for it. And furthermore, he's a deserter from the Confederacy. At least you done something right, Richards. Opening that poster that you should have opened months ago proves Devers ain't really Devers." The banker was interrupted when the door burst wide open, literally shaking the small room.

"Marshal, Marshal," said Fats Griffin, his head throbbing like mad. "I got 'im. Got—dernit, I got 'im."

"Calm down, Fats. What you got?" said Richards.

"That colored fella. The boy that brung them bank robbin' white fellas into jail. You know, the one who kilt the district sheriff's gal."

"You mean the one that was expectin'?" asked a thin, bald-headed man named Spurling Atwood.

"Yup," said Fats, his chest stuck out. "That's the one."

"Thought you said that Negra was dead, Richards," said Featherstone.

"He *is* dead. Hell, the posse kilt him yesterday out on the trail."

"If the posse kilt him, Richards, how come your deputy caught him last night?" asked Drew Murdock.

"I locked him up last night. He's in the jail right now, all of the way in the back cell," Fats said with a grin.

"Where've you been all night?" asked the marshal.

"Well, Marshal, bein' it was that I's off duty at the time of the arrest, why, I decided to go git me one a' Kate's gals. You know Heddy Sue Mabry, don't ya, she's the one with the big—"

"Never mind, Fats, never mind," said Murdock.

"I tell you, Drew," Richards cried, looking like a tallow-faced fool, "that boy's dead as he can be!"

"Only one way to find out," said the potbellied banker.

"Yeah," Murdock agreed. "And for your sake, Richards, I hope your deputy's drunk."

Drew Murdock, Marshal Cotton Richards, Hamilton Featherstone, and Fats Griffin paraded down Main Street toward the jail. And when they burst through the door, Tavares, still partially bound in his lace fetters, woke up. The marshal, the deputy, the banker, and the gambler ran

208

fast to the cells. They were empty—all of them. As one they turned and looked at Fats.

Hamilton Featherstone swelled until he looked ready to explode. He frowned, stomped to the jailhouse door, turned, and pointed his finger, which shook frantically. "One hour, Richards. One hour!" And that was that.

Marshal Cotton Richards had no choice but to obey the banker man's words. His deputy had made him look bad, but he would take care of Fats later. He stalked outside. Murdock and Featherstone were already headed toward the Lazy Day Saloon to organize a posse.

Richards went back inside to his files and pulled a blank document from the folder, filling it out as best he knew how. He supposed it was legal, to a point. He hoped he could get by with it. But if the district judge found out an officer of the peace was playing judge behind his back, he'd get twenty years or be hanged.

Every morning the folks inside LaDonna's Place buzzed like it was the last days of their lives. The victuals were on the table, and the coffee was steaming hot. Zena Beale woke up to the sound of horses' hooves and rowdy men running down the road, past LaDonna's, and onto Main Street where the dust plumed high into the sky, towering over the buildings making up the town.

"What's all the commotion?" Zena asked Dolores de Cruz.

"It iz a posse," replied Dolores, her accent even heavier than usual because she was tired. "They speak of the Negro caballero, Jonathan Shelby. They say someone found a Negro's body outside of town. They all figured it was the man you broke out of jail, no?"

"Is that all you heard?"

"Some other white vaqueros rode up, and they headed over toward Main Street. Dat iz all I hear dem say, Señorita Zena."

"I got to find him . . . if he ain't dead," Zena said.

"I thought the gringos keel heem?" said Dolores, her brown eyes sad for Zena Beale.

"They said he was dead before . . . and he was alive. They're probably wrong right now. I'll be back, Dolores, goin' out to Devers's place. Don't tell nobody where I'm at, not even Miss LaDonna."

"I don't like to lie to Señora LaDonna," said Dolores.

"Just do it," Zena said. "And stop trying to be an angel."

"I do it, I do it," said Dolores, fussing.

Zena Beale sneaked out of LaDonna's back door, into the alleyway, and onto the fresh ebony-jet horse with a blaze face that waited there. She traveled the back way toward the Circle D Ranch. Her world somehow appeared to stand still; the faster she ran, the slower her mount seemed to go. But her determination would not allow her to fail. She would not be stopped by fear.

The Circle D Ranch was beautiful in the mornings, the sun's rays glistening and sparkling as they careened off dew-covered leaves of greens and deepening blues. In the light of the new day, Sergeant Shelby confronted Montana Devers. The two men stood in the front yard, having it out.

"We got some talkin' to do."

"Sure, Shelby," said Montana Devers, all duded up in suede and silk. "Let's go take a walk over to the lake. Fresh mornin' air'll do you good."

"No time for all a' that," said Jon. "I want to know why you held out on me."

"I've been straight up with you," said Devers.

"Where are my saddlebags?"

"Don't rightly know what ya mean, pardner."

"You're lying, Devers," Jon snapped.

"Calm down, calm down. We did find some belongings in town that might have connections to you."

"I suggest you get them now."

"Hold on, boy. Nobody tells Montana Devers what to do. Why, if you waddn't my future employee, I'd let you have a mouthful of knuckle pie."

"A man who talks like that may have to back it up one day," Shelby warned, his hands near his pistols.

"I ain't no gunfighter, Shelby . . . and don't you go get-tin' no ideas, neither," Devers admitted in a hurry.

"I'd like my property now," said Shelby. Devers nodded to one of his boys. "And don't do nothin' stupid. I get shot, you get shot. Get it?"

"You'll never get out of here alive if you try me. We still got bidness, anyhow."

"Seems our business is over. You offered me a job. I'm sayin' no."

"It may be over, Jon, but it shore don't mean that it's *over*."

"Don't make me no difference if I leave here waving good-bye or runnin' for my life," Jon replied. "So ease that pistol out of your holster, just in case you get an itch to be a gunslinger when my back is turned."

As Devers eased his pistol from his scabbard and dropped it to the dust, a horse came galloping through the tree-covered rock ridges enclosing Devers's Hollow. Jon turned around abruptly when he heard the voice.

"Jonny! Jonny! . . . you're alive!" It was Zena, running fast into a trap. White men were all over the place, and they had guns—and that was bad.

"Go back, Zena! Go back!" Jon yelled.

Devers made a grab for him, and the two men wrestled across the yard. Shelby punched Devers's head into the Texas dust twice, but Devers kicked Shelby off him and landed on top of the Union man. Devers reached for his knife, and Shelby caught his hand. They rolled from side to side in a fury. Devers somehow broke from Jon and made a dash toward the pigpen. Shelby stumbled to his feet and caught Devers just as they went crashing through the wooden gate. Jon's derringer fell from him, and both men reached frantically for the weapon. Devers got his hand around it, and when he fired one of his men fell to the ground, mortally wounded. Shelby knocked the gun from his hand, and it sank into the pig's mud. The muck was more than ankle deep, and Shelby pushed Devers backward into the slime. Devers pulled Shelby's feet out from under him, and he fell. With a "splat" and a "suka" they were soaking in a pool of mud.

Devers's men looked on, enjoying a good fight. When the lookouts weren't watching for intruders, they were busy trying to see if the boss was winning. But no one was winning, not yet.

Shelby pushed Devers's face into the mud. "You bastard!" he yelled.

"Fool nigger! Ain't you got no sense?" Devers returned, muck streaming out of his mouth.

"Naw," said Jon, "I *ain't* got no sense. . . . " He paused on one knee, tired of punching. "You better give up, Devers. I ain't a-gonna let you whip me. An you"—he caught his breath—"a Rebel loser at that."

"Shut up, boy, and come let me whip your Black ass!"

"You and who else?" Jon taunted.

Devers caught his second wind and lunged at Shelby, who fell over the other way, dead tired of fighting a contrary peckerwood. Devers lay facedown in the pig slop, and he could hardly move for the mud around his ears, up his nose, and in his eyes.

Suddenly a pistol fired, and everyone stood still. Harper Fellows, Devers's horse-breaking fool, had a pretty good-looking Joslyn pistol to Zena's neck. "You settle down now, boy. I got yore nigger gal . . . and I ain't a-gonna let her go alive."

Shelby swiftly pulled out his bowie knife and threw it at Fellows. It caught him in the chest, killing him dead on the spot. Another man ran up to Zena and took Fellows's place. Three shots rang out at Shelby's feet. He wisely chose to surrender.

Wooly Samples walked out of the house and bounced over to the two men, carrying Jon's saddlebags over his shoulder. He looked Shelby up and down and walked around him, laughing.

"Well, boy, looks like the tables dun turnt. The El Paso Kid's done done it agin. I'm your master now, boy," Samples said, punching Shelby in the nose, kneeing him in the side, and knocking him down with the butt of his Joslyn. "Now talk yore bullcrap, African. I'm gon' beat you 'til the cows comes home. Ya hear!"

Devers stepped forward through the mud and stopped Wooly Samples from killing the helpless man. "Ain't no need a' that, Samples. We got more important things to do."

"Ain't *nuthin'* better than whippin' a darkie. Why you love niggers so much, Devers? You ain't one a' them abolitionists, is ya?" said Wooly.

Horses' hooves rumbled through the valley, and a lookout yelled down into the hollow. "Riders a-comin, whole slew of 'em. Looks like they mean bidness."

The roar of the posse echoed off the steep valley walls. The riders, thirty strong, arrived in a ball of dust and pulled rein; lead rider Hamilton Featherstone tipped his hat first thing.

"Good day to you, Montana. Hope we ain't bustin' up no private festivities." The banker frowned at the mud covering Devers.

"What can I do for you, Featherstone?" asked Montana, squinting his eyes in the hot sun. He pulled off his dirty hat, wiped his brow with his bandanna, and listened closely to the banker man's words.

"As you know, Montana, this here's a fine piece of property to own and work. I know you've been tryin' to get the deed for quite some time, but the war has pretty much stopped fast government action."

"What you gittin' at, Featherstone?" whispered Drew Murdock.

"Got a way, Devers," said the banker man with a laugh, "to take the bite out a' your bark!"

Chapter

Twenty-seven

The greedy banker reached inside his two-hundred-dollar jacket and pulled out the questionable papers Marshal Richards had signed. He handed them to Devers, who opened the roll quickly. His temper hit the boiling point almost as soon as his eye ran down the first page.

"Boss, boss!" A cowboy's voice rushed through the hills. Two riders came up fast. Percy Ben Stokes had his six-shooter pointed at the other horseman's gut.

Jon Shelby looked up, recuperating somewhat from the Devers fight and the Samples beating. His eyes lit up when he saw the hooded figure with an angry, cold look on her face. But Lavinia T. Gurley was the prisoner this time. Percy Ben Stokes and Vinia pulled rein. Devers was almost too preoccupied with the Featherstone business to take much notice.

"Who you got there, Percy Ben?" Devers snapped.

"That blamed bounty huntin' killer we ran outta here darn near a month ago. Says he's jes' passin' through. What ya want to do wid him, boss?" Percy Ben did not know Vinia was a "she." Vinia wanted it that way.

"I don't care what you do with him! Just get him out of my face!" Devers looked back at the papers and then into Hamilton Featherstone's eyes." Fun's over, banker man. Now you can take your forged law papers and get offa' my land. Our business is done with."

"These papers directs me to evict you from this here hollow, Devers. Pronto. I own it fair and square. The deed is in my name."

"You ain't the district judge, which means you can't tell me where to go."

"I'm a-warning you about any resistance, Devers. I've got the marshal with me. Either you vacate, or there'll be trouble," said Featherstone.

"You tangle with me, banker man, and there's a good chance them duds a' yours'll git plenty dirty on the ground."

"Ain't gon' be none a' that," Drew Murdock said, stepping forward. "The man says you got to go, you gotta go."

"Who's gonna make me?" said Devers.

Cotton Richards stepped forward, with Fats Griffin by his side. He tipped his hat and said, "I will."

The "kush-a-lee, kush-lay" call of a rusty blackbird in the distance suddenly stopped when Richards made his stand. The tension was running mighty high.

"I ain't no gunfighter, Richards," Devers said, raising his arms to show he was unarmed.

"I'm here to back up the law. You don't cooperate, I'll have to take you in."

"It'll be a cold day in the desert 'fore you take me anywheres."

"You're under arrest, Devers, for defying the establishment. I hope you'll come quiet."

A rifle cocked and fired, and the crackle and call of gunpowder on metal snapped through Devers's Hollow like invisible lightning. One of Devers's men had fired the shot, and suddenly it was every man for himself. Richards turned around to see who had fired the weapon. Devers yelled, "Take 'em, boys! Don't let 'em out of the hollow alive!"

For the next thirty seconds, men scampered around the hollow for cover, outrunning hot lead that flew everywhich-a-way. It was hard to tell whose side anybody was on. Devers's men ran to the house for cover, Featherstone's gang ran the other way. That left Shelby, Zena Beale, and Vinia to fend for themselves, to get out of the line of fire as best they could. If Jon had to die soon, he hoped it wouldn't be at the hands of greedy no-'counts like the ones he had unfortunately come to know in Clarksville, Texas. He wasn't about to let Zena or Vinia get hurt without a fight.

"C'mon," he yelled to Zena.

"I'm comin', honey," she cried. Jon grabbed her hand

and dragged her to her feet. The smell of her perfume made Jon realize how glad he was to see her. "Vinia. This way."

"My hands is tied. Can't ride no hoss right without my hands, boy," called Vinia, still atop her mount. She was the only person besides his parents who could call him "boy" and get away with it. The Union sergeant ran over to the woman's horse and jumped on the big black stallion. They raced up to Zena, and Jon reached down to snatch her up onto the giant animal. Then they raced for cover. The sergeant was amazed at how quickly the white men forgot about them.

"You better give up, Devers!" yelled Featherstone. "This here's my land now!"

"Never!" Devers screamed, shooting one of Drew Murdock's men through the eye.

"I'll make a deal with you, Montana. You pack up and move on, I'll consider the whole deal over with, the record'll be straight."

"Forget it, fat man!"

Drew Murdock scurried over to the spot where Hamilton Featherstone was hiding. "Now!" he urged.

"Let's give him one more chance. He's bound to know he can't get outta this hollow without comin' through us. Anyway, his ammunition's sure to run out eventually."

"Hell, Hamilton, we could be here for days . . . and I ain't got the time. Maybe if that coward Richards would speak up and really arrest him, this'd be all over. Hell, that photograph on that poster is surely him. With two strikes agin him, we can't lose."

"You ain't got nuthin' to do 'ceptin what I tell you. You work for *me*, Drew. Don't you forget it!"

Murdock didn't like what the potbellied banker had said, but it was true. He ran behind another tree as a bullet sent several pieces of bark flying into his eyes. He was tired of fighting, and he called to Treat Billy Slocum to proceed with the plan. Slocum signaled back.

Wooly Samples, meanwhile, was fighting on Devers's side mainly because Devers owed him money and he knew Cotton Richards would soon want his pay. He had tried his best to kill the marshal in all the commotion, but Richards still lived, to his dismay.

Steel hooves pounded on top of the rocks when Treat Billy Slocum raced from the green surrounding forestry with a blazing torch, followed by several others on horseback wielding their own flames. Devers's men fired frantically at the riders. The first torch landed inside the ranch house's front room and caught the curtains on fire. The next one hit a can of coal oil that exploded into flames. The remaining men made sure the first fires had help.

There was a loud explosion. Drew Murdock had a bag full of dynamite sticks, and he was lighting the fuses with his cigar, tossing them at the house, laughing all the while. The ornery varmint wanted to break the spirit of the man whose house he was blowing to bits.

"They's burnin' the house, Montana!" yelled Cappy Epson.

"I can see that, Cappy, got-dammit, I can see it!"

"What we gon' do, Montana?"

A thud sounded, and Cappy Epson fell backward. Blood splashed Montana's hands and face, and when he wiped the hot, greasy fluid out of his eyes, he saw his best friend ever lying on his back with blood spurting out of a large hole where his heart once was. Devers kneeled over Cappy's limp frame, cradled his head in his arms, and began to cry and to encourage the old man to live. But Cappy Epson was a goner, deader than a hog on a hook.

Devers's brain heated up. He looked around him and realized in a flash all of the bad things he'd done. He remembered Fort Fisher back in Carolina, how he'd shot . . .

Devers's memory of his crime was being voiced out loud by Vinia T. Gurley to Jon and Zena. She had found herself another bounty. Vinia spoke of Devers with more pity than anything else.

"Shot two of his commanding officers dead and deserted the Confederacy. And that ain't all he did. Rebel no-account spread havoc and death all the way from the Atlantic to Texas. Bastard stole money, cheated his 'friends,' took a dead man's wife, used her, left her for dead. I'm sure that's him. Without that mustache and beard, he's a dead ringer for Monte Devlin." She reached inside her bag, and this time she let Jon see the poster. The soldier scout could tell by the eyes that the man in the photograph was indeed Montana Devers. He had known there was something familiar about Devers when he saw him up close, and now he realized that he had been thinking of the poster he had seen briefly back inside the Clarksville jail. Monte Devlin was his real name, and he was wanted: dead or alive.

Vinia never liked killing, since death was so final, so complete. A man who committed a crime should get one chance to talk his way out of getting hung, and if he wasn't slick enough to do that, only then should he die.

Suddenly Jon mumbled to himself, "Tang Chow's in there." He looked toward the backyard amid the wood-smoke near the cistern but saw no sign of the Chinaman. He ran down into the burning house, fought his way through billows of choking black smoke to the kitchen, and there grabbed Tang Chow, who had been overcome by the heat. As he ran for cover into the thicket, Jon thought about the saddlebags with his secret documents inside. Devers had taken them from Samples and slung them across his shoulders after their fight, but there was no telling where they were now, and Devers could be dead.

"I'm gonna run down to that gully and fetch my saddle-bags," he said to Zena and Vinia.

"You be careful," Zena urged.

"I'll cover you, boy," said the bounty-hunting plains-woman. Jon took off, and the older woman looked at Zena. "Whoowee, that Devlin fella's rotten to the gizzard."

Sergeant Jonathan Frederick Shelby took off toward the clearing, where the fighting men were still wasting ammu-nition like they had an arsenal to back them up. He hid behind a bush, then slid on his belly to a nearby tree; a bullet grazed his head, causing only a trickle of blood for the moment. Without thinking of the danger, Zena ran from cover toward the wounded soldier. Vinia followed her, cursing all the while. Tang Chow, whose clothes were torn and sooty, stumblingly brought up the rear.

An earful of thunder boomed loudly overhead. Jon searched the heavens for a sign of the weather. A tall, thick, and awesome mass of fluffy white cumulonimbus clouds was headed their way. Several thin funnels formed below their tall mast. Lightning thrashed within the center, flashing zig-zag beams of bright white and golden light. To Jon it looked like hell was on its way.

A mile or two up the Red, it was raining cow chips and

hailstones. Soon the rain would reach the Devers spread—what was left of it.

Another boom broke the air, the wind speed suddenly rose, and the trees swayed violently left and right. The white men stopped their warring and looked to the sky. The whirring source of the great wind inched closer. Dust flew into their eyes, and the once-seething heat was relieved by a cooler breeze.

Zena grabbed Shelby by the arm. "What's happening, Jonny? I ain't never seen the wind blow so hard before. Let's get out of here. I'm scared." She pointed. "Look what's a-comin' our way!"

Not one, but half a dozen twisters danced their way inside Devers' Hollow, one right after the other. Screaming cowboys and running fools ran helter-skelter. The winds howled hard, blowing by almost as fast as a bullet. In spite of his fear, Jon marveled at the wonder of the natural world. What force made by man could yank a twelve-inch oak from the ground and spin it around two hundred feet in the sky? Only nature could do that, and it was doing it now.

The tornadoes roared through, destroying everything in their path. One hit a thicket of trees where a lookout tower stood. The structure imploded into a thousand pieces and crashed to the ground. The tornado behind it hovered and waited for another one to catch up. Were they actually alive, or were they conjured up by magic spells for the occasion? The third tornado spun faster than the rest, appearing to lead the others on the assault, like a general leading his men into an offensive.

"Them twisters're damn near traveling a hundred miles an hour! Gon' kill us all. Can't nobody outrun 'em," said Vinia. "Them men's fools. They should be runnin' *across* the twisters' grain. At least that way they'd have a chance."

Shelby squinted toward where he had last seen Montana Devers, and there he was still, trying to fight the wind for what it was worth. At the same time he saw Wooly Samples and Hamilton Featherstone fire at the man. Devers fell, but Jon couldn't tell which man had shot him full of lead. The terrific winds made it difficult to see or to hear anything clearly, but Jon was sure he could make out the form of his saddlebags still in Devers's hand. Jon bolted from the gully where they were hiding and fell far short of Devers's body, knocked down by the winds. He commenced to crawl toward the bags, but it was no use, the wind was too strong. The cold, hard drops of rain pounded his back, hailstones the size of small cow chips. The first tornado was only a thousand yards away from killing him dead. Finally, after what seemed like an eternity, Jon reached out for the bags. Dusty raindrops packed his eyes, and as he blindly stretched, something tore inside his shoulder. He flinched and tears stung his eyes. "What the hell you waitin' on, damned twister! You gonna kill me, blow me away, or let me live?"

At that moment a wind blew the saddlebags toward the Black man's outstretched arm. He had one chance to catch them or they would be blown to smithereens forever. He stretched as far as he could, though his chest felt like it was tearing open. A final lunge and he had them, clutched tightly in his wet hands.

Devers, still not dead but close enough to it, had his pistol in his hand. When he saw Jon take hold of the bags, he tried to squeeze the trigger, but he passed out before he could kill for the last time. Zena screamed.

"Shut up, gal," snapped Vinia. "Your hollerin' ain't gon' do him no good. Now be quiet before I belt you."

Zena's tears stopped instantly, washed away by the rain coursing over her head and face.

Jon made his way back to Vinia, Zena, and Tang Chow, and the group hunkered down in the ditch, each trying hard to cover the other. The loud booms and the twisting, whirling wind was death itself. The first tornado wiped out the remains of Devers's house. The third one hovered close, blacker in its middle where the trees and other debris swirled around and around like they were toothpicks. A cow, a calf, and even a horse had been caught up in its belly. The rain continued to fall so hard and so fast, the clearing became a river. It reminded him of the mouth of the Mississippi at the Gulf of Mexico at flood stage. The tornadoes completely ravaged the hollow and destroyed all man-made things. The hollow had only been called Devers's for a brief time, but now that would be forgotten.

Eventually the twisters moved on and away from the clearing. Men began to stagger around like zombies. Drew Murdock was lying over in the road, Hamilton Featherstone looked like he was dead. Cotton Richards had been blown away. His body was never seen again.

Slowly Jon and his fellows became aware of the distant roar of horses, maybe a hundred or so. Before too long the horses drew close, and Shelby smiled. The men in blue! He stood up and laughed as he watched the twisters fade away. The tornadoes were gone, and the rain followed suit. The sun came out, once again, and a hummingbird hovered near a flowering shrub. The men who had outlasted the storm in Devers's Hollow would never forget it. Their lives were changed forever.

"It's over, honey," said Jon, hugging Zena Beale and sassily eyeing the lace petticoat exposed from her waist up. "Now we gotta get you back to town so you can get cleaned up. Lace and Texas dirt don't look none too good together, especially on a pretty little gal like you!"

Chapter

Twenty-eight

The dazed and confused men and women worked to regain their composure after the daytime nightmare. The Union men were taking care of Samples and his boys and would take them back to town. Jon Shelby was concerned about the injured and dying men, and for some reason he could not really understand, he was bent on trying to help Montana Devers or Monte Devlin or whatever his real name was. Vinia spoke her mind in a hurry.

"After all he's done to you, I'd leave him to die," she said. She thought Montana Devers deserved to go to the devil for his wrongdoings on earth.

"I'd wake up nights wishin' I'da done him right," said Jon.

"She's right, Jonny." Zena said his name like no one else. "That white man deserves to die, or my name ain't Zena Beale."

"Color ain't got nothing to do with it. He saved my life once, at least I owe him for that. I'm takin' him into town to see the doc and then he's all yours." Jon patted the butt of his Colt and looked at some of the men standing around him. "Any objections?"

"You too good, Shelby," Vinia said. "Some good men die like fools."

"But at least they die in peace," said Jon.

Ignoring both Vinia T. Gurley's and Zena Beale's complaints, Sergeant Shelby hitched up a flatbed wagon to the two draft horses. He tied Easel and Dan'l's Appaloosa to the back of the wagon. The labor reminded him of hauling tobacco back on Dotsville Road in Tennessee.

"Gid up, here." He clicked his tongue against his side

teeth, and the horses took off. "Come up. Gid up!"

Tang Chow sat in the back of the wagon with Devers. At first Zena sat back there with him, but then she moved up onto the high seat with Jon. Lavinia stayed on horseback, flanking the wagon for protection.

The Texas sun inched slowly toward the far horizon. Something in the air still spoke of havoc, though it seemed impossible that anything worse than the preceding events could ever happen. Observing the sky around him, Shelby sensed some impending danger, but he didn't know what to do. All he could do was keep his pistol ready to fire.

Visions of twisted trees, tangled vines, and busted dreams flashed through the soldier's mind as he recalled the funnels of black air, chock full of evil, the rampant winds that had destroyed all in their way, the swirling and turbulent winds that had changed the world as he knew it. The wind! Of course! Jon laughed aloud, repeating to himself the words of a colorful man of God: "Beware, my black friend: the wind will save the day!"

Zena rolled her eyes at Shelby in the way only Black women could. "What?"

Jon laughed. "Don't you see? The preacher warned me last night."

"Preacher. What preacher?"

Jon put his arm around her, and she forgot all about her question. As long as he held her that way, she had nothing to fear.

Jon continued to muse about what they all had just witnessed. Whenever a house or a barn had burned back in Tennessee during his formative years, Jon had felt an empty gnawing in his chest. A burning home made him sad and weary. In fact, up ahead he thought he saw a house in flames burning across the plains, like a prairie fire driven by the wind. It must be my tired imagination, he thought, and he rubbed his eyes with the back of his hand.

Fires in Texas and, he had heard, in parts of Colorado and California burned for thousands of miles until they ran out of woods and tall grass. The Apaches, Hopi, Paiute, and Navajo tribes were often saddled with the blame of having started the fires, and it was true in some cases. More often than not, the fires were the fault of lightning. Either way, the fires helped to turn the whites back temporarily from the Indians' sacred ranges. White men never understood that the land belonged to God, and that no man, red or white, could ever claim it as his own.

Damn mirage, Jon told himself, as he blinked hard to clear the disturbing vision ahead of him. I'm giddy from the blood I lost. The hot sun ain't helping me none, neither.

Finally back in Clarksville, it was too quiet for Jon Shelby's nerves. He looked intently at Zena Beale, and she looked back at him.

"What'sa matter, darlin'?" she asked.

"It's too quiet."

Zena agreed that Clarksville did resemble a ghost town. It had never looked this way in the daytime, especially on a Sunday. Something could very well be awry. Where was everyone?

"Whoa, mule . . . whooaa," called Jon. He and Tang Chow, who spoke few words, picked up Devers and started toward Doc O'Reagan's office door.

Imus Wixey, himself a preacher man, too, came out of nowhere, pulled out a tape measure, tucked one end to Devers's boot and in a flash had measured the length of the tall cowpoke. "Yup. I think I've already got a box that'll fit him right nicely."

"Wait a minute, funeral man, he ain't yours yet. We're takin' him to the doc to git patched up," said Shelby.

"Patchin' up dead men's a waste of time," said Wixey as Doc O'Reagan came out into the street.

Doc O'Reagan felt for Devers's pulse, but there was none. He tore open Devers's shirt and felt for a heartbeat but there was none. Then Doc opened Devers's eyelids. His pupil were set. Lastly, he placed a small mirror under his nose. No breath. No life left. "Take him away, Imus. I'll fill out the deceased papers directly, and we can lay this man to rest."

"Ten-dollar funeral or my thirty-five-dollar special?" asked Wixey, a sneaky leer on his face.

"I think Montana Devers would want the best. Give him the works, Wixey," said Doc O'Reagan. "Looks like your business be picking up purty soon."

"What do you mean?" said Jon.

"The Honorable District Judge Mortimer Calender jes' got into town on the last stage. Says he's here to try that

224

Samples fella and his gang. He'll be cleaning up this town," said the funeral man, sticking his thumbs in the galluses of his overalls.

"Where's that trial being held?" Jon asked.

"Down in the Town Hall we calls the coathouse," said Doc O'Reagan. "Don't allow no colored folk inside less'n they's the one on trial, and since most Negroes don't git no trial, usually, I surmise ain't never no time when yore kind can go in—'ceptin to clean, I reckon."

"Thanks, doc. Mr. Wixey," said Jon Shelby, "y'awl been mighty white to me. Much obliged!"

Shelby turned fast, snickering under his breath. Sometimes he liked to say odd things to other folks, and when he looked back, both Doc O'Reagan and Imus Wixey were scratching their heads, not knowing whether to be alarmed, insulted, or both. But since neither one of them had on a gun, Jon thought it was safe to assume his irony would go unpunished this time.

Shelby left Zena and Vinia and headed down the street toward the makeshift courtroom. Arriving at a side window, he listened in as Judge Calender laid down the law:

As district judge of this here district, I am duly forced by the law of the land to pronounce sentence on the defendants before me:

Horace Lee Samples, Manfred James, III, and Paul Acedora Wiggins: I find all three of you guilty of murder, stealing, and being a general nuisance to our humble society.

Therefore, by the powers vested in me, I sentence the three of you at the earliest possible convenience of the local authority to hang by the neck until you are dead.

May God have mercy on your souls. This Court's hereby adjourned.

Scores of Clarksvillians and their relatives piled out of the Town Hall, quipping and mumbling words of praise for justice and the Confederate way. Several Black women —the ones who kept the place clean when they could get in to do the work—scurried out of the way of the exuberant crowd.

Most of the women heading now to the hanging of the Samples gang were just as riled and angry as the men. Jon thought they acted like their minds had been driven plumb loco by the howling prairie winds. They yelled out for the hangman to come forward, and when Samples, James, and Wiggins were brought out of the courthouse, the Clarksvillians led the three men straight to the gallows.

Folks had come from miles around and at a moment's notice to watch the trial of the men who had put a bullet in the belly of the district sheriff's daughter. They never dreamed they would get to hear a famous killer's trial and see him hanged on the same day! Several respected members of the community arrived on the scene, and the hangman proceeded to make final adjustments to the three nooses.

There was a festival mood in the air. Clarksvillians loved hangings, and they loved them even better when the lynchings were fast and the men didn't struggle. Little Effie McGraw wasn't allowed to see the goings-on, but her ma Annie Mae and pa Emory were there, silently supportive. Imus Wixey stood by the men after their necks were secure within the grasp of the nooses.

Samples, James, and Wiggins declined to say final words. The reverend spoke briefly some words of heaven and forgiving, words that most thought the three killers didn't deserve.

The townsfolk stood still, awaiting the final moment. Their faces were filled with expectation. The wind had stopped blowing, and a cloud covered the sun. It seemed as if the world had quit for a hanging, Clarksville, Texas style.

Jon Shelby looked on from a hundred yards back. He wasn't afraid for himself now, but he rubbed his neck and recalled when he was in a similar predicament. He wondered what Samples would do. Would he die like a man or . . .

The openings in the floor of the gallows box sprung wide at the same time, and the deadened thud of the wood falling down and the rope catching held the crowd scared. Six men stooped forward and yanked on the victims' legs to end it sooner. A fair number moaned aloud while others moved back, their eyes wide and unbelieving.

Manny James and Ace Wiggins met their death like men. Wooly Samples wet his pants, kicked, and tried to scream. An awful smell came up from the men who had taken their final breaths. All three were finally dead.

The crowd slowly turned away. Heads hung in shame. Several of the women wiped away tears, and the men removed their hats.

It was in this uncomfortable silence that shots rang out.

"Yee-hah, Yee-hah!" yelled a voice down Main Street. It was Jipson Tandy. "Come on out, coon. I seen you hiding behind that wall," he cried. "I'm a-gonna git ya if ya don't watch out."

"I ain't got no gripes with you, Mr. Tandy," Shelby said, stepping forward and hoping to calm the drunken fool before someone got hurt. Tandy wanted to shoot it out, in front of the whole town. It seemed he blamed Jon Shelby for Kate Pearson's plan to head west.

"Come on out and git shot 'tween them eyes a' yores, boy," Tandy cried, drunker than a fruit fly in July.

By now the whole town had gathered, those fresh from the hanging not overly eager to witness more killing. Tandy fired wildly again, and everyone ran for cover. Even His Honor Judge Calender ran behind a post at Flatt's Haberdashery. He watched silently while the ultimate law was carried out.

Jon hoped he wouldn't have to deal with what was called "the law of general principle"—the principle that the white man was always right and the Black man was always wrong. Under those conditions, he had to lose.

Suddenly a young boy darted across the street. Able Wilson's kid, Pooty Ray. Jipson Tandy fired on the first thing that moved, and Pooty got it in the leg. Without thinking of his own safety, Jon ran to save Pooty from certain death. He picked up the boy and handed his limp frame to his father, who had emerged from the scattered crowd. Jon Shelby was caught in the middle of the street in a white town having a shootout with a white man. There were no two ways about it. He would save himself and in the process prevent any other innocent folk from getting hurt. He would stand by no longer.

"All right, Tandy. Have it your way. I never wanted it to come to this, but I guess I have no choice."

"Brave Yankee nigger darkie soldier. You low-down son of a bitch! You gon' get kilt, boy. I'm the best with a shootin' iron in these here parts."

"Stop it, Jipson!" Kate Pearson called out from the door of the Lazy Day Saloon. Her trunk and bags stood by her side.

"See what you did, boy! Made my honey Kate pack up and head to Californey. I don't cotton to no man who takes away what's mine. Git ready to draw, boy. I'm a-countin' ta three. If you don't shoot, yore dead."

"Don't, Jipson!" yelled Kate. She had been joined by Delores de Cruz, Zena Beale, and LaDonna.

"She's right, man, it don't have to end this way," Jon offered.

"One."

"Don't do it, Tandy. I'm a-warning you."

"Two." Tandy's arm moved closer to his gun.

"Don't," said Jon, rubbing the butt of his Colt.

"Three!"

Gunsmoke billowed from the barrels of the two blokes' guns, and both Shelby and Tandy stood as if suspended in midair. They stared at each other as the thick blue smoke dispersed slowly into the sky. Tandy's gun twirled around his trigger finger as if he planned to put it away. Then the pistol fell from his hand, and he stood frozen, staring straight ahead. And then he fell backward, in slow motion, and when his head hit the ground he was stone cold dead.

Shelby fell to his knees.

"Jonny!" yelled Zena Beale, running out on the street toward her man. The bullet had grazed Shelby's left shoulder. Another flesh wound and a lot of blood. No real problem for the courageous soldier who had endured so much already.

That same eerie quiet once again stalked the town of Clarksville, Texas, as the people gathered around the Black Union soldier. The crowd parted as Judge Calender came to take the law into his hands again, now that it was safe to do so.

"What do you have to say for yourself, cowboy?" demanded the judge.

"He ain't no cowboy. He's a sergeant in the Union Army, Your Honor," explained Fats Griffin, now wearing the marshal's badge since Cotton Richards's death. "I'll vouch for him."

"This man don't need no one to vouch for him."

"What do you plan to do, Your Honor?"

"Murder's a hanging offense in these parts."

Shelby began to sweat, knowing there was almost no way to outwit death this time. The judge continued.

"But since you shot that fool in self-defense and darn near everybody saw you do it, I reckon justice done been done. After all you've done for this town—regardless of your affiliation—I say you're a free man, as long as the marshal here don't mind."

Fats Griffin smiled at Shelby as Doc O'Reagan walked up and took hold of the soldier's arm. "Follow me, Shelby. I'll fix you up. . . . "

"And then you can git outta town." Fats laughed, kidding with the sergeant whom he had grown to like. "After you's fixed up, I reckon."

"Gladly," said Shelby.

Chapter

Twenty-nine

Cinque Kele had Shelby's horse saddled and ready to hit the open trail. The soldier was glad his wound was only a scratch. He could be on his way in a hurry now. Jon patted Easel on the muzzle, and looked up to see pretty Zena Beale approaching.

"Guess you're leavin' alone." It was half a question, half a statement of what she knew to be true.

"Ain't no other way to leave, I reckon."

"All you good men thinks about is work and duty."

"Yup. Got an assignment to complete for the general, then I'm mapping my way back down the Red, Louisiana way."

"I knew it was too good to be true, you stayin' and all," said Zena softly. "My luck don't run that way."

"I don't quite know what you mean, Zena."

"I lo . . . care what happens to you. I thought I had a friend." Zena's words got stuck in her throat. A woman telling a man how she felt about him could scare him away for good. She wouldn't tell him, not just yet. "You must know how I feel about ya'."

"Don't know that I do. I'll always be your friend, Zena."

"Will you ever come back?"

"Can't rightly say."

"What *can* you say, Sergeant Shelby!" Zena Beale's temper flew. "You could at least *try* to say sumpin' I wanna hear."

"Yup, I s'posin' I could drop by. Can't make no promises."

"Is that all you can say after what we been through!"

Zena put her hands on her hips. Her breasts jutted up from within her low-cut, pink ruffled dress. "Well, I need more'n that. I reckon if I could spend some time wid ya 'fore ya go, it'd be different. I prayed you'd stay a while and we'd have a chance to get to know each other. You could tell me more of that historical stuff."

Little Petey Freeman yelled out at the top his lungs as he ran up Main Street, interrupting Zena Beale's plea for Jon to stay with her a little while longer. And just when she'd gotten up enough nerve to say the words!

Petey fell several times in his excitement, but he picked himself right up again. Folks came out of the haberdashery and the Lazy Day Saloon, and even Imus Wixey left Devers's cadaver on the slab to hear the news Petey claimed to have. The telegraph office was full of action, but Ike Ramsey left the wires for the moment to join in what he alone knew would be a celebration. People continued to pour out of their homes and onto their porches as the word spread.

Cheers and shouts of joy rippled through the crowd as the boy ran past. Folks were hugging, and some were dancing. Some women fainted, and cowboys tossed their hats high into the Clarksville sky, took shots at them, and then grabbed the first whore they could find.

Little Petey damn near ran past Jon Shelby, who grabbed him and spun him around.

"What's all the fuss, boy?"

"Ain't you heard, mister?" said little Petey Freeman. "Gen'al Lee jes' surrendered to Grant at Apomattox Coathouse in Virginny. That stinkin' war is over, mister. My pa be a-comin' home soon. My pa is a-comin' home!"

Zena jumped into Shelby's arms and hugged him tight. The sergeant felt dizzy. A weight had been lifted off his shoulders, and he squeezed Zena Beale 'til she was as thrilled as she could be.

Folks continued their yelling and hollering from one end of town to the other. Hamilton Featherstone limped from the bank with his arm in a sling. The news of the war's end did not make him happy. The Yankees were known to burn down Southern towns, every building, whenever they took over a place they could not use. Clarksville would surely be burned to the ground. Featherstone planned to steal all of the money he could from the bank and get out of town in all the happy confusion, before the Union Army could have their say.

The Kele clan had heard the good news and hurried into town to find Shelby. Safiya found her way to the soldier and gave him a hug. They savored the moment for a good while.

"I got a hog we can barbecue and a new batch of corn liquor that'll knock the colored right outta the ugliest nigger in these here parts!" Pappy Kele laughed. "That is, if you ain't leavin'."

"I've still got a job to do," said Jon.

"Whatever's inside that satchel ain't got no meanin' now. The war is over, man, ain't you heard?" said Zena, taking charge of the situation.

"Open it up and see what it says. If you don't, I will!"

"Don't get feisty with me, woman," Jon scolded.

"You gonna shoot me, or stab me with them blades up your sleeve and in your boots?"

Jon frowned. Nobody was supposed to know about those weapons. Zena knew more about him than made him comfortable.

Reluctantly opening the satchel, Jon shuffled through the various maps and clean paper included in the packet. Jon found the sealed letter and opened it.

New Orleans, Louisiana March 1st, 1865

To the Post Adjutant
Fort Belknap c/o Red River Station, Texas

Sir:

On this day of the First, about 6 A.M., I dispatched one U.S. Army soldier scout surveyer, Jonathan Frederick Shelby, a Sergeant and a Negro, to plot the area along the Red River to Red River Station and on to Fort Belknap.

Sergeant Shelby is a fine man, worthy of his rank and uniform, and I present him to you for service as you see fit.

I have heard from reliable sources in Washington that once we win the War, there will be several regiments of Negro troops both infantry and cavalry dispatched to

Fort Belknap to help keep the peace against those so-called Texas Rangers, desperadoes, and general riffraff along the Rio Grande.

Sergeant Shelby is fine officer material. Please see that he is one of the first Negroes to get a command. I vouch for him wholeheartedly. Pay and other amenities must be in accordance with U.S. law.

I had predicted this tiresome old War would end by the time he reached your command, and if I am correct, please dispatch via wire a reply; by then our battle would have been won.

If I am wrong, please send my soldier scout back the way he came. May God bless. May the scourge of war leave you in good health.

Very Respectfully,

Hollingsworth Williams
Brig. General, Cavalry
Corps D'Afrique, Commdg.

Jon looked up from the letter and laughed loud, and open. He and his people were free men and women, *and* he had been recommended for officer status. President Lincoln had used the Negroes as pawns, and the ploy had worked for both sides.

Jon stood off from his friends for a moment and thought about their personal battles still to be fought and won. He thought about Zena's brother and about Safiya's blindness. He was sure that reward money for bringing in the Samples gang was still available to him. He would give about half to Zena to buy her brother Santee's free papers, and the other half would go toward that doctor for Safiya. There would surely be some left over to get Cinque a real bowie knife, and Pappy Thaddeus could rest out his later years in warm and loving peace.

Jon looked over at Zena, his eyes bright and alive. Counting her bounty for the capture of Monte Devlin, Vinia rode up, and for the first time she smiled at Jon Shelby. The three stood together.

"What else that secret letter say, Jonathan?" Vinia asked.

"Says I deserve some time off to get drunk and raise a little hell with you and Zena Beale," said Jon.

"It don't say that!" Zena grabbed the papers and then realized she had been bluffed. She playfully punched Jon in the belly, and he picked her up in his arms and tossed her into the Keles' wagon. She bounced on the soft hay and let out a giggle. Happier than a weevil in a field of cotton, Zena winked at Jon and then kissed him on the mouth with a *smack*!

A young Black woman, Zena's friend, Nerva, raced from the crowd holding her baby tight in her arms. Handing the young-un up to Zena, Nerva hopped aboard the wagon. Zena nestled the child in her arms and burst into a beautiful smile. She cooed at the baby watching Jon untie Easel and the horse he had just won.

Jon waved his hat into the wind and motioned the jubilant band forward as they headed down the road to enjoy the Kele celebration. Pulling the roan he'd won from Devers behind him, he slowed his mount till he fell into pace right alongside Zena.

"Got a gift for you, Miss Zena, this fine-looking hoss is yourn's," Jon paused before completing his piece, "You know I can't stay here with you. I got to head out west. . . . "

"To Paradise Run," she finished.

"Yes, ma'am! But tonight, we's gon' kick up our heels a spell!"

Jon licked some spur into Easel and waved his hand to Zena Beale to follow on her brand new steed. As they rode out of Clarksville they both could truly smile. The war was over and Jon's dream was alive, far west of Paradise Run.

About

---

the Author

J.J.R. Ramey grew up in rural Tennessee and started writing at the age of nine. Since then he has worked in radio and T.V. as a reporter, announcer, disc jockey, and actor, and is an award winning video documentary producer. When not researching and writing his Jonathan Shelby Western series, Mr. Ramey anchors radio newscasts heard daily throughout America.

Mr. Ramey lives in New York City and travels extensively throughout the United States.